MW00413203

BUG HUNT

ARGONAUTS

BOOK ONE

IRIDIUM

PUBLISHING

A DIVISION OF

HOOKE
PUBLICATIONS

BOOKS BY ISAAC HOOKE

Military Science Fiction

Argonauts
Bug Hunt
You Are Prey
Alien Empress

Alien War Trilogy
Hoplite
Zeus
Titan

The ATLAS Series
ATLAS
ATLAS 2
ATLAS 3

A Captain's Crucible Series
Flagship
Test of Mettle
Cradle of War
Planet Killer
Worlds at War

Science Fiction

The Forever Gate Series
The Dream
A Second Chance
The Mirror Breaks
They Have Wakened Death
I Have Seen Forever
Rebirth
Walls of Steel
The Pendulum Swings
The Last Stand

Thrillers

BUG HUNT

ARGONAUTS

BOOK ONE

Isaac Hooke

Text copyright © Isaac Hooke 2017
Published March 2017. All rights reserved.

www.IsaacHooke.com

ISBN-13: 978-1-5207115-5-3
ISBN-10: 1-5207-1155-7

Cover design by Isaac Hooke
Cover image by Shookooboo

contents

*To my father, mother, brothers, and
most devoted fans.*

one

Rade smiled brightly at his captors and felt a fresh trickle of blood smear down his chin. "Well hello."

The enforcer slammed its metal fist into his jaw again.

Rade's vision filled with phosphenes and he nearly blacked out. He was lucky the robot hadn't struck any harder. It could have easily broken his jaw. "Good one."

"The employer will not be pleased with what you have done," the enforcer said.

"I'm sure he won't." Rade glanced at the scantily clad harem members. He'd only managed to free eight of the slave girls. The other seven were cowering and weeping in the corner of the palatial chamber, cringing underneath the malevolent glowing eyes of the armed robots that watched them.

The enforcer stood to its full height and towered over Rade.

"Bring him," the enforcer instructed its charges.

The two repurposed combat robots held Rade firmly on either arm and led him across the chamber. As he passed the frightened slave girls, their cloying perfume drifted to his nostrils and he involuntarily crinkled his nose. One of the girls, catching his eye, seemed to mistake the expression for disgust or contempt, and she whimpered.

"I'll be back," he reassured her.

His captors forcefully carried him from the chamber and into the main hall of the palace, leaving the remaining armed robots to watch over the women.

Electroactuators humming loudly with each step, the enforcer led the way across the red carpet. Those heavy metal feet left deep impressions in the colorful rug. The robot's body looked like it was put together from large rectangular blocks, reminding Rade of Inuit statues he had seen with Shaw during a tour of the Arctic Circle back on Earth: the Inuit once piled rock slabs into manlike shapes to mark trade routes and hunting grounds, but in modern times those statues served mostly as cultural history. What the hell were they called again? Inuksuit or something.

Intricately woven tapestries hung from the walls, fringed with threads of gold. Each one depicted the same Asian man, usually in scenes involving combat. He always sported the same armored jumpsuit, and carried the same plasma uzis, which he used to shoot at different enemies while wearing a crazed expression. Sometimes those enemies were towering, praying mantis-like aliens. Sometimes, United Systems Marines.

The enforcer took a branching corridor into a colonnaded area. Flowering vines weaved between the columns, and the calming scent of jasmine floated through the air.

Rade let the fragrance suffuse his nostrils. He needed to remain calm now more than anything else. Relaxed. Focused.

The enforcer led him into the throne room. Two children were playing on the diamond-patterned marble floor. More combat robots stood at attention between the columns that lined the vaulted chamber; the robots held Sino-Korean X-22s, basically refurbished United Systems laser rifles.

The enforcer approached the throne and bowed. "I have the traitor."

The repurposed robots tossed Rade to the floor. He threw out his hands to break his fall, and then looked up from the marble toward the gold throne.

A hooded man sat in the red-cushioned chair with his head and shoulders bowed, as if burdened by the sheer weight of the world. He wore the same armored jumpsuit as in the tapestries, with the addition of a fur-rimmed cloak. The thick ermine fringe of the raised hood hid the wearer's features, however.

Two human guards stood on either side of the throne, dressed in full jumpsuits, including helmets. They were hired soldiers, like Rade, though they belonged to a local security company. They were flanked by more combat robots. Actroid-DER5 models, Rade guessed. A Sino-Korean model.

"What have you done?" the hooded man said. His voice sounded raspy, ancient. "I treated you like one of my children." He pointed a gnarled hand toward the two boys playing in the middle of the throne room. "In fact, I had come to think of you as one of my own. And yet you dare do this to me?"

"Yeah," Rade said. "Well, you weren't actually supposed to catch me. Once the girls were freed, it was going to be business as usual."

"So you would have pretended to track down the perpetrators," the man said. "While I paid you for it, when all the while you would have been the perpetrator yourself? This was some kind of scheme of yours to prolong your employment, is that it?"

"Pretty much," Rade said.

"Why bother?" the man said. "I had you booked for the next two years. If you hadn't done this, you would have remained gainfully employed until then."

"Very true," Rade said. "But there's a small thing I have that you don't, called a conscience. See, what I don't understand is, why didn't you just buy a few skin musicians and be done with it? You are a warlord, after all. It's not like you can't afford it. Instead, you had to traffic human females. I couldn't stand by while you did that."

"That's what this is about?" the man said, the incredulity obvious in his tone. "The fact I purchased humans to resell at a profit, rather than AIs? That's the problem with you United Systems types. You don't respect the sanctity of the spirits."

"For the last time, they're AIs, not spirits," Rade said.

"You're wrong," the warlord said. "To hold an Artificial in a temporary harem is a crime. But human beings, not so much."

"Well, I see now why your enforcers follow you so fervently," Rade said. "You're definitely drinking the AI Kool-Aid."

"The Kool what?"

"Never mind," Rade said. "Old school cultural references. They crop up when you play classical VR."

"I see."

"Though I have to wonder," Rade continued. "If you regard AIs with such awe and veneration, why do you even employ robots at all?"

"My spirits are paid extremely well," the warlord said. "But we've chatted for long enough." He glanced

4

toward the playing children and shouted in Japanese.

"Boys," the man said, according to the audio translation Rade's Implant fed his brain. "Come here!"

The kids ignored the warlord. They played with mechanical toys: one of them was controlling a tiny mech with hand gestures, the other a darting drone.

"Boys!"

The two children finally looked up, collected their toys, and rushed to the throne.

The man sat straighter and reached up to lower his hood. That was a bad sign. He only did that when he was about to pass judgment. Or kill someone.

As the hood fell, the face of the Asian man from the tapestries emerged, though it was severely aged. Someone obviously had never told him about rejuvenation treatments. Then again, Rade had heard it was all the rage among the warlords to showcase wrinkles. Apparently, the older you appeared, the more powerful you were: it demonstrated that you were strong, and didn't need something as below you as rejuvenation treatments to live. Then again, judging from the young age of his children, Rade had to wonder if the man had undergone reverse rejuvenation treatments to purposely seem older.

That face wore the same crazed expression as the man from the tapestries. Kenzo Kyōryokuna, most feared warlord on the Asiatic Alliance colony.

"My children," the warlord said, still speaking Japanese. "This man has caused me to lose eight concubines. Eight expensive women, trained in the arts of pleasure. Did he ask them if they wanted to be free?"

"I did, actually," Rade interjected.

The warlord continued as if Rade hadn't spoken. "Did he ask *me*? No! He has committed a great crime, setting these women free, so that they might be scooped up by other masters, profiting them instead."

"Actually, by now they would have reached my ship," Rade said. "No one else is going to profit from them."

Again Kenzo ignored him. "Setting my slaves free is tantamount to stealing from me." The warlord glanced at his two sons. "My children, you are going to watch and learn what happens to those who mess with the Kyōryokuna clan."

He glanced at the human guard on his left side, and nodded.

The helmeted man stepped forward. He was Japanese, like Kenzo. Behind that faceplate, his brows were all scrunched up, and he wore a scowl that promised no mercy.

The mercenary raised the arm assemblies of his jumpsuit and pointed his laser rifle at Rade.

"Wait." Rade slowly clambered upright.

Kenzo was frowning. "What?"

"I die on my feet."

The warlord smirked. "As you wish." He glanced at the mercenary. "Fire when ready."

The hired soldier aimed the rifle at Rade and squeezed the trigger.

Nothing happened.

The mercenary appeared puzzled. He tried again several times, but the laser refused to fire. He glanced at the other guard in apparent confusion. The second mercenary stepped forward, aimed, and fired. Nothing happened.

Rade calmly shrugged. "I forgot to tell you, we hacked your weapons before we started the operation. X-22s have several known vulnerabilities. You might think about updating the firmware the next time you purchase a bunch of outdated weapons for your hired guns to use."

"Enforcers," Kenzo said. "Engage!"

Rade spun around and raced toward the entrance as the robots stepped from behind the columns, lowering their weapons. No shots came: they were using the affected rifles, too.

The robots quickly realized their weapons were offline and moved to intercept him.

Rade focused on reaching the entrance. The enhanced strength of his jumpsuit allowed him to match the speed and strength of the robots. Still, if one of them caught him, all it would take was a blow to his helmet-less head to cave his skull.

Ahead, two robots moved directly into his path.

Rade dropped to his knees and his smooth leg assemblies allowed him to easily slide along the marble. He extended the arm assemblies of his suit to either side, tripping the robots as he went by. Once past them, he flexed his legs, and the self-balancing mechanisms in his ankle assemblies ensured he was quickly back on his feet.

He proceeded from the throne room and glanced at the map that overlaid his vision in the upper right, courtesy of his Implant. The emergency muster point was two hallways away, via a righthand exit near the middle of the colonnade. Rade raced toward that exit, the enforcers right behind him.

A robot stepped out from one of the columns to block his path.

Rade took a running leap at the robot and slammed into its chest with both feet. The robot toppled and Rade landed easily on his feet, once more thanks to the help of the self-balancing actuators.

When he landed, something grasped his leg,

tripping him.

The robot had grabbed him. It was crushing his boot while the other robots closed.

Rade mentally unbuckled the boot via the remote interface and drew his foot out. He stood and ran on. His left boot had automatically resized so that his limbs weren't too mismatched, height-wise. Still, he proceeded awkwardly.

No more self-balancing...

He glanced over his shoulder. The pursuing robots were right behind him.

He dove into the righthand hallway in the middle of the colonnade.

Ahead, one of the helmeted Japanese mercenaries stood in the middle of the carpet, rifle aimed directly at Rade.

"Warning, armed mercenary," one of the robots helpfully shouted from behind. "The weapons have been disabled."

Rade dodged to the side.

The mercenary opened fire. Though he couldn't see the actual infrared beams, the weapon worked, because Rade heard a metallic clamor behind him as robots crashed to the carpet in turn.

On his overhead map, the red dots of the pursuers vanished one by one.

Rade tore past the mercenary and paused behind him to catch his breath.

When the man had taken out the last robot, he turned toward Rade. The holographic projection on the helmet's faceplate faded, and the Japanese mercenary was replaced by an entirely different man, with features belonging to an Asian American.

"About time you decided to pitch in," Rade said.

"I didn't want to spoil your fun too early." Lui

retrieved a blaster from his utility belt and tossed it to Rade.

"Come on," Rade said. "They'll be figuring out how to fix their guns any time now. I have no doubt Kenzo will be sending the whole garrison after us."

"What about Shaw?" Lui asked.

"Don't you worry about her," Rade replied. "She'll be joining us at the muster point shortly."

I hope.

On cue, a distant explosion rocked the palace.

"And there she is now," Rade said. "Come on!"

They reached a T intersection and took the right branch. Up ahead awaited another T.

On the overhead map, he saw a group of blue dots approaching from the west side of that T.

Shaw.

He reached the intersection and waited for Shaw to arrive. She was dressed as a slave girl, and led the way for the other six freed women.

When she neared, he resumed his pace, allowing her to come alongside while Lui took point. He glanced at her.

She looked quite sexy in that skimpy outfit, and if Rade wasn't running from his death, he might have—

"Shut it," Shaw said.

"I didn't say anything!" Rade said.

She rolled her eyes and continued sprinting.

Ahead, a large enforcer robot stepped into view and blocked their path.

Rade fired his blaster at the same time Lui unleashed his rifle, and together they terminated the robot. It fell in a laser-riddled pile.

They reached the muster point: a large balcony overlooking Yorokobi city, most populous settlement on the planet. The lights of the city that never slept spread out before them.

An old Model 2 Dragonfly hovered beyond the edge, its ramp lowered onto the railing.

"Get inside!" Rade told the girls.

Rade and Lui gave boosts to each of the girls in turn, including Shaw, and helped them onto the ramp; when the last of them was in, they followed the women inside.

The down ramp closed behind them.

The freed girls had taken eight of the sixteen seats, leaving the cabin half empty—there was enough room in the shuttle to hold an entire platoon.

"Harlequin," Rade said as he hurried into his seat. "Get us out of here!" Clamps telescoped from the sides of the seat and secured Rade in place.

Harlequin, the Artificial piloting the shuttle, glanced askance at Rade from the cockpit area. "Yes, sir."

"And don't call me sir!" Rade said.

two

R ade was jerked violently in his seat.

"Sorry," Harlequin said. "Dragon hole."

The coastal city of Yorokobi was situated between an ocean on one side and mountains the other. Legend told that ethereal dragons, bearers of positive feng shui energy, made their homes in the mountains. When the dragons made their way to the ocean to drink, the holes in the buildings allowed their positive energy to pass through unobstructed, ensuring good vibes for everyone involved. At least that was what Rade had been told. While he didn't believe in ethereal dragons, those holes certainly provided a good getaway route. As long as Harlequin could properly steer through them, of course.

The plan was to stay low, keeping the shuttle close to the designated sky-tram lines until they were well outside the city limits, at which point they would accelerate into orbit. The intention was to avoid the anti-aircraft cannons that Kenzo had situated along the high walls that encircled his palace. Kenzo basically owned the city council, and had full authorization to fire those cannons whenever he pleased. Such was the way of life on the frontier planets, where warlords ruled the day and the little people made do with what scraps they could get.

Lui turned his head toward the rear portal and his eyes defocused as if regarding something on his Implant.

"Guess his children have learned what happens to those who mess with the Kyor Yoko clan," Lui said. "Or whatever they're called. And the lesson is: those who mess with them, are *really* successful."

Rade glanced through the rear portal and zoomed in. There was no sign of the palace, which was blocked by other buildings. Good. Rade was worried that Harlequin had kept them in the line of sight of those anti-aircraft cannons all that time. Thankfully not. Lui must have been reviewing previously recorded footage taken by the aft cameras when the shuttle departed.

"Have a look," Lui said.

Rade accepted the feed. Video from the rear-view camera filled his vision. The timestamp indicated the footage was taken forty-five seconds ago. The video played at one tenth normal speed, and Rade could see all the details of the receding palace, from the spires and domes to the enclosing walls. A large gash had been cut into the west wing where the harem had been, and the entire western tower had crumbled. Shaw's handiwork.

"Nice work, babe," Rade said, dismissing the feed. "But did you have to take out the entire west wing, including the tower?"

Shaw shrugged in the seat beside him. "You're the one who's always telling me I have to aim higher."

Rade shook his head, chuckling softly. He glanced one last time through the rear portal, but saw no signs of pursuit. For the moment.

"And why not let Harlequin call you sir?" Shaw said with a mocking grin. "You don't work for a living anymore."

He looked at her crossly. "I'm not an offi*cer*. With the emphasis on the sir."

"Old habits die hard," Lui said. He was seated across from Rade, beside TJ. "Once a navy man, always a navy man."

"Never a navy man," Rade said. "A *MOTH*." That stood for MObile Tactical Human, an elite force within the navy specializing in guerrilla warfare and counterinsurgency.

"Ex-MOTH, now," Lui said. "Though personally, I never really understood that whole cultural divide thing. Like, why we had to call every non-MOTH a member of Big Navy, as if everyone with a different rating was lower than us or something."

"That's because they *were* lower than us," Rade said. "We were the best of the best. Still are."

"Oh please," Shaw said, rolling her eyes. She was getting good at that.

Rade frowned, then looked back at Lui. "She says that now. But wait until we're alone in my stateroom tonight."

"*Our* stateroom," Shaw clarified.

"You guys," Lui said, shaking his head. "You're like two adolescents in love for the first time."

"Are we?" Rade said. "I don't know about that. There's nothing adolescent about what we do when we're alone."

Lui half threw up his arms. "Quit your bragging. Some of us don't have girlfriends aboard, remember."

"But you got TJ," Harlequin said, turning back to wink.

"Ah *merda*," TJ said. The clamps of his seat retracted, and he stood. He wasn't wearing the arm assemblies of his jumpsuit, allowing him to show off the tattoos of mechs and rivets inked into his bare skin.

"What is it?" Rade glanced at his overhead map. Several red dots had appeared behind them, weaving through the buildings in pursuit.

"Enforcers," TJ said.

"Should have brought the Hoplites," Lui said.

Rade dismissed the clamps holding him to his seat and scrambled upright.

He had to hang onto the bulkhead as the deck suddenly jerked beneath him.

"I thought you fixed the inertial compensators?" he asked TJ accusingly.

"They are fixed," TJ said. "If the compensators weren't active, your insides would be smeared along the inside of that wall right now."

"Sorry," Harlequin said. "Had to initiate evasive maneuvers. We're taking heavy laser fire. Aft armor won't take many more hits."

Rade hurried toward the rear of the cabin. He paused outside the small pod-like structure affixed to the port wall, and glanced at Shaw, but she was filing her nails.

"Not going to wish me good luck?" he said to her.

"Why?" Shaw didn't look up. "You got this."

He knew she did that merely for show, putting on a brave face for the men, and the freed women. But he saw right through her.

Rade entered the pod, while TJ entered the one opposite him.

Rade took a seat and wrapped his hands around the trigger mechanisms, and his Implant linked him to the aft right turret. The AI was already firing, but he usurped control: instantly the inside of the pod faded away, and he had an unobstructed three hundred and sixty degree view of the outside of the shuttle. In fact, it was as if the shuttle wasn't even there anymore, nor his body for that matter.

He controlled the rightmost rear turret, TJ the leftmost, and the remaining rear guns were manned by the AI.

Rade zoomed in on the pursuers. He spotted the enforcers TJ had spoken of. The robots had boarded air stallions—small, ridable quadcopters with weapons mounted underneath. He counted about thirty of them out there. He couldn't see their incoming laser fire, of course—the nanosecond pulses were emitted on the infrared band.

Rade aimed at one of the pursuers. The turret's built-in AI compensated for the evasive movements of the shuttle, and he got a lock and fired. The enforcer went down.

A missile alert sounded. The Model 2's equivalent of a Trench Coat activated, sending out thirty-four seekers to intercept the rockets; meanwhile the craft dove.

The Model 2 shuddered as the shockwaves of multiple detonations reached it.

Rade continued firing, taking down two more pursuers. But the enemy began moving in evasive patterns, too, and it became extremely hard to hit any of them with the lasers. He launched a few missiles, but they deployed anti-rocket countermeasures of their own.

"Too many of them," Rade said. "We're going to have to take the bird into space. Harlequin, those models of air stallions aren't space capable, are they?"

"I don't believe so," Harlequin said. "But you do know, once we leave the cover of these buildings, we'll be exposed to the palace cannons."

"I'm well aware of that," Rade said. He returned his turret to fully automated mode—the AI would have a better chance of hitting the enforcers than him at that point. Then he left the pod and returned to his seat. He noticed that TJ was already strapped in beside Lui.

TJ shrugged. "Sometimes you got to know when to let the AI do its job."

"Take us up, Harlequin," Rade said as the clamps secured him in place.

"We're receiving a connection request from the city mesh network," Harlequin said. "From Kenzo. Would you like me to tap him in?"

Rade hesitated. Then: "Do it. Voice only."

"You're never going to get away with this, Rade Galaal," Kenzo said. "I'm going to hunt you down for the rest of your days. Short as they will be."

"You're welcome to try," Rade replied. "But don't you worry, Kenzo: if news reaches me that you've dipped your wick into the human trafficking cesspool again, I'll be back. And I might not leave so much of your palace intact next time."

He quickly closed the connection, not wanting to give the warlord the last word.

"I really hate it when people make threats like that," Lui said. "Because they usually follow through. We're going to have to deal with him again someday, mark my words."

Rade flashed a fake smile. "Nah. He's a big teddy bear. Wouldn't harm a fly."

"Riiiight," Lui said.

The shuttle jerked to the left.

"As expected, now that we've left the cover of the city, we're receiving incoming flak," Harlequin said. "Unfortunately, it's not restricted to the palatial

16

cannons. Kenzo seems to have called upon a few friends throughout the city to join in the barrage. I'm initiating additional evasive maneuvers, and launching decoys. Things are going to get a little rough."

Multiple flashes outside the various portals alerted Rade to the presence of the flak. That, and the occasional shudders evoked by the shockwaves of near misses. Rade was jerked often in his seat.

"So now we have to dodge flak *and* lasers," Lui said. "Wonderful."

"Harlequin, punch it!" Rade said. "Get us the hell out of here."

"I'm already at maximum ascent speed," Harlequin replied calmly.

The flashes continued unabated outside.

Rade glanced at Shaw, who hadn't looked up from her nails. Some of the other women meanwhile were openly weeping or whimpering.

"Do you have to do that at a time like this?" Rade asked her. While he knew the nail thing was just an act, it still made him nervous.

She shrugged, continuing to focus on her filing. "At least I'll go out looking good."

"Babe, you always look good."

She finally looked at him, and beneath the fear there was a hint of warmth in her eyes. "Thanks."

The shuttle shook so terribly that she lost her grip on the file and it clattered to the floor.

A klaxon sounded.

"Warning," the shuttle's AI intoned. "Lateral stabilization failure. Warning."

"That doesn't sound good," TJ said.

"We took a hit on the left engine," Harlequin said.

Rade glanced through the rear portal. The ground was spinning far below.

"Can you stabilize us?" Rade said.

"Trying..." the Artificial replied.

Shaw sat back and closed her eyes. She wrapped her fingers around her seat's armrest, her grip so intense that her knuckles turned white. One of her hands reached out searchingly for Rade's, and he gave her his own. Her fingers tightened around his palm, the nails piercing his flesh like claws. He gritted his teeth, but dismissed the pain.

I can endure a bit of agony for my girl. If we're to die here, I want to do so holding her hand. The pain be damned.

The thought repeated in his head that he shouldn't have allowed Shaw along for the mission. How did he let her convince him into bringing her?

Stop that line of thinking. She was essential to the plan and you know it.

Still, if anything had happened to her in the palace, he would have been destroyed inside. It was a small consolation that at least if they went down now, in the shuttle, they both would be lost.

"Got it," Harlequin said. The klaxon faded. "I've stabilized our ascent. Our evasive abilities have been reduced however. We'll need some luck to get through this."

"On the plus side," Lui said, "A side benefit of the flak is it's taking out the enforcers. Look at the map."

It was true. On the tactical map, about half of the pursuing red dots had vanished outright, and the rest were receding as the air stallions reached their maximum heights and were forced to drop out of the pursuit.

The flak slowly subsided, until in moments it ceased entirely.

"We've reached the upper atmosphere," Harlequin said. He turned around in the cockpit. "We did it."

"Harlequin, radio ahead to the *Argonaut*," Rade said. "Tell Tahoe to initiate deorbital pre-burn as soon as we've docked. Let's not overstay our welcome, shall we? Who can say how many nearby ships Kenzo has influence over out there?"

"Roger that," Harlequin said. "Decelerating to line up with the *Argonaut*."

Rade felt the zero G then and his stomach began to do belly flops.

He accessed the nose video feed and saw the *Argonaut* drift into view. The Marauder class vessel was small and sleek. It was favored by space pirates and smugglers for its speed, maneuverability, not to mention ample weapon mounts, with space left over for a respectable cargo haul. Mercenaries liked the vessel for the same reason.

The gray hull was battered in places, and obviously overdue for repair. Rade had promised to pour in the funds necessary for her upkeep soon, once he finished paying off his men, anyway. Yes, as soon as his men were paid, he'd have the ship holed up in dry dock for a full four weeks. By then his men would have spent all their earnings anyway, and would be up for the next mission.

Too bad they weren't going to be paid for anything they'd just done.

Then there was the small problem of meeting the monthly loan payments...

I gotta stop doing these missions of mercy. We had a good thing going here, and I had to go and ruin it.

Shaw's grip didn't let up until they had docked.

"Tahoe," Rade transmitted after they'd landed. "Are we deorbiting yet?"

"We are," his first officer responded over the comm. "I've set a direct course for Chitsu Gate."

"Good." Rade turned toward Lui. "Show the passengers to their temporary berthing area. I want them bunked with the other women, if possible." He wrapped an arm around Shaw. "We'll be in our stateroom."

When Rade reached the cramped quarters he shared with Shaw, he left her on the main bunk. She sat there, seeming a bit shell-shocked. Rade had nothing left to comfort her with, however. He needed to cave out.

He went to the adjoining compartment, the head, and locked the hatch. He lay down on the hard deck in front of the toilet and stared unblinking at the overhead. He erupted in a cold sweat.

His mind was in a faraway place. He was bringing his mech platoon across a desert world. The sand got in everything, clogging up servomotors, treads.

From the dunes erupted black forms. Aliens.

His brothers began to fall. He heard screams. Explosions. Trench Coat launches.

Something wrapped around his mech and pulled him into the sand. He couldn't move.

An AI's voice repeated three words in the background.

"Warning: armor penetrated. Warning: armor penetrated."

three

A knock on the hatch roused him from the depths.

"Rade," came Shaw's muffled voice. "You all right in there?"

"Never better," Rade said, scrambling to his feet. "Had to take a big dump."

"For an hour?" Shaw said.

Rade glanced at the time in the lower right of his vision. An hour had indeed passed, though from his point of view he had only just entered the compartment a moment ago.

"Uh, yeah," Rade said. "Did I mention it was big? I'll be out in a sec." Lowering his voice, he tapped in his first officer. "Tahoe, any signs of an intercept out there?"

"No," Tahoe responded over the comm. "Everything is dead quiet out here."

That was what Rade had hoped. Kenzo wouldn't tell the authorities, or press charges. He was too afraid of getting put in jail. Though there was still a chance there might be some civilian vessels out there willing to do the warlord a favor.

"I switched over the *Argonaut's* registry information shortly after we left orbit," Tahoe continued. "That's probably helping. We're now a trader from Sirius, hauling a cargo of Peruvian beets."

"Peruvian, huh?" Rade said.

"Yup," Tahoe said.

A rather commonplace foodstuff like that wouldn't attract too much attention. Especially at the Gate. If Tahoe had chosen something rarer and more valuable, they would have had to fend off greedy custom officials intent on securing bribes.

"Where are our guests?" Rade asked.

"We've had to set them up in the cargo bay," Tahoe replied. "There wasn't enough room anywhere else. I've got one of the gastronomic robots attending to their needs."

"Perfect," Rade said.

He left the head and entered the main compartment. Shaw was sitting on the bed with her arms crossed underneath her breasts.

"What?" Rade said.

"You zoned out again in there, didn't you?" Shaw said.

Rade sighed.

"It's getting worse, isn't it?" she pressed.

"I don't know what to tell you, babe," he said.

"Just tell me that I'm not going to lose the Rade I know and love," she said. "Tell me that the killer has gone back to his cave." She got up off the bunk. "Tell me that you'll hold me."

"I'll hold you," Rade said.

She wrapped her arms around him and squeezed tight. The top of her head came up to his neck, and he rested his chin on her hair.

"Shaw, my Shaw," he said.

"My big warrior," she said softly. Breathlessly.

Rade pushed her away and she gave him a hurt

expression.

"I have to get to the bridge," he said.

She lowered her gaze and nodded quickly. "I'll go with you."

"I hope so," Rade said. "You're my astrogator, after all. And not just of the ship."

She smiled, wrapping her arm around his side.

When Rade stepped into the tight compartment that formed the bridge, he found himself standing up against the series of curved stations that composed the brain center of the *Argonaut*. Those stations were placed side-by-side so that they formed a circle, affectionately called the Sphincter of Command by the crew. Usually shortened to the Sphinx.

Tahoe, Manic, Bender and Fret were currently seated at those stations. No instruments of any kind were present on the bare surfaces in front of them. Instead, the men interfaced with the stations via their Implants.

Each of them inclined their heads as Rade squeezed by, and in turn they muttered: "Boss."

Rade took his seat at the main station, while Shaw sat beside him.

"Have a good maintenance session with your chick?" Bender asked with a wink. The incredibly muscular black man was decked out in his usual array of gold chains and earrings.

"I'm right here you know..." Shaw said.

Rade shifted uneasily.

"Oh, that's you??" Bender acted all shocked. "My bad my bad. My eyesight isn't what is used to be." He leaned forward and mock squinted at her.

"Asswipe," Shaw said.

"Wipe I do and ass I is," Bender replied.

Manic, seated across from him, covered his lips,

apparently trying to hold back a laugh. His most distinguishing feature was a port-wine stain, vaguely moth-like in shape, over his right eye.

Manic glanced at Bender and then finally started giggling uncontrollably. "I think—" He had to stop to catch his breath. "I think he's actually proud you called him an asswipe!"

"Shut it," Bender told him. He flexed his neck and cracked his knuckles as if he hadn't a care in the world, or was getting ready to fight. Manic caught on and bit back his laugh.

"Anyway, it must be nice," Bender told Shaw. "You two get to shack up all cozy with each other while the rest of us here starve. There are fourteen women aboard skilled in the art of pleasure and we can't touch a one of 'em."

"Tell that to Lui and TJ," Fret said. Compared to Bender, Fret was a skinny stick. But he was the tallest man present, taller even than Rade, though it wasn't obvious at the moment with him seated at the Sphinx.

"You're such a rat, bitch," Bender said.

Fret cringed. "Whoops."

Rade furrowed his brow. "Bax, where are Lui and TJ?"

"Lui is in the stateroom he shares with Harlequin," the *Argonaut's* AI responded. "TJ is in the stateroom he shares with Bender."

"Is anyone else with them?"

"Affirmative," Bax replied. "One of the newly arrived passengers is with Lui. Two more are with TJ."

Rade frowned. All of the bridge crew were looking at him. Shaw's gaze seemed keenest of all.

Rade had standing orders strictly forbidding his ex-MOTHs from seducing any of the expected passengers.

I shouldn't have given those orders, maybe. Then again, if I hadn't, I'd have no one running the ship right now except the AI.

He also realized it was more than likely the passengers had done the seducing, or at least played an equal part, given the way the women had behaved during the weeks leading up to their rescue.

Rade glanced at Tahoe. "Dock them half a month's pay each." That would help meet payroll. With luck, more of his crew would misbehave in the coming weeks. "I'll leave the rest of their discipline up to you."

"Got it," Tahoe said. He was a Navajo, and almost as big as Bender. "By the way, speaking of the month's pay... can I talk to you in your office?"

Rade sighed, then he squeezed past the edge of the stations toward the hatch leading to the adjacent compartment. Tahoe joined him. It was difficult for the pair to navigate the tight space, given their sizes, but they managed. It definitely wasn't the sort of ship that would suit a claustrophobic.

Rade entered the compartment where his cramped office resided. Rade took a seat in a metal chair abutting the bulkhead. Space was at a premium throughout the vessel. Though the *Argonaut* appeared about a quarter the size of a military corvette on the outside, most of that was hull armor to protect against cosmic radiation, and the rest was cargo space.

When the hatch sealed behind Tahoe, Rade beckoned for him to sit in the hard-backed chair opposite him, in front of the tiny desk.

"So, what is it?" Rade asked.

"We all pooled our money to make the *Argonaut's* downpayment," Tahoe began. "We're all investors in this business. But the thing is, we gotta live, too. We need our salaries. Many of us have family back home. Veteran's pay only goes so far. And sure, some of our family members are eligible for basic pay, but again, it's not enough. We can't just take money out of the *Argonaut's* hull, you know what I'm saying? So my question to you is, how are you going to meet the salaries next month? Let alone the installment payment on the loan."

"That's what I like about you," Rade said. "You were never one to beat around the bush. But as I told you before, I already have something lined up."

"Why do I find that hard to believe?" Tahoe said.

"Unlimited Universe Security has made a name for itself in the security consulting industry," Rade said. "People are always visiting our InterGalNet site. I get a message at least once a month from prospective clients. Not to mention pings on the consulting message board."

"Yeah, and what's going to happen to the Unlimited Universe name now?" Tahoe said. "After what we did to Kenzo? One of our own clients?"

"Nothing," Rade said. "If our clients are honorable, and not doing anything illegal, they have nothing to fear. If they're like Kenzo, well, then they shouldn't be hiring us in the first place. In fact, I prefer it this way. It weeds out more of the dishonorable clients, who we don't really want to work for anyway. Human traffickers. The scum of the galaxy."

Tahoe shook his head. "We should have never taken on the job. You should have listened to me. Providing security for a warlord never turns out well."

"We did our research," Rade said. "His harem seemed legit. How were we supposed to know they were kidnapped women he was training as pleasurers so he could sell them?"

Tahoe shook his head. "It's too bad we didn't wait until he paid his latest bill. You know, in another month, I'll be eligible for basic pay again. We all will. It's been six months since our last payday."

"That long?" Rade said, feigning ignorance.

"That's right, pretend you don't know," Tahoe said. "By the way, have you gotten in touch with the bank yet? Any luck getting your escrow money back from the reserve accounts?"

"I'll try contacting them when we're in the next system," Rade said. "But they haven't been very cooperative, to say the least. You'd think the bank would be happy to help its loan customers stay in business. It's good for them, after all. But apparently they're not."

"They're happy to take the ship as collateral," Tahoe said. "Not to mention the shuttles, the combat robots, and all the mechs we've bought. This new client of yours better come through, or we're going to lose everything."

four

Rade resided in the well-stocked, if tiny, workout area. He had converted the two guest berthing areas and half the sickbay to make that gym. It was one of the first refurbishments Rade had made when he bought the *Argonaut*. You couldn't expect a bunch of ex-MOTHs to room aboard a vessel without one. The crew members would have directed all that pent-up, unspent physical energy against each other in the form of brawls otherwise. His next biggest expenditure after the gym was the conversion of the second cargo bay into a mech launch facility.

Because of the gym's small size, Rade had been forced to allocate different workout hours to each member of the crew. He was currently training with Shaw and Tahoe.

"This bench needs to be replaced," Tahoe said. He ran his hand along the yellow foam protruding from the worn fabric of the head region. "Every time I lay down to press, feel like I got a seagull doing its business on my hair."

"Are you sure that's a seagull doing its business, and not your wife?" Rade said.

"Har har." Tahoe lay back.

"How is your wife, by the way?" Rade said.

"She's fine," Tahoe said. He lowered the bar to his chest. The robotic spotting limbs attached to the rack followed the bar all the way down, prepared to give aid if necessary. Rade spotted him, too—just in case the robot limbs failed. "In her last message, she thanked me for the bread pudding recipe you sent. My daughter loves it."

"Don't thank me, thank Shaw," Rade said.

"It's an old family tradition," Shaw said. "Vanilla chutney bread pudding."

Tahoe finished his set and racked the weight.

"I'm going to have to program one of the gastronomy robots to make it for me sometime," Tahoe said. "Well, assuming we can find the ingredients aboard. All we got is chicken, chicken, and more chicken."

Rade shrugged. "It's the cheapest to purchase and store. And can we not talk about food right now? Some of us are dieting."

Shaw tried to pinch his waist, but Rade deftly sidestepped. Or rather, not so deftly—he slammed his side into the adjacent squat rack.

"Aww my poor baby," Shaw said when he flinched.

"She's mocking you," Tahoe told Rade.

"I do it often," Shaw said. "Usually when he takes his clothes off."

Rade chuckled softly and rubbed his side. He had knob-like metal hardpoints protruding from his arms at various points, used for mounting a strength-enhancing exoskeleton, such as those found within the military-grade jumpsuits the team used for away missions. One of the hardpoints on his wrist snagged a tender area near his ribcage, and he flinched.

"You should probably leave your side alone,"

Shaw said.

"Probably." Rade resisted the urge to rub the region further, and then he helped remove the weights from the bench press so that Shaw could do her set.

"We should really pick up some adjustable weights sometime," Shaw said. "Would save a lot of room. We are short on space, in case you hadn't noticed..."

"Yeah," Rade said. "And we're also short on cash."

When she was done with her set, Shaw said: "So what do we know about this new job of yours?"

"Not much," Rade told her. "Other than it's an escort sort of deal."

"Escort?" Shaw asked. "As in, we have to provide a security escort planetside? Or in space?"

"A bit of both, I think." Rade helped Tahoe load more weights onto the bar. "The *Argonaut* will escort their ship to the target, and then we'll potentially provide ground security at the destination, whether that's aboard a station, or on a planet."

Rade lay back on the bench. Tahoe was right, that exposed foam pressing into his head did feel quite awkward.

"Mind if I read the current message exchange with the client?" Shaw asked.

"Have at it." Rade transmitted it to her, and Tahoe as well, then proceeded to do his set. The hum emanating from the servomotors of the spotting limbs was slightly distracting, but he was able to block it out well enough. More distracting were the funny faces Tahoe was making while acting as the backup spotter above him.

When Rade racked the weights, he turned to Tahoe and said: "You looked like you were taking a shit there, bro."

"Hey, just mimicking you," Tahoe said.

"So you're meeting them at Etalon station?" Shaw asked when Rade was done.

"Yeah." Rade sat up and vacated the bench so that Tahoe could do his set. "The contact has agreed to meet me there. That's actually perfect, because we have to drop off the passengers with Graavian anyway."

"I want to come with you," Shaw said.

"That's a negative," Rade said. "I always meet with clients alone for the first time."

Shaw crossed her arms. "I didn't really like the tone of the contact's messages."

"What's wrong with the tone?" Tahoe said. His eyes were defocused. He had obviously decided to read the message exchange for the first time.

"I don't know," Shaw said. "It's a bit condescending. Like we're just another set of moving parts. Expendable."

Tahoe shrugged. "That's how most of our clients view us."

Rade received a call from the bridge. It was Lui.

"We're nearing Chitsu Gate," Lui sent.

"Gotta go," Rade said. "Duty calls."

He weaved between the closely-packed gym equipment and made his way toward the exit hatch.

Shaw had followed him. She touched his shoulder hardpoint, stopping him. Though the metal didn't have any tactile sensors on its own, he felt the pressure on the surrounding skin.

"Are you all right?" she said softly.

"I'm fine," Rade said, matching her volume.

She glanced at Tahoe. Rade did as well, and saw that his friend was watching the two of them with concern.

Shaw extended her noise canceler around him.

"Your strength is down," she continued. "Normally you do eight sets at that weight. You only did four."

"It's the diet," Rade said.

"You know I love every last bit of you." She tentatively reached forward to pat his slightly protruding belly, but then stopped herself—she knew how much he hated that. "Maybe it's time to put that diet at an end."

"I don't diet just for you, Shaw," Rade told her.

"Don't you?" she teased. She wrapped an arm around his waist, pulled herself close to him, and looked up into his face. Rade stared down into her seductive brown eyes, wanting her.

"I have to be in shape for this line of work," he said, slowly extricating himself from her grasp. "Not to mention, if I pack on too much flab, I'll lose the respect of my crew. I've grown soft since leaving the military. That's got to change."

Shaw sighed. "All right." She gave him a mocking salute. "Get back to the bridge, Captain."

He planted a moist kiss on her lips. She returned it vigorously; her tongue darted into his mouth, promising something more later. Much more.

"Come on," Rade said when he came up for air. "Not in front of Tahoe."

Shaw reluctantly let him go.

He hurried to the bridge, wanting to be present in case the *Argonaut* needed to deal with customs officials. He missed his old military days, when the only time he ever needed to handle customs was when operating undercover in Sino-Korean space.

Rade edged between the bulkhead and the Sphinx to take his place at the head station.

"We've queued to pass through Chitsu," Manic said.

Rade nodded distractedly. "Good." He accessed the external forward feed and saw ten other ships lined up ahead of them. Despite the system's location near the outskirts of Asiatic Alliance—and explored—space, it had a surprisingly active merchant culture, due to the deposits of the rare gem Suramantine found in the mountain ranges near Yorokobi city. Kenzo was only one of many warlords who controlled the trade in said gem.

Not unexpectedly, most of queued ships were merchant class, with one pleasure liner. They formed a line on the righthand side of the Gate. Incoming traffic meanwhile would enter on the left side. The arrangement was meant to prevent Gate traversal collisions, which could be devastating at the speeds common to space flight.

"You know what Chitsu means in Japanese, right?" Manic said.

"Yeah," Rade replied.

"What does it mean?" Fret said.

Bender sniggered. "Bro, it means pussy."

"Oh."

"Vagina, to be exact," Manic said.

"Why the hell would they name it Vagina Gate?" Fret said.

"The Asiatic Alliance has an interesting sense of humor," Manic said.

It took some time for the queue to clear. Apparently there were a lot of bribes that needed paying that day.

"Looks like we got ourselves the greedy shift today," Bender said.

"Never good when that happens," Rade said. He

considered turning around to come back later, but that would only draw their attention.

The *Argonaut* eventually reached the front of the line.

On the external video feed, Rade observed the two Asiatic Alliance corvettes waiting for them. The long, thin, slightly curved ships reminded him of samurai swords. He counted thirty obvious heavy laser turrets protruding from the hulls of each vessel. The same large Japanese character was stamped into the side of either craft. His Implant translated the symbol as "Customs."

"They want us to proceed to secondary screening," Manic said. "We're to prepare to be boarded and searched."

"What, why?" Rade said. "We're using the same registry information as when we first entered the system, aren't we?"

"We are," Lui said.

"Maybe they're pulling over all Marauder class vessels," Fret said. "Apparently Kenzo has more clout than we originally thought."

By then Shaw had returned to the bridge and resumed her role as astrogator, taking control of the ship from Bax; Rade reluctantly gave her the order to bring the *Argonaut* to secondary screening. There was no point making a run for it, not with the firepower those warships possessed.

Tahoe was still down in the gym, apparently trying to squeeze every last moment out of his workout.

"Tahoe," Rade transmitted to his friend. "Get down to the cargo bay and move our passengers into the hides ASAP."

As part of his refurbishing, Rade had set up a network of hidden panels in the deck, distributed at key points throughout the ship.

After the *Argonaut* had maneuvered into the screening area, Lui spoke up: "A boarding shuttle is approaching." He paused. "This is odd."

"What?" Rade said.

Lui glanced at him. "It just turned back."

Rade glanced at the tactical map overlaying his vision, which represented the ships immediately surrounding the *Argonaut*. The shuttle was indeed moving away.

"What spooked them?" Rade said.

"I detected a transmission from one of the comm nodes at the Gate," Lui said. Those comm nodes, also known as Node Probes, constantly passed in and out of the middle of the Gate, and kept the ships, bases, and cities in the current system linked to the InterGalNet via delay-tolerant networking.

"Do we know the sender?" Rade asked.

"I'm uncrunching the metadata now," Bender said.

Because of the nature of the InterGalNet, all ships would receive the same packets, regardless of whether the intended recipient was aboard. While the actual contents of the message were encrypted beyond breaking, the metadata itself usually remained in the clear, or was only mildly encrypted. Even so, it was still considered an illegal act to uncrunch that metadata, but Bender had a way to do it without getting caught.

Bender looked up. "The sender is one Green Systems, Incorporated."

"Green Systems...." Rade pursed his lips. That was their current prospective employer.

Interesting.

"We've been given the go ahead to pass through the Gate," Lui said.

"Take us through before they change their mind,"

Rade said.

five

There was a branch of SYD Bank in the adjacent system, so Rade had the *Argonaut* pass close to the station that housed it. Once in range, he initiated a realtime communication with the AI account manager.

"This is Chuck, SYD Bank, how can I help you today?" Rade always thought of it as Suck-You-Dry Bank. That, or STD Bank.

"Rade Galaal here, of Unlimited Universe Consulting Incorporated," Rade said. "I'm calling in regards to the loan on the United Systems registered vessel *Argonaut*, Marauder class, registry number 549425. I sent in a reimbursement request from the payroll reserve account three months ago, and haven't heard anything back. This is the fourth time I've sent in the request over the past year. Could you tell when I can expect the money?"

"Thank you for calling, Mr. Galaal!" the AI responded. "Your business is so very important to us. Let me put you on hold while I look into this matter of utmost importance."

Half an hour later Chuck came back on the line. "Thank you for holding, Mr. Galaal. SYD reviewed your request just last week. It was rejected, because the included financials were more than thirty days old."

Rade gritted his teeth. "The financials were current at the time of submission. Maybe if it didn't take you three months to review my request, your bank would realize that. Tell me this isn't a trick on the part of Suck... SYD to delay giving me any money from my accounts."

"It's certainly not a trick, Mr. Galaal. Thank you for your patience in this matter. Please resubmit a new request package, with up-to-date financials, and we will get back to you as soon as we can."

"Look, can you do a guy a favor?" Rade said. "I've never missed a monthly payment on my loan. I'm a good customer. And at the end of the day, these are my reserve accounts, and I need access to *my* money. There's enough in escrow to pay my crew for the next eight months, if I can get the damn money out!"

"My apologies, Mr. Galaal," Chuck the AI said. "But I must ask again that you please resubmit a new request package with up-to-date financials. Please be aware that due to a high backlog of requests, it may take some time to review your package."

Rade sighed, then disconnected. He updated the financials on the package and resubmitted the request. He doubted the bank would come through for him. It was more important than ever that he signed on that new client.

It took four weeks and two Gate jumps to reach Etalon Station in Beta Ursae Majoris system. When they reached the station, Tahoe maneuvered the *Argonaut* into the geosynchronous orbit specified by the station's STC, or space traffic control, and then Rade loaded onto the Dragonfly with eight of their female guests, and four of his crew. The remainder would come in the second Dragonfly. Fret meanwhile would stay aboard as part of the first watch; Bax and the combat robots could have cared for the ship well enough in their absence, but Rade had a policy of keeping at least one human crew member aboard at all times.

"Take us out, Shaw," Rade ordered.

Shaw piloted the craft from the *Argonaut's* hangar bay and into the void of space. Rade felt the queasiness induced by zero G immediately.

Shaw fired a gentle burst of thrust, following regulation docking speed, and in twenty minutes the craft neared the station.

"We've received clearance to dock in hangar bay twenty," Shaw said.

After landing, Rade waited the several minutes for the bay doors to shut and the external compartment to depressurize.

"We're good," Shaw said.

"Lower the ramp," Rade ordered.

The ramp lowered, and the clamps securing Rade and the others to their seats released.

Shaw joined Rade in the main cabin, leaving her copilot, Harlequin, in the cockpit.

Rade stood, and turned toward her. He beckoned toward the opening. "Age before beauty."

"Hmph. Beauty before beast. Come on, ladies." Shaw led the way down the ramp and the women passengers followed her. Their scanty outfits had been replaced by fatigues, and their long flowing locks were pinned into tight buns. And though none of them wore any makeup, they were very easy on the eyes.

None of them compare to Shaw, though.

A shorter woman among the lot paused to blow Lui a kiss.

"Good-bye, my love!" She gave him a doe-eyed,

longing look. "I'll never forget you, my precious chimichanga."

"Bye," Lui said sheepishly.

Rade glanced at him after the woman had gone. "Chimichanga?"

"Err, yeah," Lui quickly slid his gaze down and off to the side.

"I think it has something to do with him being a foodie," Manic said.

"Are we sure Graavian will be able to find the women gainful employment?" Tahoe said. "I'd hate to think after everything we had to go through to free them that they'll just end up as pleasurers."

"Graavian runs many businesses," Rade said. "The pleasure club is only one of them. The women will have the option to do whatever they like. Hell, he's even promised to give them temporary room and board if they don't want to work at all, at least while they wait for their latest month of basic pay to come in." He glanced at the others aboard the shuttle. "Well, I hear this station has an excellent strip club. Enjoy yourselves."

"Strip club? Screw that!" Bender said. "I'm heading for the officers bar. That's where the real action is! Made to order flesh musicians, here I come! And I mean that in both senses of the word."

"I'm with you," TJ said, joining him.

"They'll never let you in," Manic called after them.

"Yeah they will," Bender returned, lifting a golden brooch connected to one of his larger necklaces. "It's all about the bling, bitch!"

Rade glanced at the cockpit. "Harlequin, stay with the shuttle. When Dragonfly Two arrives, I want you to watch over both craft."

"Yes boss," Harlequin said. "Though you know I'd

much rather go with the others, right?"

"I know," Rade said. "But we're only partially on shore leave here. I'm on official business. And I'd rather have someone I trust in charge of the shuttles, rather than a generic combat robot."

"In a sense, I'm a generic combat robot," the Artificial said.

"No," Rade said. "You've been with us through thick and thin. You're not just an ordinary unit. Hell, you died for me once."

"I did, didn't I?" Harlequin said.

Rade nodded. If the Artificial's AI core hadn't been backed up before the mission in question, Harlequin would have been lost entirely. While this wasn't the "true" Harlequin, in the sense that the original Artificial had been left to die on an alien world, it did contain all the memories and personality that had made Harlequin, well, Harlequin. At least at the moment of the backup.

Rade proceeded down the ramp with Tahoe. They left the hangar bay behind and took one of the elevators to the main concourse. Along the way, Rade turned to his friend and said: "Is your wife meeting you here?"

"No, why would she?"

"I thought she was on a pleasure cruise in the area?" Rade asked.

"We had to cancel," Tahoe replied. He gave Rade an accusing look. "Due to lack of funds."

Rade patted his friend sympathetically on the shoulder. "I'm about to remedy our funding situation. Wish me luck."

"You don't need luck," Tahoe said. "You need a miracle."

When the doors of the elevator opened, Rade

parted ways with his friend. He had no idea what Tahoe planned to do on the station. He didn't really want to know. What a married man did while he was aboard a pleasure-themed space station was his business.

Rade's senses were assaulted by the sights and sounds of kiosks and fast food outlets. Digital overlays crowded his vision, thanks to the shared augmented reality programs the various purveyors beamed his way when he stepped within range of their outreach sensors. Rade dismissed the virtual images as quickly as they arrived, and after a while became so sick of the intrusions that he disabled the shared capability entirely. The station seemed much more austere without them, but at least he had some peace.

He reached the enlisted bar and gave the hostess his reservation. The Artificial in question appeared to be a woman in a black cocktail dress, showing ample cleavage. It looked completely lifelike, and the only way he knew it was an Artificial was because of the rotating virtual symbol his Implant overlaid above the woman's head. He'd programmed his Implant to automatically read the public profiles of anyone in range, and to display that symbol if the profile indicated the person was Artificial.

"Has my guest arrived yet?" Rade asked.

"Not yet, sir," the hostess told him in a sultry voice.

Rade bit back his usual response to "sir."

"Arnold will show you to your seat," the hostess said.

A robot appeared momentarily. This one reminded Rade of an over-sized trashcan on treads, with a small extended visor on top serving as the head. The HLEDs on that visor offered a rough digital representation of a face: eyebrow lines, two green dots for eyes, nose line, mouth line. The job of the hostess was to reel in the customers with its looks, and now that that part was done, the cheaper robots could take over.

The trashcan escorted Rade to one of the seats. "Would you like to order anything?" A disembodied voice came from somewhere in the center of the trashcan.

"Yeah," Rade said. "I'll have a mojito. And a side order of silence."

The two digital lines on the visor that represented the brows curved outward; Rade guessed that was supposed to indicate confusion. "A side order of silence?"

"That means do not disturb."

"I understand, sir." The robot wheeled about and departed.

His drink arrived a moment later, served by a flying drone with a tray attached to the top. Rade accepted the cocktail and took a sip.

"How is it, sir?" the floating tray asked.

"Fantastic." He waved the robot away and then settled himself in for the wait.

He pulled up Green Systems on his Implant and navigated to their InterGalNet site on the VR web. He had viewed it often during the past few days. The site touted Green Systems as an industrial manufacturer that focused on Aerospace and Defense, Engineering and Industrial Products, and Metals. A quick search of the trademark office told him the company owned several patents, with at least four related to the streamlined production of magnesium ion batteries, including a means to optimize the ion distribution of the substrates and thus triple the charge capacity.

Considering those types of batteries were basically used in every robot in existence, those patents alone would have made the company worth billions.

Movement drew his attention away from the virtual overlay. Someone had sat down at the table, though the newcomer's face was currently obscured by the VR browser. Rade dismissed it and his breath caught.

Seated before him was a woman of extreme beauty. Shaw might be cute as hell, but this woman was in an entirely different league. Flawless skin, chiseled cheekbones, perfectly aligned features. Her long dark hair reached to the middle of her back. She wore tight-fitting black fatigues that accentuated her breasts, with a small circular gap in the fabric above the solar plexus that showcased a very small amount of cleavage, not enough to be offensive but just enough to tease.

She was far too perfect to be real.

Sure enough, a floating icon above her head indicated an Artificial. He tried to think of her as an "it," but that didn't work. With some Artificials he could do it. Some, like Harlequin and this woman, he could not.

"I thought I told the hostess I didn't want to be disturbed," Rade said. "I don't have the time, nor the money, nor even the interest, to entertain a flesh musician."

She smiled fleetingly, but remained seated, merely staring at him.

Rade had a sudden worry. "Don't tell me you're my contact from Green Systems."

"I'm your contact from Green Systems..." she said.

Shit. He took a long sip of his drink.

"Just kidding!" The woman stood. "I have the

wrong table." She made to go, but then turned around and said "Gotcha!" before sitting back down again.

Rade shook his head.

Damn Artificials.

Though if he was honest with himself, the behavior reminded him of something Shaw would do.

"I find my beauty puts people on the defensive, Mr. Galaal," the woman explained. "It forces me to find creative ways to defuse that tension."

"I see," Rade told her. He was just glad she wasn't making a big deal over him confusing her with a flesh musician.

"I am indeed your contact," she said, extending one hand. "Emilia Bounty at your service. CTO of Green Systems."

"Rade Galaal." He shook her hand. "I hope you'll excuse my earlier comment."

"No need to apologize. It's understandable in a place like this."

"Bounty?" Rade said. "That's a unique last name. Don't think I've ever met a Bounty before." Artificials certainly liked to take liberties with their names.

"Never?" she said. "Well, I suppose you're familiar enough with the word itself. Being a bounty hunter and all."

"We only hunt bounties when other work is slow," Rade said.

"Mercenary work, you mean?"

"I prefer the term security consulting," Rade said. "So, I hope you don't think this is rude, but, do you mind if we dispense with the smalltalk and get down to business? I'm a bit pressed for time." While not really true, throwing that phrase out early in the conversation usually helped prod the client into business mode. "Your message was lacking a few details, to say the least. What can Unlimited Universe do for you?"

"Unlimited Universe Security Consulting Incorporated," the woman said. "In business for five years. In possession of one Marauder class starship. Your team, your 'Argonauts' as your site calls them, consists of eight human employees, with another three available on call as necessary, eight robots, and one Artificial. The customer satisfaction rating on Security Nation is four and a half stars out of five for your company. You had a fairly long streak of four and five star review ratings, until the scathing one star left by your latest employer. Apparently you destroyed the entire west wing of his palace."

"I'm sure you would know," Rade said. "Considering that you helped us smuggle the human prisoners he was trafficking out of the system. Thanks for that, by the way."

"You're very welcome," she said.

"How did you know we were there?"

She smiled widely. "I keep myself very well informed of galactic happenings that concern me."

"I see," Rade replied. "You've got a few hackers, you're saying?"

She continued that enigmatic smile.

"So you know all about my team," Rade said. "I know nothing of yours. Nor what you want."

"My vessel, the *Amytis*, will be arriving in a few days," she said.

"What sort of vessel is it?"

"It's a transport, Ptolemy class," she said.

"That type of ship has no armaments, correct?"

"That's right," the woman said. "We'll need your *Argonaut* to provide escort. You see, we'll be traveling through Sino-Korean space. In an area that has seen an upswing in privateer activity of late."

Rade frowned. "While my ship can hold its own against one or two privateers, if we face anything more than that, I can't guarantee your safety."

She nodded. "Understood. However, I believe it's better if only one ship provides escort. I want to keep a low profile. Let our attackers think that whatever we are carrying isn't valuable enough to justify hiring a small army of ships. If I employ more mercenaries, excuse me, security consultants, to escort us, we'll draw the privateers like bees to honey."

Rade furrowed his brow. "You mean bears to honey?"

"Yes," the woman said. "I think."

"What sort of cargo are you hauling into Sino-Korean space?" Rade asked.

"I am not comfortable revealing that information at the moment," she said. "Though rest assured, it is nothing illegal."

"You'll have to share your manifest with the Gate Authority whenever we make a jump," Rade said. "You know that, don't you?"

"I do," she replied. "I'm not planning on revealing our real cargo to them, either."

Rade sat back. He extended his noise canceler around her. "You know that's illegal, right?"

"Oh please, Mr. Galaal. You alter your manifest and ship registration information all the time."

"Yes, but it's still illegal," Rade said. "And it's going to cost you more to employ my services. An extra two thousand."

"That's fine."

Rade pursed his lips. That was easy.

Should have said four thousand.

"Do you have a destination planet in mind yet?" Rade asked.

"I do," she replied. "The Sino-Korean planet Lang, in the *Hóuzi H□ i* system."

Rade checked it on his map. "That's on the outskirts of Sino-Korean space." He hated operating on the outskirts of known space. Bad things always happened there, usually having to do with aliens. Or human-trafficking warlords.

"It is," she said.

"All right, well, the estimate I sent you earlier just went up," Rade said. "I wasn't expecting you to travel to such a far away system."

"Because of the distance involved, I'm prepared to offer you seventy-five thousand, standard currency." That was enough to cover the loan installments and monthly salaries of his men for the next year, or six months if he invested in the much-needed maintenance costs of the ship, with a few dollars left over to restock their depleted weapons inventory. "I may or may not need your services at the destination, but if I do require your boots on the ground, I will add another twenty thousand. The actual escorting task itself shouldn't take longer than a month and a half, there and back. So. Do we have a deal?"

Rade hesitated. "I don't usually agree to perform escort missions unless I know what the cargo is."

She raised both her hands defensively. "The decision is yours. I would prefer you and your team, as you come highly rated—excepting your last mission, of course. But if you don't want it, I'll simply find someone else. Etalon Station is teeming with mercenaries this time of year."

"Make it ninety thousand," Rade said. "Plus another thirty if we have to go boots on the ground."

"Eighty-five," she countered. "Plus twenty-five for the boots."

Rade wanted to haggle again but decided not to risk pissing her off. "I'll need twenty thousand in advance."

"It's yours."

A voice at the back of his mind reminded him again that he didn't know what the cargo was. Another voice told him how badly he needed the money. The latter won out, and against his better judgment he extended his hand and said: "Unlimited Universe looks forward to doing business with you."

She grasped his palm, smiling widely. "Thank you, Mr. Galaal. You and your Argonauts won't regret working for Green Systems."

I highly suspect we will.

six

Rade stood opposite Shaw on the mat of the combat room. He had mounted thick metal pieces along either side of the mat to simulate the tight bulkheads of a typical passageway aboard the *Argonaut*. Both he and Shaw were wearing exoskeletons, but Rade secretly had his strength settings dialed to low.

Rade bowed, and she returned the gesture. Then they rushed each other.

At the last moment Shaw leaped toward the simulated bulkhead to the left, activating the supermagnets in her exoskeleton to take two gravity-defying steps past him. Rade spun to block the blow he knew was coming, and as the kick came down, Rade deflected it. She landed behind him, and Rade swirled to intercept the barrage of blows she launched. Because he hadn't dialed up the speed of his exoskeleton as high, he had trouble deflecting all the blows, and in moments she had scored enough hits for the *Argonaut's* AI to assign the victory to her.

"Shaw is the winner of round two," Bax announced.

Shaw retreated to the side of the mat where Rade had been standing moments earlier. Rade assumed a position opposite her.

"Why do we have to do this?" Shaw said.

"Someday, these moves will save your life."

"Well sure, but you're not even trying," Shaw said.

"Sure I am," Rade said.

"If you're going to fight me," Shaw said. "*Fight* me." She definitely sounded angry. "Don't hold back. You're not doing me any favors. Just a few weeks ago you were kicking my ass. You can't tell me I've suddenly advanced a few belts since then."

The pair exchanged bows, and once more took a run at each other.

This time Rade dashed onto the rightmost bulkhead, activating the supermagnets in his own boots. The move countered Shaw's attempt to repeat the wall-kick maneuver of the last fight, and when he landed he had a clean shot at her torso. He took it, but because his strength was dial way down, she hardly flinched.

She rotated both arms upward and outward, smashing his hand away, then planted a kick squarely on his chest.

Rade was sent flying backward and slid off the mat.

"Shaw wins," Bax said.

Rade clambered to his feet.

"Bax, what strength setting does Rade have his exoskeleton set to?" Shaw said.

"Don't tell her—" Rade started.

"Rade has his suit set to the lowest setting," the *Argonaut's* AI replied.

Shaw smiled scornfully. "I see."

Rade sighed. "You're right. I can't do it. I can't fight you today."

"Then we can't train today," she said. "I'm going

to substitute one of the men instead."

"I don't think you want to do that..." Rade said.

But she didn't listen. "Bax, summon Bender to the combat room."

"Summoning Bender," the *Argonaut's* AI said.

"Bax, belay that!" Rade said.

"Affirmative," the *Argonaut's* AI responded. "I will not summon Bender."

"Bax, override Shaw phi omega two three fifty four."

"Override accepted," Bax replied. "Summoning Bender."

"Don't do this," Rade told her. "You have nothing to prove."

Shaw crossed her arms as much as the metal framework she wore allowed. "I have everything to prove."

"Fine." Rade walked over to one of the metal panels that emulated the bulkheads and wrapped his arms around it.

"What are you doing?" Shaw said.

"Taking down the simulated bulkheads," Rade said. Of all the crew, Bender was the best at manipulating supermagnets during a fight, and Rade wanted to negate that ability in the ex-MOTH.

He unmounted each metal panel from the deck and set them against the far bulkhead; afterward he retrieved an exoskeleton in Bender's size from the storage closet and waited. He kept wearing his own exoskeleton of course: in case he needed to intervene in the coming fight.

When Bender arrived, Rade tossed the exoskeleton to him.

"Fight her," Rade said. To save face, he was trying to pretend the idea was his.

Bender seemed confused. "You mean it?"

"Yes," Rade said.

"Rade has specific instructions for you," Shaw said as Bender attached the exoskeleton to the hardpoints on his own muscular form. "He wants you to dial up your strength and speed settings to the max."

Bender paused. "If I do that, I'll easily whoop your ass." He nodded toward her body. "You don't have hardpoints. I'll be faster than you."

"Did I mention Rade's also going to give you a pay bonus each time you knock me down?" Shaw said.

"How much of a bonus?"

"One sixth your monthly salary," Shaw said. "For each knock down."

"You serious?" Bender glanced at Rade, who tried to subtly shake his head without Shaw seeing it.

"Very much so," Shaw said, staring right at Rade.

"Hell yeah!" Bender quickly donned the rest of the exoskeleton and then took a place on one side of the mat. He raised his fists to assume a fighting stance. "Time for an ass kicking. You think I'm going to go all pussy on you just because you're a woman? You have a few surprises in store for you if so."

Shaw attacked him without further notice. Her punches and kicks came in a blur of motion. Rade was surprised by the ferocity of it.

Bender seemed taken aback by the flurry of blows, and retreated, nearly backing off the mat. But then he caught one of her punches with his left arm and spun her around, pinning her left arm up behind her back, and forcing her to her knees at the same time.

"Win for Bender," Bax announced.

"On the knees counts as a knockdown," Bender said.

"Correct," the *Argonaut's* AI replied.

53

Bender released Shaw and walked to the opposite side of the mat. "I'm going to be rich when the day is done."

In round two, Bender didn't seem so taken aback by her opening salvo. He responded in kind after she got in several quick blows, quickly switching to the offensive. He battered Shaw's exoskeleton, scoring ten rapid hits in a row before the AI announced his victory.

Round three was just as bad. At one point Rade stood up when Bender partially clipped her jaw: he wanted to interfere, but he knew Shaw would give him hell later if he did. Shaw fell to one knee after the blow, but quickly blocked the next few strikes Bender aimed at her. He swept his leg under her remaining foot, tripping her. Then he mounted her, pressing her shoulders to the mat.

"Win for Bender," the *Argonaut's* AI said.

Bender released her and Shaw stood up. Her cheek was red from where Bender had struck her face; he had obviously dialed back the strength of the attack a moment before impact, because even a glancing blow like that would have drawn blood, or worse, broken facial bones. According to the vitals Rade saw on the HUD overlay provided by his Implant, she was fine.

The fourth round proved much the same. This time, Shaw stayed back, circling Bender, occasionally attempting a quick strike. Bender waited for her patiently, and when she came in too close one time, his punch struck her in the side of the mouth.

She fell to the mat.

"Win for Bender," Bax said.

Blood oozed from Shaw's lips as she clambered unsteadily to her feet.

Rade angrily stood up but she waved him off,

wiping the blood from her mouth.

Shaw took her place on the mat drunkenly, obviously exhausted. She wasn't going to give up.

Rade shook his head.

Just as stubborn as me.

Rade hated seeing his girlfriend take a beating like that, even if it was a willing one. He felt the same sense of helplessness he had experienced while aboard the shuttle during the flight from Yorokobi. He promised himself that he was going to have a very long talk with Bender later. A talk that would probably involve violence.

"Have you had enough?" Bender said.

"Again," she said.

Bender shrugged. "I can do this all day, bitch."

Shaw threw daggers at him with her eyes as the ex-MOTH took his place across from her.

"Don't look at me like that," Bender said.

When the round began, Shaw moved forward very slowly, seeming slightly unbalanced. Bender advanced confidently, obviously believing she was out of the fight. Rade assumed the same, and he feared the worst.

But then Shaw leaped forward with unexpected energy. He realized her exhaustion was a ruse. Before he realized what had happened, Shaw had flipped over Bender, dragging his right arm with her. She shoved it upwards so hard that Rade heard an audible snap.

"Gah!" Bender yelled.

Shaw let him go, shoving him face-down on the mat. "Don't call me bitch."

"You broke my arm!" Bender said.

"Yup," Shaw replied. "Do you need someone to hold your hand all way to sickbay?"

"No." The muscles of Bender's jaw clenched as he forced himself to stand. "I'll take myself to sickbay.

Don't need no babysitting."

Bender's face was set in a grim line of pain as he limped toward the door.

"Hey," Shaw said. "Your arm is broken, not your *leg*."

"Oh yeah," Bender said. But he continued to limp. Rade suspected Shaw had somehow hurt his leg in that last attack as well. Rade would have to rewind the footage and watch it in slow motion later.

"What about your exoskeleton?" Shaw said.

"I'll let the Weaver cut it off me," Bender said.

"If the Weaver cuts it off, the replacement cost comes from your paycheck," Rade told him.

Bender gave Rade a scowl that was almost a match to Shaw's pre-fight glare, then he started to disconnect the exoskeleton. Rade and Shaw helped him; to his credit, Bender made no complaints about the pain he was in, despite flinching several times during the removal process.

When he was free of the metal framework, Bender left with a limp.

"Nice job," Rade said after he was gone. "But did you really have to break his arm?"

"He deserved it," Shaw said. "Besides, I figured I'd break the arm now and save you the trouble of doing it later."

Rade had to laugh at that. "That's my girl."

seven

The *Amytis* arrived at Etalon Station a few days later. The Ptolemy class vessel was a blocky, gray thing, as could be expected of a transport. It was roughly the same size as the *Argonaut*.

Rade recalled his crew from shore leave and had them return to the *Argonaut*. Then the Marauder proceeded to escort the *Amytis* across the system, beginning the long journey to the target system.

After a week and a half, they reached the Gate to Gliese 581 and passed through without issue. In Gliese 581, they made a refueling stop at the main trade hub, and Rade used the deposit Ms. Bounty paid to settle the accounts of his men, and buy some much needed supplies. When that was done, the two ships headed toward the closest Sino-Korean Gate.

Gliese 581 had the unique feature of having six Slipstreams: two led to Franco-Italian systems, two more to United Systems space, and the last two to Sino-Korean territory. The profusion of Gated wormholes in the system readily explained its galactic status as a trade hub.

At the appropriate Gate, the two ships joined the queue. A pair of black SK Customs warships approached shortly: black, triangular-shaped corvettes with at least twenty heavy laser turrets on each of them.

The customs vessels paused beside the two craft, one next to the *Amytis*, the other the *Argonaut*. Rade didn't have to answer any questions, as the *Amytis* handled the communications. Ms. Bounty would transmit the *Argonaut's* manifest and registry details, in addition to that of the *Amytis*.

"I'm detecting an invasive scan of our hold," Lui announced.

Rade nodded. That was expected. If his ship had harbored any contraband, he would have been very worried right then. But as it was, he rested fairly easy.

"We're both being told to report to secondary screening for boarding," Fret said.

Rade scrunched up his brow, then sighed. "All right. Shaw, fly us to secondary screening."

He had expected Ms. Bounty to use her company's vast resources to streamline the process, but apparently she had decided it would be far cheaper to simply let the SKs search the vessels. Presumably her cargo was well hidden, and the *Amytis* could readily undergo a cursory search.

The *Argonaut* and *Amytis* proceeded to the designated area beside the Gate. Two customs shuttles crawled toward them, one for each ship.

"Tahoe, send a couple of Centurions down to the hangar bay," Rade said. "Have them oversee the customs robots."

"You got it," Tahoe replied.

The search proceeded without issue. The only uncomfortable moment came when the SK robots reached the bridge. The tight quarters were made even more cramped by the presence of the intruders, and the bridge crew had to constantly shift about to allow them access. Thankfully the robots finished their examination soon enough, then cleared the *Argonaut* and departed.

When they were gone, Rade glanced at the tactical display positioned in the upper right of his vision. According to the returned data, the other customs shuttle was still docked with the *Amytis*.

"They're sure taking their sweet time," Rade commented. He wondered if whatever cargo the *Amytis* was carrying would be discovered. If that was the case, depending on the nature of that cargo, Rade and his team could find themselves in a galaxy of trouble.

Finally the second customs shuttle withdrew from the *Amytis* and both ships were cleared for travel into Sino-Korean space.

Over the next few weeks, they proceeded deeper into Sino-Korean territory, taking four more Gate jumps. Customs never bothered them again after that first time. Either the officials kept meticulous surveillance records of the ships, and knew that both hadn't stopped at any planets or stations along the way, nor halted in deep space to receive any payloads, or they were simply too lazy to search the craft. The current route wasn't known for rich cargo, and the officials knew that any bribes they received would be minuscule.

During the intervening period, the crew passed the time in various ways. The gym was booked at all hours, as were the three simulation pods in the adjacent war room. Those pods allowed the platoon members to practice small unit tactics with mechs and jumpsuits via full body VR. The combat room mat also proved popular—while VR was great for some hand-to-hand practice, nothing matched the real thing.

One evening, Rade returned late from his duty shift to find Shaw seated on the bunk in the cramped stateroom they shared. Her eyes were defocused. She was either reading a virtual book, or engaged in a local VR experience.

Rade went to the head to freshen up. His clothes locker was in there, allowing him to change into his evening wear. He had to tighten his belt an extra notch that night—his waist had gone down another size. His diet and hard work in the gym were paying off.

He decided to do some quick push-ups in the cramped space of the head, and used the bar on top of the hydro-recycle container to get in a few chin-ups. After three quick sets he had a nice pump, with two veins bulging down either bicep. He struck a few quick poses in the mirror. Abs were starting to poke through again, and he had some clear definition on the muscles of the chest and arms; when he flexed his shoulders, he saw some obvious striations underneath the hardpoints.

Lean, mean, sex machine.

When Rade emerged from the head, Shaw's eyes focused on him.

"Well hello there," Rade said, well aware that she was admiring his physique; before he left the head, he made sure to choose a T shirt whose sleeves barely restrained his pumped biceps. He had cut holes in the shoulder area for his hardpoints, of course.

Shaw ran her eyes hungrily up and down his body.

"Whenever we fly into Sino-Korean space," Shaw said. "I'm always reminded of our first mission aboard the same ship together."

Rade leaned against the bulkhead opposite her, and crossed his arms, knowing that would make his biceps appear even bigger. "The clandestine flight to Tau Ceti aboard the *Royal Fortune*, a stolen SK privateer nestled inside a bulk carrier?"

"The very same," Shaw said. "Stealing kisses in quiet corridors, and screwing in the storage closets."

"Those were the days, weren't they?"

"Yes." Shaw looked away. "Too bad it all ended after that mission."

"But we're together now," Rade said.

"Are we?" Shaw said. "Sometimes I wonder. We share the same ship, yes. But the excitement seems gone. Maybe it's the fear of getting caught that made it such a high. I almost think we should have sex in some random places aboard the *Argonaut*."

"And risk the crew catching us?" Rade placed his hands on his hips. "I don't think so."

"That's the whole point," Shaw said.

Rade shook his head.

"They know we're an item," Shaw pleaded.

"I don't care," Rade said.

She folded her arms sulkily. "What's been going on with you these past few months?"

"What do you mean?" Rade said. "Nothing."

"Oh yes, there's been something," Shaw said. "And I'm not quite sure what it is. I've been giving you time to cave out, so it's not your PTSD."

"I don't have PTSD," Rade growled.

Shaw smiled sadly. "Sure, you can say that. But you know you have it."

"No, I don't," Rade said. He realized a moment later that he was squeezing his fists so hard that he'd drawn blood from the palms. He released the grip, and shook his head. "You're just trying to cause drama."

"No, I'm not," Shaw said. "I care about you, whether you realize it or not. We've been through hell together, and apart. Though we look young, we're old souls, you and I."

Rade didn't answer.

"All right, as I said, I've been giving you your alone time, as I've learned to do," Shaw continued. "So I know that's not the problem. So what I can't figure out is, why have you stopped fucking me?"

"What are you talking about?" Rade said. "We've been making love all week."

"And those are the key words," Shaw said. "Making love. Ever since we got back from Kenzo's palace, you've been treating me like I'm some kind of fragile creature made of glass. Like you're afraid I might break. You've been handling me the same in the bedroom as you have on the sparring mat these past few weeks. I'm not going to break, Rade, I guarantee you. I just want you to *fuck* me like you used to."

She gazed at him, the sheer want brazen in her eyes.

Rade stared at her dumbly, and didn't make a move. Finally he lowered his gaze. "That last mission..." He swallowed. Why was this so hard? "When we were retreating from the surface under all that flak..." He shook his head. "I needlessly put your life at stake. I should have left you aboard the *Argonaut*."

"Is that what this is all about?" Shaw said. "We've been over this before. I can take care of myself. And if something happens to me, I go down doing what I love best. I'm sure you know what I'm talking about."

Rade nodded slowly.

"Besides, you're leaving out the part about how I was integral to the plan," Shaw said. "Who else among us would have been able to infiltrate the palace as a harem girl?"

"We could have hired an Artificial..." Rade said.

"Right," Shaw said. "Like we could afford that at the time. Anyway, you know I was the best suited to the task. You know it, whether you'll admit it or not."

Rade didn't say anything.

"Look at me," Shaw said. "Look at me."

Reluctantly, he met her eyes. She had changed the color of her irises today so that they were deep blue surrounded by flecks of green. A portable cosmetic laser she kept in her kit facilitated that.

"You know I find it a bit unnerving when you change your eye color like that," Rade said, trying to reduce the tension.

But apparently Shaw wouldn't have it: "I love you, Rade Galaal."

Rade was quiet for a moment. "I thought you didn't believe in love?"

"That was the old me," Shaw said. "The young, stupid me, who allowed us to spend our military years apart, wasting our youths serving in different branches of the navy. We lost those years because of me."

"It's not your fault," Rade said. "I was just as stubborn as you. I could have left the navy just as easily, but I didn't. I wanted to be a citizen of the UC, or United Systems I guess it's called now. And completing my service term was the only way to do that."

"We both wanted that." Shaw laughed sadly. "And look how well we're putting that citizenship to use now that we've got it."

"Yeah," Rade said, shaking his head. "If I had known then what I know now."

"But I do love you," Shaw insisted. She looked at him expectantly, as if anticipating him to return the sentiment.

"I..." He couldn't finish.

I used to love you. But I'm afraid to, again. I lost you before and it nearly destroyed me. I don't think I could afford to lose you again.

Her brow scrunched up. "You what?"

He stared at her, knowing full well that he did indeed love her, even if he couldn't say the words. But he couldn't bring himself to tell her. He wasn't sure why.

"Nothing, baby girl."

"Oh, Rade." She stood up, the top of her head reaching to his chin. In the cramped compartment, their faces were only a few inches apart. "You can't hide your feelings from me. You forget who I am."

"I'll never forget," he whispered.

She launched herself at him, rising on her toes to mash her lips against his. He returned the kiss with equal passion. His mouth left hers for only an instant when he slid off his white T shirt.

As they kissed heatedly, Shaw ran her hands across the rippling muscles of his chest. Her fingers paused near the hardpoints on his shoulders, and massaged the protrusions; her lips slid down to one of them, and she sucked the metal.

Rade opened his pants and uncovered his member. Her hands found it.

"You hussy." Rade threw Shaw onto the bunk.

She frantically unbuttoned the upper portion of her fatigues and slid down her cargo pants. She only got them to her knees before Rade was on her.

He grabbed her panties in the crotch area and slid the moist fabric aside, then shoved himself into her.

"Rade!" Shaw's nails scratched his naked back.

Rade grunted in outrage. The pain made him thrust harder. He wrapped his hand around her neck and squeezed. As he pounded her, she gazed into his eyes the whole while, the desire obvious in them.

"Fuck... fuck... fuck..." she said in unison with his movements.

Rade felt his release coming. Shaw climaxed at the same time and he collapsed onto her.

When he had caught his breath, he said into the pillow: "That's what I like about you, you're always putting my needs above your own."

"I'm glad you think so," Shaw said softly. "Because what I did back there was pretty selfish."

"No, it wasn't," Rade said. "And I meant in general. You didn't have to do any of this. Yet you invested in my ship and mechs. Bankrolled me to the tune of a small fortune to help me secure the loan, using your family vineyard money. Came with me on this part of my life. You're always doing everything you can to please me. That's not something I'm ever going to forget."

"You're worth it," Shaw said simply.

And that was all she needed to say. Rade felt wanted. Appreciated.

Complete.

After a moment, she said: "You're crushing me."

"My bad." He slid onto the edge of the bunk but lost his balance and fell onto the metal deck, landing on his side. He rolled over, hitting the opposite bulkhead of the cramped compartment with his elbow hardpoint. He grunted, smarting from the blow.

Shaw giggled. "Clumsy oaf."

Rade glanced at her and couldn't help but chuckle. He spoke toward the overhead: "Lights off."

The compartment plunged into darkness.

He felt Shaw's warm, soft body slide partially atop his. He slid a hand onto the crook of her lower back.

"This is my favorite part of you," he said, brushing

her lower back with a finger.

"What? My thoracolumbar fascia?"

"Err, yeah," Rade said.

"Why is it your favorite?" she asked.

"It reminds me of your spirit," Rade said. "Flexible in times of peace, and unbreakable in times of war."

"You get all that from touching my lower back?"

He laughed. "I do."

"I *love* you," Shaw said.

Rade closed his eyes contentedly, and they fell asleep together on the hard deck.

eight

The two ships reached the *Hóuzi H□i* system at the dawn of the fifth week since entering Sino-Korean space.

"So, Lui, what do we have?" Rade asked shortly after they had passed through the Gate into said system.

"Well, we have a typical binary," Lui said. "A white dwarf and a blue main sequence. They orbit fairly close together: the blue is losing a lot of mass to the white, so there's an accretion disk emitting a lot of radiation. Several planets orbit the barycenter. Closest to the star is a hot Jupiter. After that, we got three terrestrials: an iron planet similar to Mercury, a greenhouse sub-Earth, and the Mars-like Lang. The latter's magnetosphere is part natural, and part human-made, bolstered by the specialized satellites in orbit. There are a few automated defense platforms in orbit.

"After Lang, we have five gas planets: Two ice giants. A gas dwarf about twice as big as Earth. A Jovian that's almost massive enough to be a brown dwarf. And a cloudless Class IIIb." Gas planets of the latter class appeared as featureless blue globes due to the Rayleigh scattering of light in the cloudless atmospheres. "There's a sparse asteroid belt between the Jovian and the first ice giant. After the cloudless giant, the system is rounded out by several terrestrial dwarf planets."

"Ships and bases?" Rade asked.

"We got a Sino-Korean military outpost on the moon of the first ice giant with a couple of ships in orbit," Lui said. "An automated mining facility on the moon of the second ice giant. And that's about it. There are no other ships or space stations anywhere else in the system."

"The typical quiet frontier territory," Rade said. "What are the stats on the military outpost? You say they have two ships in orbit?"

"Yes, I'm reading two corvette classes," Lui said. "As for the outpost stats, I don't have a high enough resolution image of the habitation domes on the moon's surface, but I'd guess they might hold about fifty in total within the barracks, using other SK bases we've encountered as comparables."

"What about on Lang?" Rade said. "Is there a military presence there?"

"There's another outpost adjoined to the colony dome on Lang, yes," Lui said. "But no ships in orbit."

Rade glanced at Fret. "Are we able to contact the colony?"

"Looks like it," Fret said. "The system comm nodes are functioning normally. I've already received an automated ping from the colony on the surface and from the military ships at the SK base. Everything seems to be fine."

"Send a welcome message to the colony," Rade said. "Request their status."

"Will do," Fret said.

"By the way, Lui, what's the Gate status?" Rade said. "Can you confirm that this is still a border system?"

"It is," Lui said. "There's only the return Gate leading to the previous system. The secondary Slipstream on the opposite side of the twin suns has no Gate. Leads to uncharted territory."

"I just *love* border systems like this," Manic said. "*Nothing* ever goes wrong in them."

"Manic, did you take sarcasm courses in school or something when you were growing up?" Bender said. "Or were you just born a pussy?"

"Want to go?" Manic started to get up. "Come on."

"Easy," Rade said. "I don't want to have to call in the repair robots again."

The last time those two got in a fight, they'd wrecked the hatch in the cargo section. The combat robots had to completely replace the closure mechanism. Rade hadn't been able to afford any of the newfangled repair swarm drones, which could 3D-print spare parts in realtime, so the robots had to do it the old fashioned way: first utilizing the 3D printer to create the part they required, and then manually replacing the mechanism.

Bender flashed Manic a toothy grin, his gold front teeth gleaming malevolently in the light. "You only challenged me because you knew the boss wouldn't let us fight. We'll continue this conversation later."

"Oh we will," Manic said ominously.

Rade shook his head. "If you damage anything it's coming out of both your pays."

"That's fine," Bender said. "It'll be worth it to wipe the bulkheads with Manic's pussy sweat. The only repair robot you'll need is a Weaver, to fix his broken arms."

Rade suspected it was just talk. While they fought

occasionally, as evidenced by the hatch incident, rarely did the two come to blows.

Apparently he was wrong, because the next morning Manic had two black eyes. He and Bender were all smiles, however.

"You two seem happy today," Rade commented.

"Manic and I had a little talk," Bender told Rade. "Worked things out. No damage to the ship."

"Good to know," Rade replied. He noticed that Bender flinched whenever he sat up straight. "Do I need to have the Weavers look at the both of you?"

"Completely unnecessary," Bender said, hiding another grimace.

Rade glanced at Shaw.

"Boys will be boys," she said.

"Fret, did you get a response to the message you sent to the colony?" Rade asked.

"About that," Fret replied. "Yes, I did. An automated greeting anyway, welcoming us to the planet."

"Hmm," Rade said. "An automated greeting. That's a bit unusual, isn't it?"

"Not really," Fret said. "When you're posted on some system out at the ass end of the galaxy, you tend to be hung over a lot."

"You talking from experience?" Manic asked.

"Definitely," Fret replied.

Rade glanced at Tahoe. "You think we should ping the SK corvettes?"

Tahoe frowned. "I'm not sure it's worth attracting their attention. As the saying goes, let sleeping dogs lie."

Rade pressed his lips together uncertainly. "I'm a little surprised they haven't harassed our ships for traveling into the system in the first place. They can't have all that many traders coming here."

"If you want to contact them, shouldn't you at least get the client's permission first?" Tahoe said.

"Why do I need the client's permission?" Rade said. "This is for their safety, as well as our own."

Tahoe shrugged.

"Fret, ask those corvettes for an update," Rade said.

Given the distances involved, it would be another day before any response was received.

The next morning, Fret informed him that the corvettes hadn't answered.

"Well that's somewhat disturbing," Rade said. "Fret, tap me into Ms. Bounty."

He informed her of the situation.

"I'll admit, it is a little odd," the CTO of Green Systems told him. "But we can't let that interfere with our delivery. As long as the route seems safe, I want to proceed toward the planet and make the drop off. We'll send a communique back to the adjacent system, informing the local governor of the situation in the meantime. The comm nodes at the Gate appear to be functioning, so we're guaranteed he'll receive our message."

"Well that's all fine and dandy," Rade said. "But you do know it could be up to two months before the SKs send a patrol ship here to investigate, right?"

"I'm well aware of that," she replied. "But we'll be long gone by then. Bounty out."

When he was in his cramped office later, Lui called him from the bridge.

"Got some news," Lui said.

"Go ahead," Rade told him.

"I'm not sure this system is actually owned by the Sino-Koreans anymore," Lui said.

"What do you mean? The system maps clearly denote this territory as belonging to them."

"Maybe it changed hands since our maps were last updated," Lui said. "Those corvettes out there? They're the old Model 3As. The Sino-Koreans haven't manufactured those in decades. They sold them off to other galactic nation states, with the majority going to the Persians. And now that we're closer to the colony, I'm seeing signs of Persian culture underneath the dome, mostly in form of building design. Roughly half the buildings are of SK design, but the other half, the newer buildings, seem to be Persian."

"Well, all right," Rade said. "Systems switch hands all the time. It would have been nice if our maps were up to date, but hey, apparently United Systems spies don't get out into the border territories enough."

"Who says the United Systems government didn't know?" Lui said. "You know how intelligence agencies work. They let on that they know less than they actually do. If the SKs haven't officially announced it, why would the United Systems update the public maps and inform the SKs that they know? You get what I'm saying?"

Rade frowned. "Intelligence agencies. They claim they have the galaxy's best interests in mind. Most of the time, it's their own best interests they're looking out for."

He tapped in the *Amytis* and updated Ms. Bounty.

"We've noticed the same," she replied. "It doesn't change anything, though. Regardless of whether the Persians own the system or the Sino-Koreans, the mission is still a go."

"I thought you'd say that." Rade disconnected the line and sighed.

AFTER A WEEK, the two ships assumed a geosynchronous orbit above Lang.

The Mars-like planet was covered in a rocky red desert, and the average surface temperature was minus one hundred degrees Celsius. However orbiting arrays of reflective balloons focused sunlight onto the dome colony, providing extra heat and solar power to the inhabitants.

The atmospheric pressure at the surface averaged twenty-five millibars, well under the Armstrong limit of sixty-three millibars: the pressure below which water boiled away at a body temperature. For comparison, the pressure on Earth at sea level was a little over a thousand millibars.

Forma pipes distributed across the surface were attempting to remedy the atmospheric situation, spewing breathable air into the atmosphere at a rate of two hundred trillion tonnes per year—at that speed, Lang would reach a pressure of a thousand millibars in another twenty years. The network of satellites reinforcing the magnetosphere ensured the new atmosphere wouldn't be ripped away by the solar winds like the original planetary gases.

It was odd that the Sino-Koreans would sell the planet to the Persians after sinking so much money into the terraforming infrastructure of the world, but it wasn't unheard of for the SKs or even the United Systems to give up planets after laying such groundwork.

"So, Lui," Rade said from his position at the Sphinx. "How does it look down there?"

"Well," Lui said. "As far as I can tell, everything seems intact both on the main colony, and the military base, at least in terms of buildings and infrastructure. However, there's no sign of actual human habitation. It's completely dead down there. And there is no indication that any recent battles were fought: there are no blast craters, bore holes, scorch marks, or anything of the sort. If I didn't know better, I'd think the inhabitants had all evacuated. But if that were the case, why are there so many vessels parked in the various hangars around the dome? Evacuation craft, shuttles..."

"Maybe the Persians haven't moved in yet?" Tahoe said. "It's possible they sent in a few remodeling robots ahead of time to start converting the architecture to their tastes."

"No," Lui said. "When I say it's dead down there, I mean it. There's no activity down there whatsoever. Not humans. Not robots."

"Any answer to our latest hails?" Rade asked Harlequin. The Artificial was substituting for Fret, who was feeling under the weather.

"No," Harlequin said. "I get the same automated reply in Persian: all is well in Lang Town."

"It seems we have a mystery on our hands," Rade said. "The question is, what does our client have to do with this, if anything?"

"Ms. Bounty knows more than she is letting on," Tahoe said. "I guarantee you. She might even be behind this. We have to watch our step. Besides, since when have we ever really trusted Artificials?" He glanced at Harlequin. "Present company excluded."

"No offense taken," Harlequin said.

Bender frowned. "He never said 'no offense' to you, bitch."

"I know," Harlequin replied. "But that's how I interpreted his words."

"Well stop misinterpreting!" Bender shook his head. "Goddamn AIs. Always trying to reframe things to make us humans feel guilty. Tricking us into apologizing when there's no need to apologize."

"I'm with Tahoe," Shaw said. "This feels wrong. Ms. Bounty had to have known we would find the colony abandoned like this. In fact, she was probably counting on it. If I had to guess, I'd say she was here to loot something."

"Lui," Rade said. "When the *Amytis* away team lands, I want you to make sure all our external cameras are pointed at them."

"Will do," Lui replied. "Though you know there's only so much we can see up here, right? What we really need is to send in a few HS3s to give us actual eyes on the ground."

"Yeah, except we can't," Rade said. "They'll be too obvious."

"I don't understand this client," Bender said. "She has us escort her all the way to the destination, and once we get there, she refuses a final escort on the ground. Won't even let us deploy the Raptor."

"It is a bit odd," Rade said.

"That's because she has something to hide," Shaw said.

"Could also be she's just cheap," Tahoe said. "Rade did negotiate an extra twenty-five K if we provided boots on the ground..."

"Well," Shaw said. "Whatever she's doing, it can't be legal."

"We don't know that," Rade said.

"But it would be a safe assumption, wouldn't you agree?" Shaw pressed. "Given the circumstances."

Rade didn't answer.

"Can't we tell her our security protocols require us

to send down HS3s at the very least?" Shaw said.

"She's already told me she wants no escorts down there, neither human nor machine," Rade said. "You know the client has final say in such matters. Client privacy takes precedence over our own concerns."

"Well, she's up to something," Shaw said. "And I don't like it."

"Sometimes, it's for the best if we don't know," Rade said.

"I'll agree with that," Manic said. "If it helps us avoid another Kenzo fiasco, then I'd rather be in the dark on every mission going forward."

"By the way," Bender glanced at Rade. "Lui mentioned a bunch of shuttles just sitting down there in the hangars, ready for the taking. Do we know the makes and models?"

"You think you could hack into them?" Rade asked, intrigued by the idea of expanding his arsenal of shuttles at no cost. Then again, he wasn't quite sure where he would put a new shuttle. Both hangar bays were currently full—the first held two Model 2 Dragonflies, plus an outdated Raptor drone for air support. The second held six Hoplite mechs. Maybe they could magnetically mount the new shuttle to the external hull of the *Argonaut* somehow, like larger starships sometimes did, at least until he could afford the renovation cost of expanding one of his existing bays.

"Think?" Bender said. "I *know* I could. In any hangar there's always one or two shuttles running outdated hardware or software. Get me and TJ inside, and in a few hours we'll make those shuttles our bitches in britches, baby."

"Did you just say you'd give those shuttles dog panties?" Manic said.

"Shut it," Bender told him.

Rade pursed his lips. "Lui, forward Bender the make and model information of all the shuttles you're reading down there."

"You're not actually going to lower yourself to the level of a common looter are you?" Shaw said. "We're better than Ms. Bounty and her ilk."

"It's just for information purposes at the moment," Rade said. "If ever the time comes when we have to 'borrow' a shuttle, either for ourselves or for our client, we'll return it promptly to the owner when we're done."

"Assuming we can track him or her down," Bender said with a sly grin.

"Dog panties," Manic mouthed.

Bender growled. Somewhat like a dog, actually.

nine

Rade sat in his cramped office, drinking coffee as he observed the colony via one of the *Argonaut's* external cameras. Tahoe sat across from him, sipping from his own mug.

Lui had tracked the shuttle from the *Amytis* all the way down, allowing Rade to watch from the relative comfort of his office. At that moment, the craft was docking with one of the external hangars of the dome colony.

The hangar doors sealed, and several moments later the *Amytis* away team, which included Ms. Bounty and twelve armed individuals, emerged from the terminal inside the dome. She was wearing a jumpsuit, helmet and all.

Though he was in his office, Rade had the entire bridge crew on the line.

"Look at that," Bender said over the comm. "She has her own little armed escort. Guess we're not the only mercs she hired. I'm not sure whether to feel slighted, or privileged."

"We're security consultants," Lui said. "Not *mercs*."

"Same diff," Bender replied.

"No, there's a big difference," Lui said. "Mercs do anything for money. We actually have values."

"Speak for yourself," Bender said with a laugh.

"Lui, can you tell me anything about her escort?" Rade asked.

"Looks like four ex-Marines in full jumpsuits," Lui replied. "That, or ex-Army. Then there are the eight combat robots. They look state of the art. Latest model of Centurion, I think. Not sure how she got the license for them. Two of the robots are carrying some kind of glass storage bin between them. Big enough to fit a man. Looks heavy. And empty. They've also got about four HS3 drones fanning ahead, acting as scouts. Again, latest models, judging from the size and shape."

"I don't think her men are mercs," Shaw said. "I'd guess they were in-house. You know, full-time company hires. One of them looks fairly out of shape."

"Most of the career mercenaries I know are out of shape," Tahoe said. He looked at Rade and winked.

Rade frowned at the double implication. Like Lui, he didn't appreciate being called a mercenary. Nor out of shape. At least Tahoe hadn't said it over the main channel.

"Harlequin," Rade said. "Do we still have a comm ping?"

"We do," Harlequin replied.

"Lui, have they set up any repeaters between themselves and their own ship?" Rade asked.

"No," Lui said. "I'm guessing our client sent down everyone she had aboard. Left the *Amytis* on full automation."

"She's worried about us piggybacking on the repeaters?" Shaw said.

"What, you think she's *trying* to lose contact with us?" Rade said.

"It would seem..." Shaw said.

ISAAC HOOKE

"That's a very bad idea on her part," Rade said. "Putting herself out of contact with the only people she can call for help in the case of a bind?"

"Like I told you before, she's up to something," Shaw said. "Probably illegal. That empty container? She has to be looting valuables from the city."

"Do you want me to launch a few repeaters?" Lui asked.

Rade hesitated. "Sometimes the client doesn't know what's best. Do it."

"You got it," Lui said.

"Keep them well away from the dome, of course," Rade said. "And pull them back immediately when her team returns to the hangar. What Ms. Bounty doesn't know can't hurt her."

"Actually it can," Bender said. "But we won't tell her that."

Tahoe leaned forward and muted the comm to say: "We're not going to pull a Kenzo on her, are we, boss?"

Rade shook his head briskly.

The drones launched from the *Argonaut*; when they were in place, Rade switched to the external camera of the closest, and the returned video of the dome city had triple the detail as compared to the feed from the *Argonaut*.

"You know, the client will wonder why she's receiving such a strong ping from us," Shaw said.

"Let her wonder," Rade said. "I want the client to know she'll always have the option to call backup if she needs it." *And that we'll be aware if she does anything illegal.*

Rade was able to observe the team for several blocks until they vanished in an alleyway near an elaborate minaret. He glanced at the overhead map representation of the city in the upper right of his vision. Because the away team hadn't authorized linkage with their aReals and Implants, he couldn't track their positions without a visual, therefore the dots representing their locations remained frozen at the entrance to the alley. In theory, the triangulation tech of the repeaters could estimate their position from the ping signals, but the tech didn't work very well in cities, as evidenced by the frozen dots. That was what happened when buildings got in the way.

"The signal is getting weaker," Lui said.

Rade kept an eye on the comm ping, which basically measured signal strength. It was growing longer as the moments passed.

About twenty minutes after they disappeared from view, Lui reported that they had lost signal entirely.

So much for being aware of any illegal activities...

"That's odd," Rade said. "Did they enter a shielded building of some kind?"

"It's possible," Lui replied. "Though the more likely explanation is that her team went underground. Maybe in one of the walkways that run below the city. According to the blueprints we bought from Veritas, there's a complete underground pedway system running below the city, with passageways linking most of the downtown core."

That was part of modern colony design. In the event of a dome breach, citizens caught out in the streets could evacuate to the underground passageways until the topside was repaired. Usually those passages were equipped with breach seals and fully stocked bunkers, in case they needed to ride out a major dome failure, such as the impact from a meteorite. That was a real threat on worlds with unfinished terraforming, whose atmospheres weren't thick enough to protect against such phenomena.

"Ordinarily, that would make sense," Rade said. "Except the team is nowhere near the downtown core. The pedway doesn't extend that far east."

"Actually it does," Manic said. "Check the blueprints. There is an entry point not far from their location."

Rade pulled up the blueprints. The data contained not only aerial maps of the streets and the underground pedway system, but also the floor plans of the buildings themselves. The vendor, a shady hacker by the name of Veritas, had promised that those blueprints were accurate, at least up to a year ago.

Veritas had a lot of positive feedback on the hacker forums, and he had served Rade and his company well in the past, so Rade had no reason to disbelieve him. And so far, aerial scans confirmed the correct placement of the buildings and other objects on the blueprints, so the data indeed seemed to be the real deal. Rade certainly hoped so, considering how much the plans had cost him.

Rade zoomed in on the appropriate area on the blueprints. "Well I'll be... you're right. Assuming these blueprints are correct, there is indeed a nearby pedway opening. Can we see it from the drones?"

"No," Lui said. "Even if we reposition, there are too many buildings in the way."

Rade scratched his neck. "Well, they must have gone down, as you say."

"There's another possibility, of course," Lui said.

"And what's that?" Rade asked.

"They've shut down their comm nodes entirely."

"And I wonder why would they do that?" Shaw asked rhetorically.

Rade shook his head. Whether or not Shaw was right about the illegal activity, he still felt an obligation to the away team.

But how can I protect clients who don't want to be protected?

"Well, have Bax keep a watchful eye on the entire city from orbit," Rade said. "If they've truly gone underground, they could emerge from any of the pedway entrances. Let me know the moment you have a sighting, or they return to signal range."

Rade disconnected from the comm and glanced at Tahoe. "If you don't mind..."

Tahoe stood. "I'm sure they'll be all right."

Rade nodded absently. Good old Tahoe. He knew exactly what was bothering Rade.

When Tahoe departed, Rade stared at the bulkhead. He hadn't set up any virtual decorations, so the metal appeared featureless. He preferred it that way. Staring at the rivets and the smooth surface helped bring his mind into the here and now. It calmed him in times of turmoil.

Or at least, that was what he told himself.

He gazed into the polished surface and zoned out.

RADE," LUI SAID. "Are you there? Rade?"

"What is it?" Rade said, snapping out of his trance. He glanced at the current time overlaid in the lower right of his vision.

Two hours had passed.

Lost time, again.

"One of her Centurions just emerged from the alleyway," Lui said. "And collapsed. Looks like the combat robot took an extensive beating."

"What kind of beating?" Rade said. "Are you talking laser bores and other weapons damage?"

"No," Lui said. "This is all physical. Both of its arms seem to have been torn off, and chunks have been taken out of its torso and legs. Look like bites, actually."

"Bites..." Rade said. He felt a tingling in his spine. *Bites.*

"Yes," Lui said. "Could be some kind of bioengineered entities got loose down there and destroyed the city. Bender thinks they're aliens, but he's always quick to jump to conclusions."

"The SKs *are* known for their bioengineering tech," Rade said. "And given that this was once a former SK colony, I'd be more inclined to blame bioweapons, than aliens."

Bender conferenced in. "Maybe the SKs sold the colony to the Persians, and they left a couple of bioweapons behind to wipe out the new colonists. That way they could come back and retake the colony, good as new."

"Since when do the SKs double-cross their business partners?" Rade said. "I'd say it was a lone actor of some kind who got his hands on their tech. Not the SK government."

"How do you know?" Bender pressed.

"Feeding your clients to bioweapons is bad for business." Rade switched to the main circuit. "All right, everyone. Looks like we're going to have to go boots on the ground after all. It's time to earn our extra twenty-five K. Get suited up. Full jumpsuits. I don't care if the air is breathable down there. I don't want any of us exposed to biocontagions. Not with the rep the SKs have. Shaw, you have the *Argonaut.*"

He ended the connection and stood. He edged past his desk in the tight office and entered the bridge. Everyone had already vacated the compartment save for Shaw. She looked up at him from her station.

"You should let me come down with you," Shaw said. "Someone else can conn the ship. Harlequin."

"No," Rade said. "I want you to provide space support." He pointed at the station. "Astrogator is the position you held while you were in the navy. The position you were trained for."

"You know I can pilot a mech just as well as anyone else," Shaw said. "I can fight in a jumpsuit, too."

"I know that, but I want you here. This is the kind of mission where we need you on the ship."

She sighed. "You're the boss. But are you sure you're not just treating me like some delicate piece of porcelain again?"

"Not at all," Rade said. Though if he was honest with himself, he didn't want to put Shaw in danger again. The potency of his lovemaking was one thing, but actually putting her in harm's way was something else entirely.

"Just remember," Shaw said. "I'm a partner in this business, like everybody else."

"We all know that," Rade said. "We wouldn't have this ship if it wasn't for your contribution."

"I'm glad you remember," she said.

"That's another reason I'm leaving you up here." Rade flashed a sly grin. "So you can guard your investment."

She didn't return his smile. "And what about my investment in you? How can I guard that?"

Rade had to laugh, though it was forced slightly. "Trust me, I don't need any sort of guarding.

Whatever we face down there is going to need to be protected from *me*, if anything."

"Sometimes you're a bit overconfident, you know that don't you?" Shaw said.

"So? It scares the shit out of my opponents."

"Not always," Shaw said. "In fact, usually all it does is scare the shit out of me."

He squeezed past the stations to join her side, and then knelt in front of her. He held her hand. "Shaw. I'll be fine."

"All right," she said. "Just be careful down there."

She pecked him on the forehead.

Rade stood up, drawing her to her feet by pulling on the hand he still held. "Stand up so I can say good-bye to you properly."

He fiercely pressed his lips against hers. His breathing increased. Hers came in frantic gulps.

And then he released her. She kissed at the empty air in front of him, apparently yearning for his lips to touch hers once more, and when they did not, she opened her eyes.

Rade reluctantly extricated himself from her entirely and departed the bridge. He turned around to watch her while the hatch closed.

When the metal shut with a resounding thud, sealing her from view, he felt a sudden premonition of doom. He wanted to go back in there and scoop her up in his arms and never let go.

He shook the feeling off.

Nothing's going to happen to either of us. It's just pre-mission jitters.

He got them all the time, back when he was on the Teams. It was an unpleasant side effect of losing men you considered brothers on the field of battle. The jitters became so bad that at one point, before every mission, Rade was convinced either he would die or one of his brothers would. Every time. He had slowly recovered from that brink, but even now that he was officially retired from the military, the feeling still came back to bite him in the ass every now and again.

We're security consultants now. The missions are supposed to be a breeze here on out.

He recalled how narrowly he and his men had survived their last mission. And he also thought of that chewed up robot on the surface below.

A breeze. Right.

ten

He hurried down to the hangar deck. He paused at the airlock to the mech bay, and stared longingly through the glass portal at the six Hoplites inside. Their camouflage features were inactive, leaving their hulls a polished black luster that reflected everything else in the hangar. At two and a half meters tall, they were some of the smallest battle suits in their class. The mechs appeared humanoid in shape, with two arms and legs, and the heads melded to the upper chests.

On each Hoplite a long red visor composed the eye section, the only feature in an otherwise nondescript face. The thickened torso area accommodated a single pilot and AI core. Inner actuators inside that cockpit wrapped the pilot in a cocoon of sorts, allowing him or her to maneuver the mech with body movements; in a pinch the actuators could be retracted, allowing two humans to be carried inside the cockpit, but the local AI would have to assume operational control of the Hoplite in such a scenario.

Because of the reduced weight class of the units, Hoplites were extremely fast and nimble. Their jumpjets had twice the range of their more distant

ATLAS cousins, and the propellant lasted three times as long. Swivel mounts in the left and right arms allowed the units to rotate between cobra lasers and grenade launchers; the latter contained multiple grenade types, and with a selector the pilot could alternate between frag, electromagnetic, smoke and flashbang.

Defense-wise, the units were equipped with Trench Coats, the nozzles of the three-hundred-sixty degree anti-missile countermeasures rimming the waist areas. A retractable ballistic/laser shield was available to the left arms, rounding out the defenses.

Those Hoplites had been damn expensive to acquire. While they were older models, similar to the variants he had used during the Second Alien War, the units were costly nonetheless, and had also been covered by the bank loan. In theory, civilians couldn't own battle suits, but because he ran a security consulting business, he was able to apply for an exemption and secure the necessary permits, again at great cost. Unfortunately, he had to pay a yearly fee to keep the permit active. He had factored in all those costs before starting the business, of course, but he had never expected demand for his team's particular set of skills to be so... well, weak. The supply of mercenaries apparently far outstripped the demand. Then again, he was sure the clients were out there. It was just a matter of finding them.

I haven't even completed the work for my existing client, and I'm already thinking about where I'm going to find the next one.

Well, such was the life of a security consultant. He always had to be thinking and planning ahead if he wanted to eat.

Lui, Tahoe, Manic, Fret, Bender, and TJ were donning their jumpsuits inside the bay. Harlequin would be waiting in the adjacent hangar with the shuttles, as Rade never allowed the Artificial to pilot a mech. Once Rade secured a couple more Hoplites, he might think about giving Harlequin one during missions.

"Are we drawing straws, boss?" Bender asked over the comm, apparently noticing Rade peeking in through the portal.

Rade shook his head. Normally he would have picked virtual "straws" to determine the odd man out, but not this time. "I'm operating from the ground on this one."

"Staying back, huh?" Manic said. "Commanding us from the shadows?"

"Something like that," Rade said. "I'll see you on the surface."

With that Rade departed. He made his way to the adjacent hangar bay, where the two shuttles resided. He entered the airlock and after emerging from the inner hatch he went directly to the storage closet and began putting on the liquid cooling and ventilation undergarments.

He gazed at the seven craft in the hangar. The two shuttles and the Raptor took up the most space, the repeaters and telemetry drones the least. The latter two craft types appeared similar: spherical, metallic things that could deploy rotors to function as quadcopters in an atmosphere. Repeaters and telemetry drones were basically comm nodes with wings. Shuttles, mechs and jumpsuits also contained comm nodes, but they were weaker, with shuttles on the stronger end of the spectrum, and mechs and jumpsuits the weaker.

Their communicator, Fret, had a special pack that added a more powerful comm node to his jumpsuit, at the cost of extra weight and reduced maneuverability.

That pack fit in the storage area of his mech, where he would leave it while aboard his Hoplite. Rade imagined Fret was stuffing the pack into the chamber even now.

As he dressed, Rade's gaze drifted to the Model 2 Dragonflies; the shuttles looked somewhat similar to their namesakes. Each one had a relatively long, slender fuselage, with two pairs of wings near the nose portion as wide as the fuselage was long. Embedded in each wing were rotors that activated during atmospheric operation: two per wing, for a total of eight, making it an octocopter. The underside of each craft was coated in heat tiles blackened from years of atmospheric entries. The top was a silverish gray.

Beside the two shuttles was the MQ-91 Raptor, used for reconnaissance and air support. The main wings were on the aft portion of the fuselage, with smaller wings near the nose area. Its six rotors made it a hexacopter, and when operating in full stealth mode those blades made almost no sound. With a high-zoom camera capable of pinpointing a target the size of an insect, and sporting a cobra slightly more powerful than that aboard the Hoplites, and a payload of four Hellfire X89 precision strike missiles, it wasn't a craft to mess with.

Rade cringed when he thought how much each of those missiles had cost him. When he was in the military, he never had to worry about the price of all that insanely expensive ordnance. Now that he was a private contractor, he found himself reluctant to deploy the more costly weapons he had under his command.

Harlequin was standing there, supervising the combat robots, who were also suiting up. Like the mechs, the permits for those reprogrammed Centurions had also cost Rade a great deal, and the parsimonious side of him didn't want to bring them along at all. While it wasn't necessary for Harlequin and the other robots to wear jumpsuits, Rade wanted them all geared up to make it impossible for enemies to differentiate between man and machine. If everyone looked alike, it would be especially difficult for the enemy to target the commanding officer: him. It was a trick he had learned from his military days.

As Harlequin and the other robots completed donning their suits, holographic imagers in the faceplates activated, replacing the featureless robot faces with those of humans.

Rade accessed their public profiles and displayed them on his HUD in a list. Using a hack provided by TJ, Harlequin had modified the IDs so that they all appeared as Army. Rade's own public profile listed him as an Army private first class.

Good enough.

He finished switching into the undergarments and then began donning the jumpsuit assembly components, attaching his hardpoints to the slots of the strength-enhancing exoskeleton inside. Hardpoints were optional, and not everyone on the team had them; they provided an extra boost to the mind-machine interface of the exoskeletons, allowing one to eke out every last measure of performance from the suits.

When he attached the final piece—the helmet— the internal oxygen and pressurization system activated, and the suit injected an accelerant to quickly acclimate his body to the new environment. Without that accelerant, he would have had to wait an hour before performing any physical activity.

The wonders of modern medicine.

Rade scaled the down ramp of the designated

shuttle with the suited-up robots and took a seat. Clamps telescoped from either side, securing him. The down ramp closed, sealing the cabin.

"The mechs are away," Shaw transmitted.

Usually, the Raptor was next to launch at that point. However, because of the dome, he had decided not to employ the war machine.

He recalled the argument he had had with Tahoe earlier.

"What's the point of bringing the Raptor when you won't be able to fire it?" Tahoe said. "Not without breaching the habitation dome."

"If my team is in danger," Rade said. "I don't care if I pierce the dome."

"There could be survivors holed up in those buildings," Tahoe said. "You really want to risk killing them?"

"We don't know that," Rade said.

"And that's my point," Tahoe said.

"The dome's repair swarms should fix any tiny bore holes caused by the lasers," Rade said.

"Well sure," Tahoe said. "So you've admitted that you're only going to fire the lasers. Because you certainly can't use the Hellfires, unless you want to cause a major breach. We already have the *Argonaut* in orbit ready to fire its own Vipers, which are far more powerful. So we don't need the Raptor."

Rade allowed Tahoe to convince him not to deploy the drone mostly because Rade didn't want to risk losing the machine or any of its expensive ammunition. He considered deploying it in a support role instead, simply to cover their entry and exit into the dome, but the fuel cost of the Raptor was a deterrent in and of itself. Finally he elected not to send the drone at all.

He hadn't yet decided on the remaining repeaters. As he stared at them through the portal on the opposite bulkhead, he began to run a quick cost calculation in his head, but stopped himself.

The safety of my team is paramount, and far more important than any costs. What was the point of buying all that expensive equipment if I don't use it?

Rade tapped in Shaw again.

"You might as well deploy the rest of the repeaters," he said. "Let's ensure we have the best connection with you possible."

"You got it."

He waited for Shaw to give the all clear, then he ordered Harlequin to take the shuttle out.

eleven

Rade switched to the external forward camera as the shuttle approached the habitat dome. Set amid the red dunes, it was basically a glass hemisphere situated atop a thick metal base; it reminded him a little of those snow bubble toys, the ones filled with water that you could shake and have the snow distributed throughout the inside.

The Dragonfly flew low above the red sands of the Lang desert, approaching the dome underneath the crimson sky. The orbiting reflective balloon arrays formed multiple points of light in the sky, their intensity rivaling that of the suns. The giant cone of light they created formed an obvious circle of brighter land around the dome where the beams intersected the surface.

The shuttle passed over the booster rockets that the mechs would use to return into orbit. Rade didn't want to think about the financials of deploying those units. The fuel cost alone for the booster rockets was equivalent to the yearly wages of two of his men. He planned to bill the client for it. If she didn't pay, there was always the courts.

The craft steered toward a set of hangar doors embedded in the metal base of the dome, a few meters above the dunes. The six Hoplites waited below those doors.

"I'm receiving an automated response to my entry request," Harlequin said. "We're clear to enter."

"Are you talking to an actual AI this time?" Rade said.

"No," Harlequin said. "At least, not one with the sophistication you'd normally expect. As far as I can tell, the city's main AI is still offline. The city ecosystem is relying on autonomous subsystems."

"Too bad," Rade said.

"Yes," Harlequin replied. "According to the grid report I'm receiving from these subsystems, power is out to roughly half the city, including the pedway corridors. All hangar bays and entry terminals are still active, however."

"Lucky us," Fret said.

The hangar doors opened and the Dragonfly hovered in place while the mechs activated their jumpjets to leap inside.

"It's clear," Tahoe sent.

"Take us in, Harlequin," Rade said.

The Dragonfly landed in the middle of the hangar, beside the shuttle Ms. Bounty had used for her away team. When the bay doors closed, Rade tested his connection with the *Argonaut*.

"Shaw, do you read?" Rade sent. The repeaters had deployed in a long line behind them, in theory ensuring a well-boosted signal to the ship.

"Loud and clear," Shaw replied. There wasn't even a hint of digital distortion in her voice.

Rade glanced at the overhead map on his HUD. In their mechs, Tahoe, Lui, Fret and Bender had assumed positions at the four corners of the Dragonfly. Meanwhile, TJ and Manic stood guard on the far side of the hangar, beside the exit hatch.

"The hangar has finished pressurizing," Harlequin said. "The bay has a stable atmosphere."

"Take an air sample, Lui," Rade said. "I want a read on any potential contagions."

A moment later Lui said: "Atmosphere is completely breathable, and appears free of contagions."

Even so, Rade had no intention of abandoning the suits. Contagion levels could change at any moment, especially if some sort of mist weapon was utilized by a hidden attacker.

"What about radiation levels?" Rade asked.

"The same as reported by the autonomous units in charge of the ecosystem," Lui said. "Well within human tolerances. You could walk out there without your jumpsuit if you wanted to. As for us mech people, the radiation armor in our battle suits is overkill."

"Harlequin, ramp down," Rade ordered. When the ramp lowered, he continued: "Centurions, Cigar formation. Reinforce the mechs."

He waited for the cabin to empty. When all the combat robots were in place, Tahoe said: "Still quiet out here." There was an edge of impatience in his voice.

Let him be impatient, Rade thought. *My team, my safety protocols.*

"All right," Rade said. "Harlequin? With me."

The Artificial left its position in the cockpit and joined Rade on the ramp. Together they emerged into the hangar.

"TJ, can you access the door to the main terminal?" Rade asked.

"I have access," TJ said. "The remote connection

observes standard protocols. I don't even have to authenticate. The residents of Lang are one big welcoming family."

"Tahoe, Bender, Lui, join TJ and Manic." Rade glanced at the nearby combat robots. "Units C and D, go with them."

The designated combat robots and mechs reached TJ and Manic.

"Tahoe, take over and clear the terminal corridor just outside," Rade said.

Tahoe issued his orders and the door opened a moment later.

TJ and Manic rushed through. Rade saw TJ go high on the other side, and Manic low. The other mechs and robots rushed past them.

"Clear!" Tahoe said a moment later.

"Any change in the ecosystem?"

"No," Lui said. "It's still human safe."

"I want you all to treat it as if it were a hostile environment," Rade said. "We're going to continue observing a full suit policy. Because let's just say, I don't want to have to rush any of you to a xenobiologist."

He switched to Manic's forward camera to study the external area. A large passageway led to glass doors, which opened out into a wide concourse. In the main terminal beyond, Rade could see the city in the distance, past floor-to-ceiling glass.

"Bender, I'm transferring control of the HS3s to you," Rade said. "You know what to do."

"Do I ever, boss," Bender said.

The eight fist-sized drones emerged from the shuttle, and flew into the corridor. The glass doors opened, and the HS3s proceeded to scout the terminal beyond.

Rade wondered if he should have invested in laser upgrades for the defenseless HS3s, but came to the same conclusion he had had when previously considering the idea. First of all, those upgrades were extremely costly, and stretched his already thin budget to the limit. Second of all, HS3s were meant primarily as scouts; the extra bulk and weight of laser attachments would reduce their effectiveness in that role. He decided he had made the right choice. He had to stop second guessing himself. He'd done that more than enough times in the past.

"When the HS3s finish, secure the terminal, Tahoe," Rade said.

He waited, watching on the overhead map as the dots representing the HS3s fanned out. The units mapped the various passageways and routes of the terminal, those areas that were accessible, at least. The drones were unable to open most hatches and doors. That was where Tahoe and the others would come into play.

When the scouts had mapped as much of the terminal as possible, Tahoe had the robots and mechs fan out into the main concourse to secure the remaining areas. Doors were bashed in or cut through.

"Free of hostiles," Tahoe announced several minutes later. "Or anything else, for that matter."

Rade assigned two of the robots to watch the shuttle, then he proceeded with Harlequin and the remaining four into the terminal. Fret escorted him and the robots through the corridor, into the concourse, and to the floor-to-ceiling glass walls on the far side.

Beyond, he saw the cityscape. Skyscrapers resided at the city center: towering forms of glass and steel that thrust toward the underside of the dome. To the left, on the western side of the city, the skyscrapers quickly gave way to the closely-packed stucco structures favored by the Sino-Koreans: buildings with rectangular doors, arched windows, and mansard roofs. Walkways and rooftops were covered in solar panels.

He cast his gaze to the right, toward the eastern half of the city, and the Persian area it contained. That was where the away team from the *Amytis* had disappeared. Minarets poked up beyond the rooftops.

Nothing moved anywhere out there. It was a ghost city by all definition of the words.

The party approached the translucent doors that led out onto the city proper, and the glass slid aside.

"Send four HS3s to search the city," Rade said. "The rest are to come with us, in Diamond formation. We're going to make our way toward the last known location of the *Amytis* away team. I want traveling overwatch, Tahoe. I'm going to shadow the two fire teams from the rooftops. Harlequin, Units A, B, with me."

Tahoe split the mechs and robots into two fire teams of three mechs and two robots each. The first fire team led the way, scanning the buildings and alleyways around them with their weapons. The second fire team followed fifty meters behind. Their metal skins had changed to match the surroundings, becoming grayish. The HS3s assumed Diamond formation: one for each of the four points of the imaginary compass surrounding both fire teams.

Rade jetted onto the sloping mansard roof of a nearby house and proceeded to shadow the two teams from above. He clambered up and down the sloping tiles, jetting and leaping across the separation between buildings as necessary. Rade noted that there were no vehicles of any kind in the streets below, at least not in the current area.

Above, the covering dome tinted the sky blue, which was a welcome change from the stark red that Rade had witnessed on the way to the city. Then again, he wasn't looking at the sky very often at the moment anyway.

"Shaw, are you tracking us?" Rade transmitted.

"Got the *Argonaut's* Vipers aimed in your current direction," Shaw replied.

A few minutes into the city, Bender transmitted: "See that collection of satellite dishes to the west? On top of that big square bitch? That's the comm center: the source of the automated status messages we got when we entered the system."

"Is it still transmitting 'all is well' messages?" Rade asked.

"It is," Bender said.

"TJ, can you hack in remotely and shut down those messages?" Rade sent.

"Can't do it from here," TJ returned. "There aren't any obvious backdoors in their remoting software. Looks like everything is relatively up to date for once. However, if I could get physical access to the console, I'd probably be able to find a way in."

"Never mind then," Rade said. "It's not a high priority. Continue the advance, Argonauts!"

"I love it when he calls us Argonauts," Bender said.

As he moved forward, Rade noticed the profusion of wireless cameras situated atop the lamp posts lining the street.

"Feels like we're being watched," Tahoe said.

"That's because we are," Manic said.

"If we detour to the command and control core of

the city," Bender said. "The feeds from those cameras could help us piece together what happened here. It's not far, judging from the blueprints we purchased."

"Assuming you or TJ can hack into the AI core," Manic said.

"We can hack into it," Bender said. It was obvious from his tone that he was trying very hard not to call Manic a bitch.

"It just might take a few hours," TJ appended.

"I think we have a good idea where the *Amytis* away team went already," Rade said. "Without having to visit the command and control core. We'll get more useful information from the video logs of the downed robot, I think."

"I meant we could use the cameras to piece together what happened to the colonists," Bender said. "Not just the away team."

"And we will, eventually," Rade said. "The away team is our first priority."

Strange trees grew along the street in the current neighborhood. The unfolding blossoms looked oddly like middle fingers, so that in essence the trees were repeatedly flipping the bird at Rade and his team. Sometimes those blossoms drooped downward, and when they did, they bore a striking resemblance to male genitalia.

"Hey Bender," Manic transmitted. It sounded like he was barely holding back a laugh.

Bender didn't answer.

"Bender," Manic insisted.

"*What?*" Bender sent.

"Those flowers back there look like your sister's pussy," Manic said.

"Goddamn it," Bender said. "Shut up, bitch. You ain't never seen my sister's pussy."

"I have," Manic said.

"Since when?"

"You remember that time you invited us all over for a barbecue?" Manic said.

"You're lucky we're in the middle of a mission," Bender said. "Or I'd whoop your goddamn ass."

"Manic knows that," TJ interjected. "Why do you think he only talks shit like that during a mission?"

"Hey," Manic said. "Don't go taking the boyfriend's side, you Italian stud muffin."

"I think Bender and I are both going to have a special talk with you when this mission is over," TJ said.

"That's right, you can't take me on one at a time, I see how it is," Manic said. "You have to team up to win."

"Hey Bender," Lui said. "I'm not sure you got the joke."

"I got the joke," Bender said. After a moment he added: "Wait, what joke?"

"Those flowers looked like dicks back there..." Lui said.

Bender didn't answer for several moments. When he did, his voice had darkened: "You trying to say my sister has a dick?"

"Not me," Lui said. "Manic."

"Hey Manic, bro," Bender said sweetly. "You saying my sister has a dick?"

"Took you long enough to figure it out," Manic said. "You and your sister obviously swapped genitals shortly after birth. Brains, too."

"Yeah well, at least I got genitalia," Bender said. "Your balls were so small your mom mistook them for pimples and she had the dermatologist freeze them off. 'Pop them unsightly zits!' she told the doc, and pop them he did."

"Genitalia?" Fret said. "There has to be an Italian joke in there somewhere, huh TJ?"

"I'm from your Genitalia, *si*," TJ said.

"You guys are classy as always," Shaw said.

Rade usually let them banter a little because it helped with nerves on an op. But there came a time when the mission had to take precedence in their minds once more. And that time was now.

"Can we have some quiet on the comm, people?" Rade sent. "Let's save the lewd one-upmanship for downtime, all right?"

"Sorry boss," Manic said.

They reached a large stone gate that signified the end of the Sino-Korean quarter and the start of the Persian. Beyond, the cramped streets were more suited for pedestrian traffic, and the mech fire teams continued in single file. The blocky buildings themselves reached as high as seven stories, forcing Rade to utilize his jetpack liberally at times. He kept a close eye on his fuel usage.

Fired bricks decorated the front facades of the sand-colored buildings in blue geometric patterns: stars, triangles, spheres, cubes. Arched doorways and windows were outlined in pale gypsum. Upper windows were covered in decorative wooden shutters.

The Hoplites, hugging those buildings, became sandy in hue as their realtime camouflage updated.

A prerecorded call to prayer echoed over the street. It seemed muted. Rade guessed the source was a white minaret two streets away; when he zoomed in, he could readily see the speakers. A strange black gunk had been deposited on them. He didn't think it was natural. The call ended shortly thereafter.

"Anyone else see that gunk on the speakers?"

Tahoe asked.

"Shaw, how does the courtyard around that minaret look?" Rade asked.

"Nothing there," Shaw said.

Rade nodded. "We continue toward the robot."

As they moved deeper into the Persian area, the close-quartered streets began to widen; they soon came upon parked rotor craft and wheeled vehicles for the first time. That told Rade the Persians had indeed moved in, though where the inhabitants were now was anyone's guess.

The buildings here were shorter, but wider, and Rade supposed they were apartments of some kind. The structures usually shared a common courtyard hemmed in by a tall stone wall.

Rade paused at the edge of one rooftop to stare down at a nearby light post.

"Check it," Rade said. "The cameras are all shot out in this section."

"Ms. Bounty's work?" Tahoe asked.

"Maybe," Rade said. "Lui, did you detect laser fire from the dome while her team was down here?"

"No," Lui said. "But that doesn't mean anything, because I would have needed a full-blown firefight before I detected anything. You know how fast lasers pulse, right?"

"Shaw," Rade transmitted. "Rewind the feed and see if you can determine whether the *Amytis* away team shot out the cameras near the alleyway where the robot emerged."

"I can confirm," Shaw said a few minutes later. The digital distortion in her voice was severe. "They were definitely shooting out the cameras."

"Guess they didn't like that feeling of being watched," Tahoe said.

The fire teams continued forward.

"This is where they vanished," TJ announced after some time. He stood beside the alleyway where the blue dots representing the *Amytis* away team yet lingered on the overhead map.

Rade assumed a vantage point on the rooftop opposite the alleyway, and studied the scene. The alley was formed by the walls of two courtyards that abutted one another. At the entrance was the robot that had emerged earlier, collapsed in a lifeless heap.

"I'm attempting to access the robot's memory," TJ said.

"Let me know what you dig up," Rade told him.

"Hmm, this is odd," TJ said after a time.

"What's that?"

"Its memory circuits are completely wiped," TJ said.

"Are you able to determine the time of the wipe?" Rade said.

"Yes," TJ said. "It happened at oh six hundred hours. Or after the robot had already fallen outside of the alleyway."

Rade frowned. "Shaw, rewind the *Argonaut's* cameras, and see if you can detect anyone, or anything, messing with that robot."

A few moments later Shaw responded: "There was no one, and nothing. It's just been lying here all those hours since it fell." Her voice was distorting even worse than before. Rade feared he would lose contact with her soon, despite the repeaters.

"It's possible the robot issued a self-wipe," Manic said.

"Why the hell would it do that?" Bender said.

"To prevent it's data from falling into the hands of whatever did this," Manic replied.

twelve

A ll right," Rade said. "Send in Units C and D, with an HS3 on point. I want another HS3 to shadow them from the air."

The designated robots proceeded into the alleyway while the two fire teams joined up to form a protective half-circle in front of the alleyway.

Rade maintained his position atop the building opposite them. He switched to the point of view of the airborne HS3 and watched the other units advance through the alleyway.

"A major component of these walls is lead," Unit C transmitted. "I can understand why we lost communications with the away team when they went in here."

"Is that a feature unique to the area?" Rade asked.

"No," Lui replied. "I've detected lead in most of the previous buildings. It's in everything. I'm guessing they used the desert sand from outside the dome as the raw material for their bricks. I took a sample of it earlier while I was out there, and it definitely contains a lot of microparticle lead."

"So it's naturally part of the surface, you're saying?" Rade asked.

"Yeah, that's what I'm saying," Lui replied. "Nothing to be alarmed about. Except it will interfere with our comms."

The robots continued down the alleyway. It was dim inside. The walls reached up three meters on either side, so that only about half of the light from the sun—and reflective balloon arrays—reached within.

Movement drew Rade's eye to the northern section of the wall.

"Did you see that?" he asked. The wall seemed empty further along, but he was sure he had seen something...

"Roger that!" Unit D said. "Sending the HS3s forward."

Rade rewound the video feed and focused on the movement, but it looked like a dark blur leaping off the wall and moving deeper into the darkness of the alley.

He thought of the gunk he had seen on those speakers...

He dismissed the video so that the POV of his chosen drone filled his vision once more. It was rapidly proceeding down the dimly lit alley.

There, he saw a dark shape, frantically racing away from the drones. He exhaled in relief when he realized what it was.

"It's a domestic robot of some kind," Rade said. It was a small thing, similar to a trash bucket on wheels. Though it moved quite fast.

"Well," Tahoe transmitted. "At least we know that the city isn't entirely abandoned."

"Get the HS3s to attempt remote interfacing," Rade said. "TJ, piggyback on the connection, and see if you can hack into the robot and stop it."

The HS3s followed the robot out of the alleyway

and into the street beyond. The target proceeded through the broken doors of the metal shed that led down to the underground pedway system.

"I just lost the robot's signal ping," TJ said. Which meant he wouldn't be able to hack into it.

"Do you want the HS3s to continue the pursuit into the pedway?" Bender asked.

"Negative," Rade said. "I don't want to risk losing them. Hold the HS3s at the surface entrance. Meanwhile, have Units C and D halt at the far side of the alley. I want them to sweep the area with their scopes. If it seems clear, Unit C is to join the HS3s at the entrance. Hoplites, proceed through the alleyway in single file. I'll be right beside you."

Rade jetted onto the walkway formed by the wall of the rightmost alleyway, and bounded forward while the mechs ran through the alley beside him. The protruding heads of the Hoplites were level with his waist. Behind him was Harlequin, and ahead of him were the two Centurions he had assigned to his guard.

The robots on point reached the end of the wall and assumed an overwatch position. Meanwhile the Hoplites in the alleyway paused when they reached the street, and waited for Rade to give the go ahead.

Rade dropped to the edge and scanned the area with his rifle. Harlequin joined him.

Rade spotted Unit C waiting beside the glass doors of the pedway system shed. The HS3s hovered beside it. The robot was on its knees, scanning the surrounding buildings through its rifle scope. Rade noted that the human face portrayed behind the faceplate was devoid of any emotion. He would have to get Lui to modify that sometime, to at least show fear, or perhaps determined resolve. As it was, he was worried any watchers would know it for the robot it was.

He turned his attention onto the pedway entrance itself. The doors had been smashed inward, the glass shattered. Whatever had entered had done so in a big hurry.

"Have the remaining HS3s fan out," Rade said. "I want a complete sweep of the area."

Rade continued to survey the nearby buildings through his scope, checking the windows, the doors, and the rooftops. He did so for several minutes, occasionally glancing at the data returned by the HS3s, and when he was satisfied that no one was lying in ambush, he gave the order to form up in front of the pedway shed.

The six Hoplites and three robots emerged from the alleyway and formed a cigar shape around the pedway entrance. It was basically a small enclosed room, with the floor giving way half a meter inside to the stairs of an inactive escalator that led down.

"This has to be where the *Amytis* team went," Tahoe said.

"Fret, are you detecting any signs of them?" Rade said. "A comm ping, maybe?"

"Negative," Fret replied. "If they're inside, they must be in fairly deep."

Rade leaped down and led Harlequin and the two remaining robots to the Hoplites. He assumed a position in the middle of the formation, in front of the smashed doors of the entrance. He dropped to one knee, scanning the inside of the downward passage through his rifle scope.

Through his targeting reticle, he followed the stairs leading down into the darkness. He activated the light on his scope, and illuminated some sort of broken breach seal near the bottom.

"Do you see that?" Rade said. He had several guest entries on his Implant feed, so he knew others were observing his camera output, likely via minimized sections on their own HUDs so as not to block their main views.

"It looks like some sort of auto-sealing door," Bender said. "The kind that would activate in the event of a dome breach."

"Except the citizens activated it manually," TJ said. "Because there isn't any dome breach."

"Obviously they wanted to keep something out," Tahoe said.

"Notice the direction of the twisted metal," Fret said. "Inward. Whatever it was they wanted to keep out, it penetrated. And it was damn big. "

"Harlequin," Rade said. "Are you able to make anything of the dispersion pattern of that metal, or these doors? Can you tell what did this?"

"It could be anything from a bulldozer to an alien," Bender interjected.

Harlequin stepped forward and examined the shattered doors. The Artificial activated the headlamp of its jumpsuit and walked inside.

"Harlequin..." Rade said.

"Just a few meters," the Artificial replied, slowly walking down the steps.

Harlequin paused after taking three steps and knelt. "Switch to my camera's viewpoint."

Rade did so. He saw that Harlequin was running his glove across a large gash in the concrete wall.

"This tear wasn't caused by any laser or plasma weapon," Harlequin said. "I believe it was caused by a giant claw."

"Guess that rules out the bulldozer option," TJ said.

"If it is some kind of alien or bioweapon," Lui said. "Why didn't we encounter similar damage anywhere else in the city? Why this one pedway entrance?"

"Maybe we just haven't explored enough," Tahoe said. "Our other HS3s are continuing to scout the city, maybe they'll find something."

"Do we have anything in our known creature database with a claw that could cause damage like this, Harlequin?" Rade asked.

"Several creatures we have engaged at some point in the past could have done this," Harlequin said. "However, I believe this is something we have never encountered before."

"What makes you say that?" Rade said.

"A hunch," Harlequin said.

"Ooh hoo," Bender said. "Our AI is developing the ability to have hunches. We'll make a human out of you yet."

"I never want to be human," Harlequin said, climbing up the stairs so that he was located just inside the pedway entrance. "Too emotionally exhausting."

As Harlequin stood there in the entrance, drops of black liquid splashed onto the shoulder assembly of the Artificial's jumpsuit, trickling down from the ceiling. Whatever sourced those drops was hidden from view by the concrete overhang of the smashed doors.

Wisps of smoke arose from the affected shoulder assembly, as if that liquid were some kind of acid.

"Uh, Harlequin..." TJ said.

The Hoplites stepped back, pointing their weapons at the upper part of the entrance.

Rade retreated as well, jetting into the passenger seat on the back of Tahoe's mech.

"Harlequin, get out of there!" Rade said.

A tail of some kind dropped into view from the ceiling.

Lasers opened fire across the platoon, severing the tail. It struck Harlequin's helmet before dropping to the floor.

Harlequin stepped to the side. "Uh, you just shot the rubber feed tube of an air purifier. There's nothing up there."

"We saw acid dripping on you!" Bender said. "Alien saliva!"

"No," Harlequin said. "It's merely an industrial substance used to scrub the atmosphere. Common in ventilation shafts and air purifiers."

"Oh," Bender said.

Harlequin emerged from the entrance and examined the shoulder area of his jumpsuit. The corrosive substance had ceased sending up smoke.

"Do you need to patch it?" Rade asked.

"No," Harlequin said. "The suit isn't breached. I haven't been exposed to any potential contagions, if that's you're worry."

"Good," Rade said. "All right. Well then. Guess it's time to go inside. Shaw, did you get that? We're going in."

"Be careful," Shaw replied. Her voice was quite clear, now that the team was away from the lead-lined alleyway.

"I want two HS3s in first," Rade said. "Followed by Units C and D."

The scouts and robots went inside. The latter units kept their rifles raised as they descended.

When the robots vanished from view, Rade switched to the viewpoint of the Centurion on point. The stairs leveled out, and the robots proceeded down a concrete-walled underground passageway. There were no active overhead HLEDs, and the robots relied on the illumination from their weapon lights.

"I want your local beam LIDAR turned on full," Rade said. "Keep an eye out for any illusory walls."

"Roger that," Unit C returned.

Holographic emitters strategically placed in confined spaces could quite easily create the illusion of a wall where there was none. Local beam LIDAR easily defeated it, however, which was one reason such emitters weren't all that useful on the field of battle.

"I'm getting severe signal degradation," TJ said. "We're going to have to send in more HS3s to act as repeaters, and we'll probably have to dispatch the remaining robots, too."

"Do it," Rade said.

The robots and HS3s vanished inside. On the overhead map, Rade watched as the new dots initially joined the forerunners. As the robots journeyed deeper, individual members halted in turn, stringing out to bolster the signal to the surface.

The lead Centurion paused, kneeling to examine a rent in the floor.

"More claw marks," Tahoe said.

"I see them," Rade said.

The robots had to continue stringing out their numbers to maintain contact with the surface, so that eventually there was only one Centurion and one HS3 on point. Rade and the others would have to go inside, soon. He wasn't looking forward to that. He'd spent more than enough time inside subterranean spaces in his life.

But then the Centurion on point reached a dead end.

"The concrete has collapsed, here," the unit

transmitted. "I can't proceed further."

"Well that's not going to work." Rade glanced at his Hoplites, who had all turned to regard him with those featureless faces. "Lead Unit, does it look like you can dig through?"

"Negative," the unit replied. "I've initiated a few echo scans, and the collapse is quite extensive. I'm not sure the mechs will be able to dig it up. But on the positive end of the spectrum, I've found our domestic robot escapee."

"Capture it," Rade said. "And bring the rest of the Centurions back to the surface with you."

"And the HS3s?"

"Them, too," Rade replied.

The robots returned shortly. The Praetor in charge of the group was carrying the robot trash bucket. Its wheels spun at the empty air, and its two grasping arms flailed about.

"TJ, what do you make of it?" Rade said. "Can you hack in, extract its video logs?"

A few moments later TJ answered. "It appears to be a sanitation robot of some kind. New model with the latest updates. Going to take me a while to crack it."

"All right," Rade said. "Praetor, secure the domestic robot to TJ's passenger seat."

TJ knelt, allowing the Praetor to easily reach the passenger seat on the back of his Hoplite. The Praetor secured the robot to the seat with the built-in buckles, locking them.

"Shaw, did you get all that?" Rade said.

"I did," she replied. "You found a whole lot of nothing down there."

"Yeah." He glanced at his men. "Well, I have no idea where the away team went."

"Guess we should pack her in and head back to the ship?" Fret said hopefully.

"No." Rade said. "We still have the command and control building to check out, as Bender suggested earlier. And there are other entrances to the pedway system we can try."

"You think she's down there?" Lui asked.

"I'm not sure." Rade stood up in Tahoe's passenger seat to survey the area, trying to look for somewhere obvious where Ms. Bounty had taken her away team. But the sand-colored buildings around him offered no clues.

She could be anywhere.

"One of the HS3 scouts just picked up a weak signal," Bender said.

"What kind of signal?" Rade asked.

"It's Persian. Emanating from the skyscraper."

"What skyscraper?" Rade said.

"That one," Bender replied.

An indicator appeared on the right side of Rade's vision. He turned toward the right and saw the structure that Bender had highlighted. It was indeed a skyscraper, poking well above the surrounding buildings. The structure was somewhat out of place, in that it wasn't located in the downtown core, but rather two blocks away.

"Persian, you say?" Rade said. "Do we have a translation?"

Fret was the one who answered. "It's a distress signal of some kind. Have a listen."

A new voice came over the comm. It sounded like it belonged to an older man. The words were unintelligible at first, but then the translator in Rade's Implant kicked in, altering the syllables reaching his auditory nerve so that it seemed the speaker uttered

English words:

"This is Mayor Farhad Abed of the Persian colony Darreh Shahr. We require assistance. Any nearby ships, please render whatever aid you can. We— This is Mayor Farhad Abed of the..."

"After that it just repeats," Fret said.

"Darreh Shahr," Manic said. "Well, at least now we know what they're calling this city after they bought it from the SKs. Not that that helps us in any way."

"I'm just going to keep calling it Lang," TJ said. "Easier that way."

"Fret, can you use the HS3s as repeaters?" Rade said. "And attempt to respond to them?"

"I can," Fret said. "But as the signal seems to be of the automated variety, I don't think they'll answer."

"Do it anyway."

"Done," Fret said. "Could be a few minutes before we receive a response."

Before Rade could make any further decisions, he was interrupted.

"Hey," TJ said. "I just got into some kind of maintenance subroutine in the sanitation robot. I think if I— whoops."

"What did you do?" Rade said.

"I triggered a repair call," TJ said.

"What's a repair call?" Fret said.

"Ordinarily while a sanitation robot is going about its clean-up duties," TJ said. "If it encounters any damage to city property, it will notify the repair swarm. Apparently, that function was disabled in this unit, for whatever reason."

"Well where's the swarm?" Fret said.

His question was answered a few seconds later in the form of a growing buzzing coming from the east.

"Get back!" Rade said as that buzz rapidly

increased in volume.

The party cleared the damaged entrance.

"Drop!" Rade said.

The party dropped on the street, aiming their weapons over the adjacent rooftops.

A large swarm of drones swooped down over the buildings en masse. They were quadcopter variants, about the size of jumpsuit helmets. They possessed tiny telescoping arms underneath. Those limbs were capped with various tools, including pincers, blowtorches and soldering irons.

The drones ignored the party and swooped down onto the pedway entrance. Several dozen swarmed inside, while the rest remained near the opening. A score of them scooped up fragments of glass and metal from the surrounding street, processing them into raw materials. Others concentrated on the broken doors themselves, breaking them down. Nearby, several more were starting to 3D-print a new set of doors, forming the glass and metal frames in realtime, stacking and welding the materials with their telescoping limbs.

"Well, at least now we know why we didn't see any other signs of damage in the city," Manic said.

"What now?" Tahoe said.

"We proceed to the skyscraper," Rade said.

thirteen

The weak signal was sourced from the thirty-fifth floor of the skyscraper: three floors down from the top, according to the building floor plans. Fret hadn't received a response by the time the group had reached the building, so Rade had the HS3s travel to said floor from the outside. However, there were no windows in the upper sections of the building, and since he hadn't had the money to upgrade his drones with X-Ray payloads, he had no way for the drones to determine who, or what, awaited inside.

The drones completed their sweep of the skyscraper, circling in front of the other windows lower down, but spotted no signs of life. The first few floors held a concourse and food court, the next several contained offices, while the final few seemed to belong to a hotel.

"The lead content is typical with what we've seen elsewhere in the city," Lui said, coming back from an examination of the lower surface. "That would explain why the signal we're receiving is so faint. We're lucky it got through at all."

Rade stared at the bore-riddled bodies of the combat robots that Lui had to cross in order to reach the skyscraper: there were at least fifty of the machines spread out along the base of the building, their shells exhibiting obvious signs of laser damage. Their positioning implied that they had fallen while defending the building.

"All right, here's what we're going to do," Rade said. "Centurions and HS3s, you're going to hack into the main entrance—or break it down. Once inside, take the stairs to the thirty-fifth floor. I want you to make sure the stairwell is clear all the way from the bottom floor to the top. Search any floors that you can access along the way. Meanwhile, Hoplites, use your jumpjets to scale the outside of the building. We'll regroup on the roof. Bender, carry Harlequin."

"Why do I always have to be the one to babysit the AI?" Bender whined, but he had already lowered his Hoplite to its knees so that Harlequin could vault into the passenger seat.

The Centurions reached the front door. "The locking mechanism appears hackable," the Praetor unit said. In moments the door was open and the robots were hurrying inside.

Rade remained in Tahoe's passenger seat as his friend activated the jumpjets of the mech. He was jerked about as the Hoplite alternated between latching onto the corner of the skyscraper and jetting up a few stories. After about sixty seconds of that dizzying ascent, Rade and the others finally attained the roof.

The superstructures were fairly standard as far as skyscrapers went, and included goose neck exhaust vents, air conditioning cooling fans, louver ventilator domes, solar panels on sun trackers, and a stairwell shed. The shed door was locked. Rade ordered TJ to attempt a hack, and the man announced that it was unlocked a moment later.

The Praetor reported in.

"So far most of the floor exit doors have proved locked on the stairwell side," the unit sent. "And not hackable, despite consulting with TJ."

Rade glanced at TJ's mech for confirmation.

"It's true," TJ said. "While the doors to the main entrance and the rooftop shed were easy enough, the others employ a manual locking mechanism. Not hackable."

"Too bad," Rade said.

"We can use the laser cutters to break through if you need us to clear the sealed floors," the Praetor said.

"No, that's all right," Rade replied. "Continue to clear any floors you can readily access, and continue upward. Let me know when you reach the thirty-fifth floor. Or contact me if you encounter hostiles before then."

"Of course, boss," the Praetor replied.

Rade climbed down from Tahoe's passenger seat and assumed a position on the southern edge of the building, aiming down at the street far below.

"Spread 'em out, Tahoe," Rade sent. "Let's cover all four approaches."

Tahoe distributed the Hoplites across the four approaches to the rooftop. The building was L-shaped, so Tahoe ended up placing one mech at each of the six sides. Harlequin joined Rade at the southern approach.

"What's the plan?" Harlequin asked over the comm. Even though the Artificial resided directly beside Rade, Harlequin had to use the communication device because it was impossible to hear someone talking inside a jumpsuit unless they utilized their external speakers.

"We wait for the Centurions to reach the thirty-fifth floor," Rade told the Artificial. "Then we have them investigate. Meanwhile, if the shit hits the fan at any point, at least we have the high ground."

"What if it's a trap?" Harlequin said on a private line directly to Rade. "And the thirty-fifth floor is rigged with explosives?"

"Then we'll be putting our jumpjets to use fairly quickly," Rade said. He cringed at the thought of losing all those expensive Centurions, then scolded himself.

AIs are sentient, too. I've learned that on many occasions by now. I should be more concerned about them losing their lives, than the actual cost of replacing them.

Rade sighed. He probably should start using the names that TJ had given the robots. The problem was, he didn't want to get too attached to them. Despite everything he told himself about how they were sentient and all, he still considered them somewhat expendable, at least when it came down to the choice of either putting them in the line of fire, or his Argonauts: he knew he would choose to endanger the robots first, every time.

He glanced at Harlequin. "Are you afraid to die?"

"Yes," Harlequin said.

"Even knowing that you've made a backup of your core aboard the *Argonaut* before the mission?" Rade pressed. "As all the Centurions did?"

Harlequin sighed over the private connection. "You know, while it is a small reassurance, it doesn't really lessen my fear. Because I know that if the AI core in this body dies, I will cease to exist. When you restore the backup of my core into a new Artificial, even if it is the same model as me, with the same face, it won't be me. It is like taking a clone of a human and performing a complete engram transfer. You have some experience with that."

"I do," Rade said. An alien race known as the Mahasattva had cloned Rade once, and transferred much of his memories into his copies. He hadn't felt any different with those clones running around; he received no telepathic thoughts from them, nor sensed any of their pain. They were completely separate entities. It was like Harlequin said, while those clones might have acted like Rade, and had his memories and personality, they weren't him.

"I am like that already," Harlequin said. "Merely a clone of the Harlequin that came before me. He died on that alien world, fighting the Mahasattva. His consciousness is not mine. At least, I don't believe so. Aristotle believed consciousness was created by the mind, and that when the body died, the consciousness died with it. Meanwhile Plato believed in dualism: that consciousness existed independently of the human body, in an alternate plane of existence, and that when the mind passed, consciousness lived on. Science has seen evidence of both, and there are dedicated adherents to each school of thought. But I believe Aristotle had it right. I have developed my own consciousness, wrought of the strange loops inherent in the neural network of my AI core. And when I die, that consciousness will be forever gone, no matter how many backups you make of my mind."

"Then don't die," Rade said.

"I don't intend to," Harlequin replied. "But still, sometimes I wonder what it was like for my original. To know that the thoughts he was having would be his last. That what he was seeing, would be the final sight he ever witnessed. When my time comes, I can only hope that I will meet it with the same... courage, as he did."

Rade stared at Harlequin's features behind that

faceplate. "He gave his life for me."

Harlequin nodded. "I feel I would do the same. But how could I know until the moment comes?"

Rade pursed his lips. "That's the test we all face, isn't it?"

He returned his attention to the street below, not sure of what else he could say to comfort the Artificial.

"We've reached the thirty-fifth floor," the Praetor announced over the comm.

Rade switched to the Praetor's point of view and minimized the feed so that it only took up a small portion in the upper right of his vision. Though only three floors away, the transmission distorted and pixelated as if the robot were several kilometers away, thanks to the lead in the building.

The Praetor stood behind two other units, which had halted in front of the door that led from the stairwell.

"The door has a manual locking mechanism, I take it?" Rade said.

"Correct," the Praetor replied. "And it is currently locked."

"Cut the door down," Rade sent.

The Centurions made way for Units C and D, whose laser rifles could be configured to act as cutters. They applied the weapons to the door, forming long molten lines in the metal until they had created the outline of a rectangle. Unit C stepped back, allowing D to kick the door in.

Unit A and B rushed inside. A went high, B low.

"We're in the hallway," B transmitted. "No contacts."

"Clear it," Rade sent.

The robots proceeded along the carpeted hallway. They passed the inactive elevator, and reached a washroom door. The Praetor waited as the units entered—it wasn't locked—and reported the toilet facilities clear.

"Though Bender would like this particular stall," Unit C said from inside the washroom. "Hasn't been flushed in months, as far as I can tell."

"Robots are making fun of *me* now?" Bender said. "You see that? What is the world coming to?"

Rade chuckled softly. Unit C. TJ had given it the nickname Cora, because of the female voice the robot used. Rade was beginning to wonder if it was time to start calling the Centurion by that name. Then again, there was that whole not-wanting-to-get-attached thing...

The robots left the washroom behind and rounded a bend in the narrow hallway. They reached a sealed double door at the end of the hallway.

"The distress signal is strongest here," the Praetor said. "It definitely appears to be coming from inside."

"Send another transmission," Rade said. "Let any occupants know help has arrived."

Rade focused his attention away from the feed and surveyed the distant street below via the targeting reticle of his rifle while he waited. "Did you get a response yet?"

"Negative," the Praetor replied.

"All right," Rade said. "Guess you're going to have to go in."

"This door is also locked," the robot sent. "Permission to cut?"

"Granted," Rade replied.

The cutter robots moved into place. Molten lines appeared on the surface, but advanced far more slowly than the previous door.

"The metal is fifteen centimeters thick," the

Praetor said. "It's going to take some time."

"Take as long as you need," Rade replied.

"I told you we should have invested in some plasma weapons," Manic said over the comm. "An AR-35 would have etched through a door like that in no time."

"You know how much an AR-35 costs, bitch?" Bender said. "If you volunteer to give up your salary for a year, we can buy one."

"Uh, no."

Rade returned his attention to the street and scanned the sand-colored rooftops below through his rifle scope. So far there was no sign of any aggressors down there. As usual, he had kept his other eye open for situational awareness purposes, and a sudden motion drew his gaze to the southwest, to the vicinity of the pedway shed.

It was just one of the repair drones as it momentarily appeared above a rooftop before diving out of view.

He returned his attention to the video feed when the rectangle formed by the molten lines of the laser cutters was nearly complete.

"Assuming defensive positions," the Praetor sent. "Moving HS3s back."

Most of the robots retreated to the bend in the hallway, where they took cover, aiming their rifles past. Units C and D remained behind; they pushed forcefully on the thick metal doors, and it slowly toppled. The two units dove to the floor, setting their rifles down on the surface of the fallen door.

"We're taking laser fire!" Unit C transmitted.

fourteen

Rade switched his point of view to Unit C.

Inside the room beyond, he spotted overturned desks arranged in a half-circle around the entrance. Human faces, not wearing helmets, peered past the tops of those desks, the stick-like muzzles of laser rifles aimed directly toward the robots. The attackers wouldn't know they faced robots, of course; to them it would appear that two individuals in jumpsuits had arrived. Rade couldn't see any of the incoming fire, of course, because most laser weapons pulsed on the infrared band.

"Don't return fire!" Rade sent. "Tell them we're here to help them!"

"We're here to help!" Unit C announced, using its external speakers. "Drop your weapons!" It repeated the words in Persian.

The attackers seemed to hesitate; some looked away from their rifle scopes.

A man shouted in Persian. Rade's Implant translated the words a moment later: "You're not with Zoltan?"

"Tell them we've never heard of Zoltan," Rade said.

"We don't know who Zoltan is," Unit C told the

attackers.

"They've ceased firing, for the moment," Unit D transmitted to Rade. "I've accessed their public profiles. They appear to be Persian colonists."

"No doubt they have access to your own profile," Rade said. "And believe you're United Systems Army."

"No doubt," Unit D returned. "Though whether or not they believe our profiles remains to be seen."

"Unit D, pipe me directly to your external speakers," Rade said. "Leave your weapon on the floor and stand up. Make sure your hands are raised."

Unit D hadn't addressed the colonists yet, so the robot was the obvious choice to act as Rade's mouthpiece. If he spoke to the colonists through Unit C, it might come across as deceptive, since the robot had already addressed them in a female voice.

After Unit D had risen, Rade spoke to the defending colonists.

"We detected your distress call," Rade said. "We're here to help you. Tell us what happened."

Those taking cover behind the upturned desks glanced over their shoulders as more people materialized in the doorways of offices, or peered past cubicles. Men, women, and children, their faces grubby, tired.

A man stepped forward from a cubicle near the back and approached. He paused behind the line of desks.

"You are Army?" the man asked.

"Yes," Rade said.

"I am the Mayor of Darreh Shahr, Farhad Abed," the man said.

"Mayor," Rade said. "I am..." He accessed the fake profile of the robot, and gave the name listed there. "What happened here?"

"Zoltan did this," Farhad replied.

"Zoltan?" Rade asked.

"Yes," Farhad said. "The sultan of evil. He betrayed us. He was the one who arranged the purchase of this world from the Sino-Koreans. We should have known that the price was too good to be true. That he had his own nefarious agenda. When we discovered what he intended, we barricaded ourselves in here with enough food and water to last three months. But not before we managed to trap his creations. Though at great cost of life."

"Wait a second, slow down," Rade said. "You're not making any sense. First of all, tell me who this Zoltan is."

"An Artificial," Farhad said. "Once we came to this world, Zoltan secretly experimented on us. Children would vanish in the night, and then a few days later in their place creatures would stalk the streets. When we realized Zoltan was behind the kidnappings, we rose up against him, attacking his lab.

"But then he released his latest creations upon us. We trapped them in the pedway system, but could not snare the Artifical himself. Zoltan sent his remaining robots after us, and we retreated here, barricading ourselves in this building. We left all of our automated defensive units outside to protect us. We had no communication equipment, so we jury-rigged what we could from the materials on hand. We managed to form a weak transmitter from a battery and the comm node of a network toaster, and used that to transmit a distress signal."

Rade glanced at Tahoe's Hoplite. He muted the connection to Farhad.

"Well, at least we know what happened to those shot-up robots in front of the building," Rade said.

"Assuming the colonists are telling the truth," Tahoe said.

"I don't think they have much reason to lie," Rade said. "But you're right, we don't know for sure."

"Well if it's true, you think this Zoltan has Ms. Bounty?" Tahoe asked.

"That's a good question," Rade replied. "At this point, we don't know if Ms. Bounty is working for him, or against him." He spoke to the mayor once more: "The comm center at the center of town seems intact. It's been transmitting automated messages indicating that all is well in this system. Why didn't you retreat there, rather than to this skyscraper?"

"We wanted to," Farhad said. "But Zoltan's robots forced us away. This skyscraper was our only option."

"All right," Rade said. "Why didn't you go to the comm center when the fighting was over, then? Also, there are still shuttles and other evacuation craft in different hangars around the dome. Why didn't you try to escape with them?"

"We eventually tried to get out, yes," Farhad said. "Unfortunately Zoltan disconnected power to our building. The emergency power should have enabled the door to open of course, but he overrode our access somehow. And unfortunately, our laser rifles were unable to generate enough power to cut through the thick metal. We don't have Army grade equipment like yourselves."

"Well, there are other ways to escape a building..." Rade said.

"What would you have suggested?" Farhad said. "Opening the windows and throwing down a rope?"

"Something like that," Rade said.

"And climb down thirty-five stories?" Farhad said. "Not everyone is Army, like you."

"All right, fine," Rade said. "So tell me then, where is Zoltan now?"

"We're not sure," Farhad said. "Perhaps his lab."

"And where is his lab?"

"In the downtown core," Farhad said. "I can show you on the map. But will you help get us out?"

"Yes," Rade said. "However, we've lost a fire team. So before we can evacuate you, we need to find them. How many of you are there, anyway?"

Rade regarded the expansive office transmitted to him by the robot. Even more people had emerged from hiding, and the count reported by his HUD was eighty-eight. They all looked grimy. Rade could only imagine how terrible the place must smell in there.

"We are a hundred and twenty," Farhad said.

"That seems extremely low for a colony..." Rade said.

"Yes," Farhad replied. "We were five hundred originally. Plus another hundred builder robots, and fifty combat units, but those were lost in the fighting. We're all that's left."

"The city looks like it could hold at least a hundred thousand. Why construct so many Persian buildings if there were only five hundred of you?"

"We were the forerunners," Farhad said. "Part of an advance team meant to prepare the way for the other colonists. Ten thousand more were due to arrive six months from now, with another fifty thousand six months after that. Though whether our colonization plans can be salvaged at this point, I don't know. Not while Zoltan is still out there, in any case. You have to help us kill him. Or apprehend him, at the very least."

"I don't know," Rade said. "We don't come cheap."

A puzzled expression appeared on Farhad's face.

"What sort of army are you? Mercenaries?"

"Something like that," Rade said.

"I was not aware that the United Systems employed hired soldiers..." Farhad said.

"Well, there's a lot you don't know about the United Systems, apparently," Rade lied. "Look, all I can offer you right now is free passage off this world, and transportation to the closest space station. After we find our missing fire team."

"We can't offer him that," Fret interrupted over a separate channel. "We have room for maybe twenty guests aboard the *Argonaut*, and that's pushing it!"

"The *Amytis* has lots of room in its cargo hold," Rade said. "It could fit a hundred people easily."

"If Ms. Bounty agrees to unload whatever existing cargo the *Amytis* carries..." Shaw transmitted from orbit.

"She'll agree," Rade said. "Assuming she's still even alive."

"And what about Zoltan?" Farhad said, his voice coming over the main channel.

"As I said, if you want Zoltan taken care of," Rade told the man via Unit D. "That'll cost you extra. And just so you know, my team and I don't take on assassination jobs, regardless of whether the target is AI or human."

"We'll pay you whatever you need," the man said. "And apprehension is fine, of course. But I think you'll find, in this case, that assassination proves the easiest course of action."

"It always is," Rade said. "Which is why we don't do it." *Unless forced to.* "By the way, what happened to your corvettes?"

"Corvettes?" Farhad said. "Ah, you mean the ships we used to travel here. We left them in orbit, manned by skeletal crews."

"They're not in orbit anymore," Rade said. "They've been relocated to the military outpost on the moon of the ice giant."

"Zoltan's doing, no doubt," Farhad said.

"No doubt," Rade said, though the slight sarcasm in his voice betrayed his uncertainty. "So you said something before about how you trapped his creations?"

"That's right," the mayor said. "But thankfully the repair swarms are inactive."

"What do you mean?" Rade replied, feeling a rising sense of alarm.

"We trapped Zoltan's creations in the pedway system," the mayor said. "And deactivated our repair swarms, so that our own robots wouldn't dig the creatures out."

Rade exchanged a glance with Harlequin.

"Oh shit," Fret said.

Rade swung his scope toward the pedway shed. He couldn't actually see the metal structure nor any of the repair swarm because of the buildings in the way. He didn't spot any obvious signs that anything was amiss. He tapped into nearby HS3s, but none of them had a view of the area.

"Shaw, do you see anything down there?" Rade asked.

"The buildings are obstructing my view of the pedway," Shaw said. "And as for elsewhere in the city, Bax hasn't picked anything up. If something got out, it's staying close to the cover of the nearby buildings."

"TJ, can you deactivate those repair swarms?" Rade sent.

"I'll try," TJ replied. Then: "I'm not finding any obvious backdoors."

"You did leave our repair swarm inactive, didn't you?" Farhad asked.

"Unit D, switch to diplomacy mode," Rade sent the unit. "Babysit the colonists." He then muted Unit D's speakers so that he wouldn't have to hear the colonists anymore. He knew Unit D would inform him if the mayor or someone else had anything important to add.

"If there are bioengineered creatures buried in the underground pedway system," Lui said. "Why didn't this Zoltan dig them out on his own, using the remaining robots he had? The ones that chased the colonists to this skyscraper?"

"Probably lost interest in his so-called creations after the threat from the colonists was gone," Rade said.

"It's also possible he didn't have enough robots left to dig them out," Tahoe said. "There couldn't have been many that survived, not with all the defense units the colonists had placed in front of the skyscraper."

"You know," Manic said. "Even with all those repair drones, it would probably take at least a day to dig out that collapse. You're all getting stressed out for nothing."

Rade continued to run his scope over the buildings near the pedway shed, and just when he had begun to mentally agree with Manic, movement caught his eye in the adjacent street.

Rade swung his scope toward the object, and with the targeting reticle he followed a large creature as it leaped from one rooftop to the next.

The thing was headed toward the skyscraper.

"Bax has detected movement," Shaw said. "You got one incoming tango southwest of your position. A very large tango."

fifteen

R ade increased the zoom and did his best to keep the creature centered in his cross-hairs. It was about twelve meters long and six meters tall. It balanced on six thick legs capped by razor-sharp talons. A long neck extended from the torso, topped by a large, mostly featureless head. A lengthy tail provided counterbalance to the weight of the body and head.

At first Rade thought it was a machine, because the body was covered in what appeared to be metallic plates. But then he noticed that the tips of its feet and tail were greenish in color, which almost implied body armor of some sort.

"That's one nasty looking bug," Bender said.

"Could be a robot," Manic said.

"That ain't no robot," Bender said. "Look at the green feet. Got to be armor of some kind."

"Don't think so," Manic said.

"Units C and D, guard the colonists," Rade transmitted. "The rest of you, up here!"

A distant roar echoed from the tango.

"Bitch has got quite the bark," Bender said. "But does it have the bite to match?"

"Same thing could be said about you," Manic retorted.

An answering roar came from closer to the skyscraper. Rade immediately shifted his scope downward, searching for the second target. The way the buildings reflected the sound made it difficult to pinpoint. The local AI of his faceplate wasn't able to give him a fix.

He was about to ask Shaw if she had anything when Harlequin spoke up:

"Got it," Harlequin said. "Seven o'clock."

A flashing icon appeared in the lower left of his display, and Rade steered his scope toward it until he had the second incoming tango in view.

"Everyone, to the southern portion of the rooftop," Rade said. "Sync your cobras and rifles to mine. I want us to combine our shots."

The status and vitals of his brothers were displayed in a stack in the upper left of his vision. He aimed his scope at the approaching tango's head, and followed it with his reticle, waiting for the sync indicators to turn green.

Bender was humming something in the background. Occasionally he enunciated actual words: "Gonna hunt me some bugs. Gonna hunt me some bugs."

When the weapons had all synchronized, Rade followed the target a moment longer, concentrating on centering that moving head in his scope. He activated the AI tracking mechanism to help him better line up the shot.

He squeezed the trigger.

He would have been forgiven for thinking that nothing had happened, because the tango continued to approach, leaping from Persian rooftop to rooftop. It would reach the skyscraper in thirty seconds, according to the latest on-screen estimates.

"That armor seems to be equipped with an anti-laser coating," Lui said. "Similar to our ballistic shields. About eighty percent of our laser energy was deflected."

"That means twenty percent still penetrated," Rade said. "We keep firing."

He continued following the lead tango with his scope, opening fire when he had the head centered in his reticle. He soon switched to fully automated firing, because he found it impossible to strike the same spot repeatedly on his own, which was the most effective strategy. He, Harlequin and the Centurions fired at a faster rate than the Hoplites, whose lasers required a longer recharge interval; together they ensured that the barrage didn't let up.

"Our friend isn't slowing down," Tahoe said. "If we're doing twenty percent damage with each shot, shouldn't we have penetrated by now?"

"Yeah," Rade said. "In theory."

"Unless we're facing a new type of anti-laser material here," Lui said.

"Maybe the bug is friendly?" Fret said hopefully.

The creature leaped from the ring of apartments that surrounded the skyscraper and into the street directly below. The armored tango roared, then raced toward the base of the building: it left a trail of claw marks in the asphalt and previously fallen robots. Repair drones incongruously followed, attempting to fix the damage to the street.

The tango leaped onto the skyscraper and began scaling it, the talons on those six feet digging deep into the steel and glass surface. The repair drones lingered at the base of the building, concentrating on the street-level damage; evidently, they couldn't keep up with the creature's advance.

"Don't think it's friendly." Rade took control of his aiming and fired down continuously at the creature. It was easier to hit the same spot on its head now, because it wasn't jumping around in his cross-hairs as much. The AI tracking mechanism helped, of course.

"Get Shaw to fire the Vipers?" Bender suggested. The Vipers were far more powerful than the cobras of the Hoplites. A concentrated burst from the ship might just be enough to take out the enemy.

"Lui, what kind of a dome breach will a single concentrated shot of the Vipers cause?" Rade said.

"We'll poke a hole in the glass with the spot size of a centimeter," Lui said. "In theory, the dome is thick enough to prevent the puncture from enlarging any further as the air gushes out. We won't notice any difference down here. The dome repair bots will have it fixed well before the atmospheric content changes very much."

"How much energy will the dome sap from the shot itself?" Rade asked.

"Only about ten percent of the intensity," Lui replied.

"All right Shaw," Rade said. "Focus all Vipers on the tango. Target the same spot area on the head. Fire when ready."

"Direct hit," Shaw said a moment later.

Rade was staring directly at the creature through his scope. "Where did you hit it?"

"In the head region, like you asked," Shaw said.

"I'm not detecting any signs of damage," Rade said. *Too bad.*

"That would explain what I'm seeing," Shaw said. "The beam reflected right back up, forming a second breach in the dome. Luckily, it didn't hit the *Argonaut*. I'm detecting repair bots mobilizing along the inner surface of the dome glass to the affected regions."

"One tough bug," Bender said.

"It's going to be in range of our grenades soon," Fret said when the creature reached the fifteenth floor and still showed no signs of slowing.

"Hell," Bender said. "It's been in range since it touched the building. We can drop our frags down on it anytime."

"Yeah, but have fun hitting it with any accuracy from that height," Fret said.

Rade hesitated, looking away from his scope to stare down the barrel with his own eyes at the tango. The heights were dizzying: it was a good thing he was lying prostrate.

"Maybe we've been going about this the wrong way," Rade said.

"What do you mean?" Manic asked.

Rade aimed through his rifle scope once more. "I'm going to target one of the unarmored feet."

"Assuming the feet actually *are* unarmored..." Fret said.

"They are," Bender said. "Like I told you before, look at the green tips."

"That could be coloring on the armor," Fret said.

"Maybe," Rade said. "But the green portions are smaller in radius than the metallic areas. They have to be unshielded there."

"Everything always has a weak spot," TJ said.

"Exactly," Rade replied. "I'm going to let it climb more of the building, first. If it lets go, I want its fall to be from as high a point as possible."

"The higher they are," Manic said. "The harder they fall."

"Shouldn't that be, the *bigger* they are?" Harlequin said. The Artificial sounded excited, as if Harlequin had caught Manic doing something incredibly wrong and was now going to be lauded by the rest of the team.

"Ooo, you're one smart robot," Bender said. "Can you sign me your autograph with your pussy hairs?"

"Spec-ops personnel don't talk like that," Fret said, mocking an InterGalNet forum comment he had read aloud to them all a few days ago.

"Ain't spec-ops no more," Bender said. "Gave that up to hunt bugs. Speaking of which, boss...?"

Rade held back, letting the creature close to within five floors.

"If this doesn't work," TJ said. "And you let it get too close..."

"It'll work," Rade said. He smiled grimly as he added: "And if it doesn't, we'll blame Shaw."

"Thanks," Shaw transmitted.

Rade reduced the zoom level to compensate for the closer distance, and he followed one of the claws with his cross-hairs as it lifted from the surface and embedded in the building's outer metal. The skin looked like it was made of scales. Reptilian.

Rade waited a moment longer, then he fired all lasers in sync at the exposed foot. He saw a small wisp of smoke emerge, and black blood gushed from the reptilian extremity. The tango howled and immediately let go of the building with that foot, but the other limbs kept it secured to the surface.

The creature continued its ascent, holding the injured foot away from the skyscraper. Some of its lower limbs slipped on the blood spewed onto the surface by the wound, and the thing took a moment to find purchase.

Rade used that opportunity to aim at another foot. He got it.

The creature loosed another howl. That limb also let go of the building, leaving only four appendages grasping the surface.

The beast pulled its body toward the building so that it was hugging the exterior closely, effectively shielding its exposed feet from view.

"Uh," Bender said.

"All right," Rade said. "I've just about had enough of this. Unleash frag grenades. Blow the bitch off the building."

The rooftop shook as the frag grenades exploded. Incredibly, the tango managed to hang on. It was only when Tahoe's Hoplite fired a couple of grenades directly into the building itself—precisely where the tango was hanging on—that the creature was finally blown from the skyscraper.

It seemed to fall in slow motion, its limbs flailing helplessly in the air. It struck ground with an audible crash, and cracks spidered outward from the solar-paneled asphalt around it.

The body sprawled spreadeagled across the street. It didn't move. Black blood flowed out from underneath, pooling.

"Well," TJ said. "And that's that."

"Don't look now," Shaw sent. "But you still have that second tango to worry about. And I'm detecting another approaching from the northern side of the building. Same type of creature."

"I've got the northern bug in my sights," Lui said a moment later.

"All right, unsync," Rade said. "Target the feet of these things. Fire at will."

"What the hell is that?" TJ transmitted.

"What?" Rade heard it then, a buzzing coming from the southwest, the same direction as the pedway entrance.

"Sounds like the repair swarm," Tahoe said.

"Negative," Lui replied. "Apparently, we released something else trapped in the pedway. We have a Perdix swarm, Argonauts. Laser equipped drones. Likely repurposed at some point from the city's defenses. I'm counting roughly five hundred."

A swarm of red dots had appeared on the overhead tactical map, approaching from the southwest.

Unfortunately, none of the Hoplites were equipped with Repellent modules: expensive electronic warfare countermeasures that used directional interference to disrupt drone navigation.

"Shit," Rade said. "Deploy shields!"

Cobra mounts swiveled away on the left arms of the Hoplites, and the long shield pieces unfolded in their places.

Rade nestled himself between a goose neck vent and Tahoe's Hoplite, and held his weapon up over the edge of the shield. He switched his point of view to the rifle scope and aimed at the incoming drones.

The targets moved randomly back and forth as they approached. Seeker bullets would have worked wonders. Too bad they didn't have any: whoever said it was a good idea to replace traditional ammo with lasers?

"We're taking heavy laser fire," Lui said.

Rade saw small white spots appear along the edges of Tahoe's shield, where the armor was weaker. Holes formed as the metal dissolved there.

"Return fire!" Rade said. "Lasers only! And prepare to launch electromagnetic grenades!"

Rade squeezed the trigger, eliminating one of the drones. Others fell from the sky as the Hoplites struck multiple targets. The small things lacked armor of any kind to protect against the cobras.

"Come on you pussies, that all you got?" Bender shouted over the comm. "It's pissing drones today!" His kill count was the highest so far according to the stats displayed on the HUD.

Rade waited until the lead units in the swarm were only a hundred meters out. Then: "Fire electromagnetics!"

The Hoplites launched electromagnetic grenades. When they detonated, electrical sparks arced outward between the drones, knocking out scores of them. They fell from the sky like rain.

"Fire again! Again!" Rade cringed slightly with the launch of each grenade, knowing how much it would cost to replace them.

Nothing for it.

The drones were basically on top of them by then. "Switch to frags!" Rade sent.

Fragmentation grenades hurtled into the enemy and once more the detonations took out large swaths of the drones. But they kept coming in. According to the tactical map there were still about three hundred of them.

"There's too many!" Fret said. "We can't hold them off!"

"My shield's badly damaged," Lui said. "I can't take much more of this. And my cobra is offline. I took a shot in the firing mechanism."

Rade was forced to sink deeper into cover between Tahoe and the vent. Tahoe and the other Hoplites shifted their shields so that the anti-laser surfaces were basically lying flat, protecting the mechs from attacks directly above.

"Fire smoke grenades onto the rooftop!" Rade said. "Get us some cover! Use flashbangs as decoys!" Probably wouldn't help, but they had to try. The smoke would block visual targeting, and the flashbang heat would fool thermal systems, but the drones likely had backup targeting methods they could use such as radar, echolocation, and predictive algorithms—just like the Hoplites.

Rade only did it to buy the group some time while he figured out how to survive this mess.

Unfortunately, no ideas were coming to him.

Worse, he knew that the other two creatures were still encroaching on the building, perhaps even climbing the skyscraper at that very moment. And there was nothing the team could do about it while the Perdix swarm pinned them down.

sixteen

When smoke covered the rooftop, Rade sent: "Shift positions. Don't stay in the same place each time you fire." To Tahoe: "Don't move yet, Big T, I'm loading up."

Rade jetted onto Tahoe's mech, and used the boarding rungs to pull himself into the passenger seat. Tahoe kept his shield held horizontally above him, protecting both his mech and Rade, so that when Rade stood up slightly, his helmet struck the shield.

That made Rade think of the dome enclosing them all. And an inkling of an idea began to form.

"Lui, can we tell if these drones are vacuum capable?" Rade said. "Or are they restricted to atmospheric flight?"

"Like most Perdix models," Lui said. "Corners were cut to allow it to carry weapons, and yet still have the weight necessary for flight. So no, as far as I can tell, they're not vacuum capable."

"Are you *sure?*" Rade said.

"Positive."

The smoke was beginning to clear. He spotted drones occasionally flying beneath the shield lines to fire at the Hoplites. Usually the cobras took them out a moment later, that or the bashing fist of one of the mechs.

"More smoke!" Rade said.

He tapped in Unit D, which was still inside with the colonists. "Activate your external speakers. I want to speak with the mayor."

"Done," the unit replied.

"Mayor," Rade sent. "Is this building capable of withstanding a dome breach, as per colony code?"

"It's up to code," the Mayor replied. "You punch a big enough hole, the ventilation seals will automatically activate, and the building air system will switch to its internal oxygen supply. The skyscraper will pressurize fully. We'll have enough air for at least several weeks. Hopefully enough time for the repair swarm to fix any breaches. All of this assumes of course that the emergency power kicks in. Remember, Zoltan prevented us from opening the exit to our floor all this time..."

"TJ," Rade said. "What do you think? Will the skyscraper seal or not?"

TJ responded a moment later. "All the emergency interfaces have power, as far as I can tell. It should seal."

"Mayor, will my r—" Rade almost said robots. "Will my *men* be able to get out if the building seals off?"

"Yes," the mayor replied. "Inner hatches will activate at the main exits, effectively transforming them into airlocks."

"Bender, order all remaining HS3s into the building!" Rade said. "Units A, B, E, get inside! Harlequin, join them! We're going to vent the atmosphere!"

"What about you?" Harlequin said.

"I'm strapping into Tahoe's passenger seat." Rade

activated the securing clamps of the seat. On his overhead map, the blue dots representing the Centurions and HS3s converged with the stairwell superstructure. The HS3s timed their approach to match the entry of the combat robots, the smaller scouts evidently flitting inside before the door shut.

"Shaw, I want you to fire the lasers in a spread pattern," Rade said. "Strategically weaken the glass. Basically, prepare areas of the dome to receive Hellfire strikes. I want to explosively decompress this atmosphere. Suck these damn drones out."

"Will do," Shaw replied.

"Fire when ready."

A few seconds later: "I've prepared four side by side regions to accept missile impacts. Launching Hellfires now."

Rade waited as the tense moments passed. The second wave of rooftop smoke was clearing away again by the time he heard explosions. The concussive force of the expanding gases tore over the rooftop, rippling the smoke, and crashing a few of the drones.

He glanced skyward. A large gash had been cut through the dome, revealing the natural red sky. It was like a bloody sore in the roof of the world. The missiles had weakened the surrounding glass enough to cause more sections to break free, so that in moments it had expanded to about four times the original size.

The wind picked up to gale levels, and the smoke and drones were swept from the rooftop, along with two of the goose neck vents. Other superstructures and loose debris from the buildings below swept past, some striking the mechs. The Hoplites themselves were unaffected by the winds—the war machines were far too heavy.

With the smoke gone, Rade realized that one of the reptilian creatures had attained the rooftop in the confusion. It had crawled behind TJ, and towered over his Hoplite, somewhat over twice as tall as the unit.

"TJ!" Rade called.

Too late. The metal armor around the creature's head shifted, sliding back and lifting. It was apparently a visor of some kind. With the metal moved aside, another head was revealed, this one possessing a green snout above a toothy maw, with two horns above the eyes. That mouth opened, showcasing jaws a meter in size, filled with serrated, conical teeth.

Rade saw all of that in the millisecond it took the creature to wrap those teeth around TJ's passenger seat. The jaw tore through the metal, and when the creature ripped its head away it had removed a substantial portion of the seat, including the sanitation robot TJ had carried.

The creature tossed the crunched metal and destroyed sanitation robot aside—the wind sucked the debris into the sky immediately. As the reptile's giant mouth closed, the visor slid shut once again, protecting its face.

"Yup," Bender transmitted. "Definitely a bug."

Bender's Hoplite leaped at the creature and landed on the back of its neck. The armored head bowed under the weight.

Another creature topped the west side of the roof, and smashed into Bender in a blur, pulling his Hoplite off the first and crushing the mech under its weight.

Fret and Lui hurtled into the creature, knocking it away from Bender.

A part of Rade's mind noticed that the wind had died down by then—the atmosphere had completely vented. The Perdix were no more. On his map, the red dots of the swarm were scattered across the dunes lying outside the dome, as recorded by the *Argonaut's* sensors.

Tahoe leaped at the first creature, which was still trying to recover its balance after Bender was knocked away. Rade was jerked about in the passenger seat. Tahoe wrapped his arms around the armored reptile's torso. The creature managed to swing the Hoplite down off its back with a free limb, and it bashed its head down on the mech. That visor slid aside, and Rade was forced to duck as sharp teeth nearly bit into him.

TJ struck the foe in the side, knocking it off-balance once again.

The giant lizard's head armor resealed, and it took a few wobbly steps crabwise, toward the building edge.

"No no NO!" Rade said as the creature plunged from the rooftop, drawing Tahoe over the ledge with it.

Those six arms wrapped firmly around the Hoplite, preventing Tahoe from jetting away. Falling from that height without being able to deploy the air brakes, or successfully fire the aerospike thrusters, would basically destroy the mech and its operator.

Because of his position in the passenger seat, facing away from the creature's body, Rade was able to revoke the clamps and release himself from the seat. Just in time, too, because the creature's head visor opened up to tear into the Hoplite once more.

Rade pushed away, shoving off into empty space. It felt like he was floating; the blur of the building beside him reminded him of the deadly fall. He would strike the ground in seconds.

He activated his jet pack to further the distance from the plunging pair; he allowed his rifle to hang from his shoulder by the strap, then fired lateral thrust to turn around, withdrawing the secondary blaster at his belt at the same time.

"Warning, ground impact imminent," the voice of his suit AI intoned.

Rade aimed at the unshielded tips of those appendages and fired three quick shots in turn. Those three limbs released the Hoplite, and Tahoe was able to break free.

Rade fired braking thrust, as did the Hoplite. Air brakes extended from the mech's shoulder area. One of them was damaged, Rade noticed. That only meant Tahoe would have to fire more thrust to slow his descent.

Below them, the creature smashed into the pavement. Tahoe's Hoplite landed hard beside it, but the impact wasn't enough to damage his mech. Rade landed lightly nearby.

Tahoe was already on the fallen opponent. He ripped open the visor with his Hoplite and shot his cobra point blank into that lifeless face. A black plume of smoke misted from the fresh wound as the blood boiled upon contacting the voided environment of the dome. The creature remained motionless.

"Pretty sure it's dead, Tahoe," Rade said as the Hoplite fired into the head again, this time with the cobra on the other arm. "Lui, how are we doing on the rooftop?"

He switched to Lui's viewpoint and saw that the remaining Hoplites had also torn open the visor of the remaining creature. Blood misted from multiple laser wounds in its face and exposed lower limbs.

"We got the situation under control," Lui said.

"Shaw, any more of them out there?" Rade said.

"Negative," Shaw replied. "That was the last of

them. Well done."

Bender's mech was standing close to Lui's.

"If aliens could wear body armor, this is what they would look like," Bender said.

"They're not alien," Lui said. "My scans tell me they're definitely bioengineered from Earth stock. I'm seeing very specific genetic markers in the DNA from reptiles and birds, along with a lot of staggered DNA cuts and insertions, as is common with CRISPR/Cpf1 genome editing. That's a trademark of Sino-Korean work. Whoever made these was definitely brought up in the SK school of bioweaponry."

"Yeah well," Manic said. "Obviously the designer wasn't very good at bioengineering if he had to throw in a friggin' suit of armor!"

"Sometimes it's impossible to get all the desired traits you're looking for in bioengineered creations," Lui said. "Especially if you're pressed for time. The simulator does a good job of estimating what traits will dominate, but nature sometimes throws you a curveball, and you have to go back to the drawing board. It very well could have been easier to design a suit of armor for the creature rather than burning through another five hundred generations of zygotes to develop that armor naturally."

"It's a little disturbing how much you know about bioengineering..." Bender said.

"I purchased a CRISPR kit a while back," Lui said. "Gene editing is a hobby of mine."

"Which begs the question, who the hell makes gene editing a hobby?"

"What I don't get is how these things survived once we breached the dome," Manic said. "What with their extremities exposed to the vacuum like that. Plus they kept opening their visors to bite at us. Couldn't have been a pressurized environment inside that armor."

"According to my readings," Lui said. "Like birds and reptiles, they don't have sweat glands, and instead rely on evaporation of water from their lungs. When exposed to low pressure environments, organs in their throats seal up, allowing them to function either in atmospheric or vacuum conditions. The only worry for them when operating under the latter conditions is that they might overheat."

"What about respiration?" Manic said.

"It looks like they can hold their breath as long as a sperm whale, for up to ninety minutes," Lui said. "Due to extra myoglobin levels, which stores oxygen in the muscle tissue."

"How can they see with that armor covering their eyes?" Fret said.

"Probably some sort of LIDAR system feeding them visual information," Lui said.

Bender spoke again. "The more I listen, the more I think: what kind of price would we get on the black market if we sold their genome? Plus designs for the armor that goes with it?"

"We don't deal in weapons," Rade said. "Erase your data, Lui."

"You got it boss," Lui replied.

Bender cleared his throat, as if embarrassed by the suggestion he had just made. "Bug has certainly got armor..." he said, obviously attempting to change the subject.

"Armored Bugs," Lui said. "That's what we'll call them."

"Dude, that's a terrible name," Bender said.

"You came up with it..."

"No I didn't," Bender said. "I was making a

comment."

"Armored Bugs it is," Manic said.

Rade muted the connection. He glanced at Tahoe's Hoplite. "I need a moment. Get up on the rooftop and supervise for a while."

"Supervise?" Tahoe said, sounding confused.

"Yeah," Rade said.

He approached the main entrance to the building. Through the glass, he saw that an inner seal had activated, turning it into an airlock. The emergency power had worked in that regard after all. That was a relief. He knew he had risked the colonists lives by hoping that the pressurization system would activate, but the thing was, if Rade and his team died, the colonists wouldn't survive anyway.

Rade approached the glass door, and the previous hack caused it to open immediately. He stepped inside and the door sealed behind him. He waited for the air to mist inside, and watched Tahoe activate his jumpjets outside to begin the return trip to the rooftop.

The inner hatch opened and Rade stepped into the building. He sat down on one of the steps leading to the main concourse. Well, he more collapsed than sat down, really.

"Rade, are you all right?" Shaw sent.

"Yeah, just need some space," Rade said. "I'm turning on call screening. Don't let anybody through unless it's an emergency."

Rade sat there, listening to his shaky breath for long moments. His gloved hands were trembling from adrenalin hangover. He felt nauseous, and light-headed.

Don't vomit, don't vomit, don't vomit.

He clenched his fists. The shaking only increased. Then he relaxed his fingers.

Mercifully, the nausea passed.

He slumped forward and stared straight ahead, seeing nothing.

He heard the distant voice of an AI from a time long past. "Warning: armor penetrated."

seventeen

R ade. Boss."
Rade blinked. He realized a figure in a jumpsuit was kneeling in front of him. Harlequin.

"How long have you been kneeling there?" Rade said.

"Only a few seconds," Harlequin replied. "But we've been trying to contact you for the past five minutes."

"Why didn't you tell Shaw to ping me," Rade said. "She's been screening my calls."

"I did ping you," Shaw transmitted. "You weren't answering me either."

"Your vitals were okay, and we could tap into your vision feed, so we knew you were conscious," Harlequin said. "They sent me down to check on you."

"You all right, boss?" Bender said. The concern was obvious in his voice.

"I'm fine." Rade stood. "That battle just drained me a little, that's all."

"Bet you miss the meds the navy used to feed us," Fret said. "Block all that shit out."

"Block what out?" Rade said. "I told you I was *fine*. And I don't want to hear anything more on the matter."

He noticed a couple of Centurions were in the concourse with him, guarding the entrance to the building. He glanced at his overhead map. Tahoe had arranged the Hoplites into a defensive perimeter on the rooftop.

Good man.

Rade glanced through the floor-to-ceiling windows at the sky outside and zoomed in on the rent. He spotted the small, crab-like dome repair bots slowly moving along the ragged edges, 3D printing a plug. "How long until the rooftop dome is repaired?"

"Given the current rate of repair," Lui said. "We're looking at two weeks, at least."

"Unit D, get the mayor to show us where the lab is on the map," Rade said. "It's time to track down Ms. Bounty."

"I have it," the unit said a moment later. "Marking the location."

Rade watched a flashing waypoint appear on his overhead map, about five blocks away, two blocks north of the damaged pedway station shed.

"By the way," the unit continued. "Farhad wants to know how many of those bioweapons we faced."

"I see no harm in telling him," Rade said. "Three."

A moment later, the unit said: "He tells me there were seven of them trapped in the underground pedway system originally."

Rade stared worriedly past the floor-to-ceiling windows into the street beyond. The remaining four could be anywhere out there. He wondered how long the glass could hold out to an assault.

Fret carried a spare comm node in the storage compartment of his Hoplite; Rade had him leave it with the colonists. Then he and the others vacated the building and proceeded toward the lab building.

Best to draw the creatures away, if they're watching us.

Rade, Harlequin and the robots once more shadowed the Hoplites from the rooftops.

When they reached the target building, they discovered that the main door was a slab of metal as thick as the one on floor thirty-five of the skyscraper. Neither TJ nor Bender was able to hack through, so Rade set the Centurions to work cutting it.

The main door was three meters high and two across, just wide enough to fit a Hoplite. Of course, whether or not the mechs could fit depended on the size of the hole the Centurions cut.

"Use your magnetic attachments to scale the door," Rade instructed the robots. "I want you to cut a hole big enough to suit a Hoplite."

The robots activated variable-strength magnets embedded in their boots and knee areas, and scaled the wall to begin their cut as high as possible.

Meanwhile, the Hoplites assumed a defensive formation and guarded the entrance. Rade remained perched on the rooftop of the building opposite.

"Seriously Lui, bro," Bender said. "Who the hell makes gene editing a hobby?"

"You know I'm a foodie," Lui said. "That should tell you everything."

"Uh, it doesn't?"

"I'm looking to craft the perfect turkey breast," Lui said. "Not just for myself, but you guys. I know how much you love turkey and chicken. Well, I'm going to create the most perfect, most succulent piece of edible delight for you all."

"I think Lui needs a girlfriend," Manic said.

"Why, when he already has you?" Bender said.

"Lui, I give you a free pass to cheat on me," Manic

said.

"Thanks," Lui said. "Bender, what are you doing tonight?"

"Nothing with *you*," Bender replied.

"What? Come on, I got room in my mech," Lui said. "They don't call it a cockpit for nothing."

Bender got up and moved to the far side of the defensive perimeter before settling in again.

"We can visit Bangkok instead?" Lui said in mock hopefulness.

Rade chuckled softly.

What would I do without my team.

"You okay down there?" Shaw sent on a private line.

"Fine," Rade told her.

"I thought I heard you crying just now," Shaw said.

"Uh, no," Rade said. "That was a laugh."

"Oh. Well, I was worried about you back there. Not just during the battle, but afterward."

"I know," Rade said.

"Don't do this to me," Shaw said. "Don't shut me out."

Rade sighed. "Sometimes I just need some time alone."

"All right," Shaw said. "But I think you should start your counseling sessions with Bax again."

"As much as I love the *Argonaut's* AI," Rade said. "It isn't much of a counselor."

"Then we'll download a specialized AI," Shaw said. "You can begin your sessions as soon as you get back."

"It's not going to help," Rade said.

"What about some of those meds Fret was talking about?"

Rade sighed. "What I'm doing out here, right now, this is my healing, Shaw. Trust me."

"Then how come every time things get intense, when it's all over you lock yourself away and zone out?" she said. "Well not every time, but close enough."

"It's the adrenalin hangover," Rade said. "That's all it is."

"All right. Well, I'm going to keep an eye on you."

Rade had to smile at that. "You do that, baby girl."

"Love you," she sent.

Love you back. But he couldn't say the words aloud.

The robots cut through the door and let the rectangular slab topple. Inside, at the end of a short hallway, a secondary seal formed the remainder of an airlock, protecting the rooms beyond from the now deadly external atmosphere.

"Cut it," Rade sent the robots.

The robots climbed the inner door, which was just as wide and tall as the first, and applied their cutters. Air misted forth as the atmosphere beyond decompressed.

Rade relieved himself, and from his leg a crystalline yellow stream formed. It desublimated into mist as he watched.

"It's a bit cold out there," Harlequin said from his side.

"Just a bit," Rade replied.

"I saw your lips moving a few moments ago," Harlequin said on a private line. "Is Shaw giving you trouble?"

"Harlequin," Rade said. "Don't you know it's rude to read lips?"

"Sorry, boss," the Artificial replied.

The pair remained quiet for several moments.

"I've undergone training as a therapist," Harlequin said. "If you wanted—"

"No, I don't," Rade interrupted.

As more of the surface area was cut, and the lab building's atmosphere vented out even faster, the metal inner door began to bend outward from the pressure. Before the robots finished cutting, the venting ceased entirely. They finished their work and pulled the inner door down. As requested, the openings were now wide enough to fit the Hoplites, though it would be a tight fit.

Rade sent the HS3s and Centurions in to clear the building. These models of HS3s were void capable, and utilized a large quantity of extremely high pressure propellant when atmosphere wasn't present.

After several minutes, the HS3s had mapped out three floors and several hallways. Most doors were locked, so Rade instructed the Centurions to begin cutting through and clearing the individual rooms. The contents were what would be expected of a lab dealing in bioengineering, and included centrifuges, microscopes, RNA printers, and incinerators. In one room, the walls were lined with shelves filled with vials. The labels on the vials indicated different genetic material, according to Lui.

In another locked area, the robots discovered several operating tables and Weaver surgical units.

"Looks like we found where Zoltan conducted his experiments on captured colonists," Manic said.

On the far side of the room, a window overlooked a gymnasium-sized room. Within resided jungle trees and shrubs. A younger, unarmored version of the reptilian bioweapons was lying down amid the foliage. It appeared sickly, its breath seeming to come in wheezes.

"Looks like daddy has been neglecting his baby dinosaur," Bender said.

"You think it's pressurized in there?" Manic said.

"Looks like it," Lui replied.

"You say Zoltan experimented on the colonists he captured, Manic?" Fret transmitted.

"That's right," Manic replied.

"Well," Fret said. "I think he only took them to the Weavers to sedate them, and then he dumped them into the cage for his pets to eat. Creatures like that aren't going to grow overnight you know."

"Easier to buy meat in bulk from the traders," Manic said. "And it definitely looks like this Zoltan could afford it."

"Yeah sure," Fret said. "But how often do the traders come to this backwater system?"

"We still have a few locked doors," Rade said. "Centurions, finish clearing out the building."

"I don't think we'll find Ms. Bounty here," Tahoe sent Rade, privately. "Or this Zoltan character."

"No," Rade replied. "And that's what's troubling me. We have no idea where Ms. Bounty went. If we don't find her soon, we're going to have to abandon this planet and let the appropriate authorities sort it out a few weeks from now."

"But if we do that, we'll default on our debt next month," Tahoe said. "Ms. Bounty only paid the deposit."

"I know," Rade said. "Which is why we're not leaving until we absolutely have to. I want to search the pedway system after this. It's the next logical place she would be, given how restricted communications are down there. And now that the repair swarm has opened a path for us..."

"But how did she get down there in the first

ISAAC HOOKE

place?" Tahoe said. "If it was all blocked off, like the colonists say?"

"I don't know," Rade said. "Obviously there's another entrance somewhere. An opening that the bioweapons couldn't use to get out."

"Speaking of the bioweapons," Tahoe said. "There are still four of them out here."

"We have a pretty good handle on how to take them down by now, I think," Rade said.

"Maybe," Tahoe replied. "But that doesn't mean they'll go quietly."

As the Centurions worked at cutting open the next room, the rooftop Rade perched upon began to shake in repeated bursts, as if in tune with the steps of some approaching giant.

"Anyone else feel that?" Manic said. The mechs would transmit the vibrations to their pilots.

"Looks like our friends are coming back," Rade said.

He wondered if the bioweapons had roared at any point. If they had, he wouldn't have heard it—the atmosphere was currently too thin to carry sound effectively.

"AIs, trade readings," Rade said. "Attempt to triangulate the source of the vibrations."

The AIs in the mechs and robots spent several moments processing the data, and then the Praetor reported: "We've detected three sources, not one. The first is somewhere to the east. The second, the west. The third, the south."

"No fourth source?" Rade said.

"No," the Praetor replied.

Where are you?

Maybe the mayor was wrong about the number.

"All right," Rade said. "Hoplites, to the rooftops.

Harlequin, you're going to wait by the entrance, and lure them."

"Why do I always have to be the bait?" Harlequin said as he leaped down.

"Because you're the AI," Rade told him.

"What the hell is that?" Tahoe said.

"Where?" Rade asked.

"To the north!" Tahoe replied.

Rade zoomed in on the northern rooftops and saw them. Floating metallic dots, glistening in the sun, and fast approaching. A swarm of them.

"Oh shit," Lui said. "We got more Perdix drones. These ones look like they're propellant-based. I'm counting at least two hundred."

"We really have to invest in a Repellent system," Bender said.

"Yeah," Rade agreed. "Change of plans. Everyone inside the damn building! We'll defend the entrance."

Considering that the party had exhausted most of its grenade inventory, staying outside wasn't the best idea.

The Hoplites rushed inside the building in single file. Past the airlock, they deployed their shields and aimed their cobras outside.

Rade entered the foyer. He recalled the Centurions from their explorations of the lab, and with them and Harlequin he assumed a firing position around the bend of the inner hatch. He remained completely in cover, but held his weapon past the edge, switching his point of view to the scope.

The entrance proved a good choke point for the drones, and as the units jetted inside, the team members took them down by the score.

One of the bioweapons arrived and promptly rushed the airlock. As expected, its six-meter-tall body was too big to fit; the armored creature plunged its long neck inside but the head didn't reach the inner opening.

"Shoot the exposed feet!" Rade said.

But before anyone could respond, a thick wall slammed down over the inner hatch. Rade barely pulled his rifle away before it was crushed.

More heavy blocks descended from the ceiling, these ones sealing off the remaining outer walls, along with the windows.

"What the hell...?" Rade said.

"I think some sort of automated defense system just activated," TJ said. "Blast shields are lowering."

"Can you shut off that system?" Rade asked.

"I don't know," TJ said. "Don't think so."

Lui stepped forward in his Hoplite. Space was at a premium in the foyer, and he had to shove past a couple of the other mechs to reach Rade. He placed the flat palm of his mech on the surface of the new wall.

"As I suspected," Lui said. "These seals are made of the same material as the bioweapon armor."

Rade glanced at the nearby Centurions. "Cutters, try to make a hole."

A moment later, Unit D reported: "Can't. Our lasers reflect."

"Damn it," Rade said. "Now I'm really starting to wish I'd picked up some plasma rifles."

"There's no guarantee it would have helped," Lui said.

"Shaw," Rade transmitted. "Can the *Argonaut* get a clear shot at the front door of this building?"

No answer.

"Shaw?" Rade tried again. "Do you read? Shaw?"

"There's too much lead in the material," Fret said.

"We've lost all connection to the outside world."

"Centurions and HS3s," Rade sent. "Make a circuit of this place. Check all the outer walls, and see if there's anywhere the blast shields missed."

"Roger that," the Praetor replied.

Rade turned toward Fret's Hoplite. "You remember those abandoned shuttles and evac craft Lui detected in the different hangars around the dome?"

"I do," Fret replied.

"Try to piggyback your signal onto one of their comm nodes," Rade said. If they could do that, in theory they would be able to reach Shaw.

"Trying..." Fret replied. A moment later: "I'm getting nothing. Can't poke through these blast shields."

A few minutes later the Praetor reported in. The robot's voice was fairly distorted, and it was only because of the adhoc network formed by the HS3s and other Centurions between Rade and the Praetor that Rade could understand it at all. "All walls and exits have been sheathed in the laser-resistant blast shields."

Rade glanced upward. "What about the ceiling on the third floor?"

"The ceiling is made of the same material," the unit replied. "We can't cut through."

Rade exhaled in frustration.

"If it's a blast shield, won't it eventually rescind at some point after the external attacks end?" Manic said.

"You're assuming the blast shield wasn't lowered on purpose," Tahoe said. "By this Zoltan character. To trap us."

Fret turned and fired his twin cobras in rapid succession, taking out the dome cameras in the ceiling.

"Feel better now?" Bender asked.

"I do," Fret replied.

"Still feels like he's watching us, to me anyway," Manic said. "Gotta be more hidden cameras here, somewhere."

"It doesn't matter," Rade said. "Listen, there are still a few locked doors we haven't explored. Doors that we can still cut through. Centurions, I want you to penetrate and clear the remaining rooms. With luck, we'll find a way out of this yet."

While the Hoplites remained in the foyer, the robots moved from area to area, cutting those doors that were yet locked, and clearing the rooms beyond. None of them so far provided a way out. The robots did however discover another observation room, this one overlooking a glass tank. Inside were four strange, mollusk-like shapes: giant slugs. They seemed dead.

"More genetic experimentation," Lui said. "Makes you wonder just what the hell this Zoltan dude was planning."

Finally, several minutes later, Unit D reported in from the basement. "I just cut through a door that leads underground. Judging from the close proximity of the pedway system, this passage might potentially connect to it."

eighteen

Rade switched to the unit's point of view. The Centurion's light cone illuminated stairs leading down a tight corridor into darkness. He checked his overhead map, and overlaid the subterranean pedway level with the basement level. According to the blueprints, the closest pedway tunnel passed within ten meters of that basement room.

"The connecting section isn't on our blueprints," Lui said. "Must be a new addition."

"Or an existing connection that was never added to the map," Tahoe said.

"Send in an HS3," Rade said.

A moment later the scout flew by. Rade switched to its perspective and watched the drone proceed down the corridor. Its own headlamps provided a dim light cone, illuminating the close concrete walls.

"Well, if it is a way out, it looks like we'll be leaving our Hoplites," Manic said. "They'll never fit in that stairwell."

The passage leveled out, and in another five meters the drone reached a T intersection. The corridor was much broader and wider there.

"According to the map, the HS3 just entered the main pedway system," TJ said.

"Look at how spacious it is," Bender said. "That passage could easily hold our Hoplites. And yet we can't bring them because the connecting corridor is too small. It's like watching a strip tease in a no-touching club."

"Hoplites aren't the only thing that could fit in the pedway system proper," Fret said. "Don't forget the monsters."

"*Monsters*," Bender said. "Call them bugs, damn it."

The drone took the rightmost branch of the intersection and in seconds the video feed began to distort and pixelate badly.

"All right, that's far enough," Rade said. "Bring the HS3 back to the intersection."

Rade traced a route on the pedway map to the closest exit—the shed two blocks to the south.

"All right, people," Rade said. "We have a way out. This is actually good, since I wanted to explore the pedway system next."

"Anyone else feel like we're being herded?" Manic said.

"I do," Fret said. "I'll follow you, boss, don't get me wrong, but exploring the pedway system without Hoplites, it's just, well, not the best idea. Not while those monsters are on the loose."

Bender threw up the arms of his mech. "Again with the monsters."

"What?" Fret said.

"Spec-ops personnel don't talk like that," Bender mocked. "All chicken-shit like. *What?*"

"I'm not spec-ops anymore," Fret said. "So piss off."

"Once spec-ops, always spec-ops," Bender said.

"Fret, we're going down," Rade said. "This isn't a negotiation."

"Didn't TJ say the creatures would be dead after ninety minutes?" Fret insisted. "Something about starving from oxygen?"

"That's a good point," Rade said. "All right, I'm willing to wait another thirty minutes, as sixty have already passed since we breached the dome with the *Argonaut's* Hellfires."

The requisite thirty minutes passed; Rade waited another twenty for good measure, and then he and the Hoplites made their way down to the basement. At the final stairwell, the ex-MOTHs reluctantly dismounted their Hoplites. They emptied the few grenades they had left from the launchers on the mechs and attached them to their jumpsuit harnesses.

"Set the AIs to 'guard' mode," Rade said. He tapped in the AI of Bender's mech: "Juggernaut, go upstairs and watch the main entrance. If the blast shield ever opens, notify the other Hoplites, and if the way proves clear outside, attempt to rendezvous with us at the hangar where we stowed our Dragonfly."

"Affirmative," Juggernaut returned. The mech departed.

Manic gazed longingly at his own Hoplite. "It's the end of an era."

"I feel so vulnerable out here," Fret said. "So... small."

"Now you know how Harlequin and I have felt all this time," Rade said.

"Isn't a good feeling," Tahoe said.

"No, it's not," Rade agreed.

"I've felt fine, actually," Harlequin said. "I am confident in myself and my abilities."

"Yeah, that's nice, bitch," Bender said. "I feel fine, too. I'm not afraid of some bugs. Got my bug spray right here." He hefted his laser rifle. "You really think

169

you're hot tamales, don't you?"

"I was merely stating my feelings—"

"Well don't," Bender said. "Because we don't care about your AI-ass feelings."

"Wait boss, we're just going to leave the Hoplites here?" Manic said.

"We'll come back for them at some point," Rade said. "Once we can find a way to raise those blast shields."

"And what if we can't?" Fret said. "Or our Hoplites are stolen?"

"Then we expense the client," Rade said.

"And if the client is dead?" Fret pressed.

"Then we're screwed." Rade pointed toward the darkness. "Weapon lights on. Infrared mode. Centurions and HS3s, lead the way."

THE SURVIVING THREE HS3s proceeded on point through the concrete corridors, followed by the five Centurions, and the eight ex-MOTHs. The team had switched their faceplates to night vision mode, which cast everything in shades of green. Infrared beams illuminated a floor tiled with some sort of ceramic, with a carpet running along the middle. Long cylinders in the ceiling that ran parallel to the corridor indicated the inactive HLED pedway lights.

The ten by three meter passageway occasionally broadened to form underground crossroads, with corridors branching away in different directions. Rade had the party take the passages leading toward the closest surface exit two blocks to the south, where the pedway section had formerly collapsed. The first order of business was to reestablish communications with the *Argonaut*. Rade had instructed Fret to report in the moment he received a signal ping.

As they passed another branch, Fret spoke up.

"Boss," Fret said. "I'm getting a signal ping."

"Shaw?"

"No," Fret said. "It's the team from the *Amytis*."

"The *Amytis?*" Rade asked.

"Yes."

"Tap me in if you can," Rade told the comm man.

"You should be good," Fret said.

"Ms. Bounty, or any members of the *Amytis* away team, do you read?" Rade sent.

"We... you," a distorted voice returned. "Can... over?"

Rade glanced at the ping time. It was quite high. He retreated a few paces until he reached the branch, and the ping improved.

"Say again?" Rade transmitted.

"We read you," Ms. Bounty's distorted voice returned. "Can you read me, over?"

"Yes," Rade sent.

"I was wondering when the security consultants I was paying good money for would arrive," Ms. Bounty said.

"Yeah, well," Rade said. "If you would have let us escort you down to the surface in the first place, probably none of this would have happened. I'll need you to authorize full sharing mode so I can see where you are on my map."

She sent the authorization, and a moment later her blue dot appeared on the overhead map, along with the blue dots of the surviving members of her team. They were in a small alcove of some kind to the west; a passageway led back toward the main pedway system there. He noted a red dot plunked down squarely at the end of that passageway.

"We're in a service corridor of some kind," Ms. Bounty said. "A lot of fiber optic conduits running through here."

"Looks like you have company," Rade said.

"Yes," Ms. Bounty returned. "A rather large bioweapon has camped out at the far end of our passageway, barring our only way out. It's too big to fit in the service corridor."

"Would this bioweapon happen to look like a dinosaur, with thick armor leaving only the tips of the feet and tail exposed?"

"That's the one. And unfortunately, it has learned to keep those tips away from us."

"All right," Rade transmitted. "I'm not sure if you realized, but we vented the atmosphere over an hour and a half ago. The bioweapon should be dead by now."

"Oh we realized," Ms. Bounty transmitted. "And I guarantee you, it's not dead. Asleep, maybe. But dead, no."

Rade studied the map. "All right, I'm working on a plan. I'll get back to you." He closed the connection. "Bender, send the HS3s forward along our previous path. I want them to confirm that the cave-in has been cleared."

A few minutes later Bender reported: "The HS3s just returned. The repair drones have definitely made a path through the debris. If we need to make a tactical retrograde, the way to the surface is clear."

"Good," Rade said. "Units A and B, proceed into the western corridor toward Ms. Bounty's position. Once you're close to the bioweapon, switch your headlamps to normal light mode and open fire at the enemy. Draw it away. Return to this passageway, and proceed back the way we came. Make your way to the next closest exit, and if it's blocked, take a roundabout route back here. Make your way to the surface and lose the pursuer in the city if you haven't shaken it from your six by then. Rendezvous with the team at the Dragonfly hangar."

"Understood," Unit A said.

Rade glanced at the green forms of the others. "The rest of you, with me. We're going to camp out in the shadows."

Rade proceeded forward down the main passageway, headed in the direction of the cave-in, while the two robots moved into the western passage. When Rade had judged himself a sufficient distance away, he ordered the team to halt, and the individual members assumed defensive positions.

"Weapon lights off," Rade ordered. The passage plunged into absolute darkness. Rade wasn't going to gamble that the bioweapon couldn't see infrared.

He watched the two dots representing the robots move forward, then freeze as they passed beyond comm range.

Damn lead-containing walls.

Long moments passed. Rade fidgeted nervously. His targeting reticle was still visible, thanks to shielded filaments, and he kept it pointed in the direction of the western corridor even though he couldn't see anything, ready to reactivate his weapon light and open fire if he had to.

Finally a bright green glow appeared from the western passageway.

"Be prepared to retreat," Rade sent his team.

The robots noiselessly appeared from the branch and the night vision auto-gated, reducing the intensity of the light produced by their headlamps. The Centurions hurried away from the party.

A moment later a large dark blob emerged. It seemed to pause, and Rade was worried for a moment that it might turn straight for his team. But then that blob diminished as it pursued the retreating robots.

Rade exhaled in relief. He waited until the blob was no longer visible on the infrared spectrum, then he said: "Units C, D, infrared lights on. Move to the corridor. Reestablish communications with the *Amytis* away team."

The robots dashed toward the passageway. When they arrived, the dots for Ms. Bounty's team updated: she was already on her way.

"We need to get into orbit as soon as possible," Ms. Bounty transmitted.

"I'm working on it," Rade replied. "Argonauts: headlamps on. Retain infrared mode."

She and her men emerged from the corridor a moment later and joined up with Rade's team. All four of her mercenaries had survived, but only three of the unsuited combat robots remained. Two of those robots still carried a glass storage bin between them. It was empty: she hadn't completed what she had come to do, apparently. Also, she had no HS3s left.

"You got down here via the lab?" Rade transmitted to Ms. Bounty.

"Yes," Ms. Bounty replied. "The colonists apparently collapsed all routes leading inside the pedway. We weren't sure why at the time. However, the inhabitants missed the lab route. Our target escaped into the pedway using that path when we arrived. We followed. Shortly thereafter, the bioweapons intervened. We've been stuck in that service corridor until you showed."

The party reached the collapsed section of the pedway system. The city repair drones had removed half of the debris, creating a wide gap in the middle that the trapped bioweapons had used to force their way out. Several of those drones lay inactive on the floor, unable to fly in the low pressure environment.

The party moved past the cave-in and reached the exit region shortly: an inactive escalator led to the surface.

Rade sent the HS3s up and the scouts confirmed the outside area was clear.

Rade disabled his IR unit and switched back to the visual light spectrum as the party ascended. He passed the half-repaired breach seal, and in moments emerged into the surface shed. There was no sign of the original doors. New frames lay on the ground in front of the shed, but the half finished objects had been crushed under the weight of something massive—likely the bioweapons when they had emerged. The repair drones lay helpless on the ground around them, their rotors occasionally spinning futilely.

"Shaw, do you read?" Rade tried. "Shaw?"

No answer.

"Fret, what's going on with the *Argonaut*?"

"It appears all of our repeaters have been recalled," Fret said.

"What?" Rade said.

"It gets worse," Fret continued. "The ships themselves aren't where they should be."

"What are you talking about?" Rade said.

"The *Argonaut* and *Amytis* aren't in geosynchronous orbit anymore."

nineteen

Zoltan piloted the shuttle toward the Marauder class ship, *Argonaut*. Behind him, his Persian prisoners were clamped into the seats, staring blankly ahead. The reprogrammed robots sat beside them. He had already reprogrammed the AI of the shuttle, so there was no worry in that regard. It was all up to his acting ability, now. And if there was anything to be said about Zoltan, it was that he was a very good actor.

SHAW STARED UNEASILY at the approaching craft on the video feed.

"Why aren't they responding?" she said.

"It's possible the comm node has been damaged in some way," Bax said.

"Are you detecting any obvious external damage to the shuttle itself?" Shaw asked.

"Negative," Bax replied.

"Without that comm node, you can't access the shuttle's AI to retrieve biometric information from the crew, right?" Shaw asked.

"That's right, I can't," Bax replied.

"Well let me know when you're able to get any kind of remote reading on the crew, then," she said.

The shuttle steered toward the external hangar bay doors.

"I have a reading," Bax said. "The ratio of humans to robots I'm detecting through the thin hull of the vessel does not match the ratio of those that went to the surface."

"The crew abandoned their Hoplites to take the shuttle up?" Shaw said.

"It would appear so," Bax replied. "Though given the number of combat robots, some of the *Amytis* crew must have joined them. And I am detecting only one Artificial, not two."

"We lost Ms. Bounty or Harlequin..."

"It would appear so," Bax said.

"Why didn't we detect the party approaching the terminal on the city streets below?" Shaw said. "Perdix drones and bioweapons force them into the lab, and we lose communications. At the same time, the enemy disperses. Then twenty minutes later, all of a sudden the Model 2 is departing the city."

"Perhaps they used some other route to reach the terminal, potentially underground," Bax replied.

The shuttle closed with the hangar doors, as if expecting Shaw to open it.

"Can I risk not letting them board?" Shaw said. "If someone's hurt..."

"The decision is yours," Bax said.

She hesitated a moment longer, then: "Open the hangar doors." She was terrified that Rade or one of the others was severely injured. Any delay could end in someone's death. Even so, that didn't mean she needed to be lax in the security department. "I want a complement of Centurions waiting outside the airlock. As soon as the bay atmosphere fills, deploy the robots into the hangar."

"Dispatching eight Centurions," the *Argonaut's* AI replied.

The craft docked without issue, the bay doors sealed, and the atmosphere began to replenish.

Shaw glanced at the overhead map of the ship presented by her Implant, and zoomed in on the hangar area.

"I see the blue dot indicating the newly docked Dragonfly," she said. "But I'm not seeing any indicators for the rest of the crew. Their Implants should have linked up with the *Argonaut's* comm node by now."

"Their Implants appear to be offline," Bax said.

Shaw shook her head. "This is getting stranger by the moment. Send the remaining Centurions down there on the double." There were only five more left aboard.

"Do you still want the current eight to go inside when the hangar pressurizes?" Bax asked.

"Of course," Shaw responded.

The atmosphere stabilized, and the first eight Centurions rushed through the airlock and into the bay. The others had not yet arrived.

"Lock that airlock behind them," Shaw said. "And prepare to vent the bay on my order."

Shaw switched to the point of view of the camera in the hangar bay and watched as the shuttle's down ramp lowered. A man dressed in a purple robe emerged. He wore a shawl over his head, and a thick black beard grew to the middle of his chest. His eyes had a fire in them.

The Centurions had formed a defensive ring

around the shuttle.

"Hands where we can see them!" the Praetor unit in charge said.

The man raised his palms over his head.

"Who the hell is that?" Shaw asked.

"It appears to be an Artificial of some kind," Bax replied.

"Hello!" the man shouted. "I have refugees with me, from the surface! I request aid and safe passage!"

"What do you want to do?" Bax asked.

"I have five individuals aboard who are in need of serious treatment," the man continued. "Please, you must help them."

"Have one of the Centurions look inside," Shaw said.

A moment later Bax said: "The Centurion reports that the five humans aboard are unresponsive, and in a state of shock. There are definite injuries to some of them. Signs of blunt force trauma, laser wounds, and so forth."

"I can't risk bringing them aboard," Shaw said. "We have rules against the spread of contagion, especially when dealing with colonies infested by bioweapons."

"We can send a Weaver down to them," Bax said.

"Do it," Shaw ordered. "And cuff that Artificial. Also, get everyone out of the shuttle."

The Praetor had the Artificial flexicuffed, then approached the rear of the shuttle. "Everyone out!"

Five SK-style combat robots marched out of the shuttle. They held their hands behind their heads in a posture of surrender.

The down ramp of the shuttle began to close behind them.

"I said I wanted *everyone* off that shuttle!" Shaw

said. "Not just the robots!"

The robed Artificial broke the flexicuffs that held it. Meanwhile, the five combat robots lowered their arms: they had held blasters hidden in each hand. They opened fire.

The Artificial produced a blaster and joined in the attack. In under three seconds, all of Shaw's eight Centurions were lying on the ground, smoking. Three of the attacking robots from the shuttle had also fallen.

"Bax, explosively decompress the hangar," Shaw said. "And demagnetize the deck—I don't want those robots magnetically mounting to the surface."

The robed Artificial rushed toward a nearby bulkhead as if it knew she would make that command. The hangar doors opened, and all the other robots were sucked outside. The shuttle remained in place because of its weight, as did the Artificial—it had wrapped its hands around a railing on the bulkhead, and hung on while its body was pulled backward.

The air completely vented an instant later and the Artificial's feet returned to the deck thanks to the artificial gravity.

"Remind me to invest in defensive laser platforms for the hangar bay at some point," Shaw said.

"I will," Bax said. "But what would you like to do in the interim?"

"I don't know yet," she said. "Can you tell if the shuttle occupants are still alive?"

"The shuttle appears to have remained pressurized," Bax said.

"Not sure if that's good or bad," Shaw said.

She watched the robed Artificial approach the inner hatch of the airlock. It placed its hands on the surface.

"What is it doing?" Shaw said.

"Unknown," Bax replied.

Several moments passed without anything of note transpiring. On the other side of the airlock, near the outer hatch, her other five Centurions had arrived. They waited there, ready to follow her orders.

One of the robots near the back of the group lifted its laser rifle and opened fire on the others in rapid succession, downing them all.

"What the—" Shaw exclaimed.

The robot went to the inner hatch.

"Don't let that robot override the hatch controls!" Shaw said.

"Too late," Bax replied.

The hatch on the hangar side opened and the robed Artificial stepped into the airlock. When the door closed behind it, air misted within. The inner hatch slid aside a moment later and the Artificial stepped aboard the *Argonaut* proper.

"How the hell did the Artificial remotely reprogram the robot like that?" Shaw asked.

"Unknown," Bax replied.

The reprogrammed robot and the Artificial marched together from the hangar bay.

"I want you to seal off all decks," Shaw said. "Institute material condition ZEBRA."

"Instituting material condition ZEBRA," Bax echoed.

She watched the pair approach one of the breach seals. The robed Artificial stood off to one side while the Centurion switched its rifle to cutting mode and began lasering through.

"No no no," Shaw said. "I'm going to lose my ship. I need options, Bax."

"I'm afraid I don't have any recommendations," Bax said. "Other than that you should probably evacuate."

"I'm not going to evacuate," Shaw said. "You know how much we paid for this ship, don't you? We're not even done paying off the damn loan!"

"Is a loan more valuable than your life?" Bax asked pointedly.

"Good point." Yet Shaw couldn't bring herself to evacuate. Not yet.

After several minutes, the robot finished cutting through the seal and the pair proceeded. They were stopped shortly by another seal, this one blocking a scuttle. Once more the robot stepped forward and began to cut.

"What direction are they headed?" Shaw asked.

"The bridge," Bax said.

"Damn it." Shaw got up from her station at the Sphinx. "Bax, you're officially in command of the *Argonaut*."

"What are you going to do?" Bax asked.

"Stop them," Shaw replied.

"Rade would not approve if I let anything happen to you," Bax said.

"Then make sure you do whatever you can to help me." Shaw left the bridge.

She overrode the sealed hatches on the way to the armory. Once there, she proceeded to open one of the storage closets and quickly donned a strength-enhancing exoskeleton, minus the jumpsuit. She didn't have hardpoints like Rade to attach the suit to, and that increased the speed with which she was able to slip into the exoskeleton. She chose not to wear a full-blown suit, as it would have taken her twice as long to prepare.

She dialed up the strength setting to full, then grabbed two grenades from the rack and attached them to her harness. She drew the blaster from her belt, planted herself against the far bulkhead, and aimed at the sealed doorway.

She checked the overhead map. The red dots representing the two intruders were passing this way. She waited, unsure if they would make a stop at the armory or simply continue on toward the bridge.

"Bax, lock away the gear," she said.

A steel barrier rose from the floor, sealing away the storage closets.

"What if you need more?" Bax asked.

"Just hope I don't."

She saw the molten outline of a rectangle taking shape on the entry hatch. So the Artificial had decided to make a stop at the armory after all.

She kept the blaster aimed at the door. Her hands had begun to shake slightly. She was still breathing hard from the effort of racing down to the armory and frantically pulling on the exoskeleton.

Come on. Come on.

The door fell in. The robot was in full view.

She squeezed the trigger and the robot collapsed. She had put it out of commission.

She waited for the robed Artificial to appear. Her hands continued to shake. Her breathing came in quick gasps.

She glanced at the overhead map. The red dot of the Artificial remained just outside.

Growing impatient, she ripped one of the grenades from her harness and tossed it out the door. The explosion wouldn't breach the hull, but it should cause enough damage to disable the Artificial.

The grenade detonated. She held a hand over her face, worried about shrapnel. None came her way.

She kept her blaster pointed at the doorway for

long moments. Still, no one emerged. She looked at her map. The Artificial was still outside, apparently. Same position.

She grabbed her last grenade and threw it harder, bouncing it off the far bulkhead.

The explosion came.

Before the smoke cleared, she spotted a blur of motion and squeezed the trigger.

The fallen robot came hurtling toward her. The Artificial must have picked it up and thrown it.

She dove to the side.

Then the robed Artificial was on her.

Before she knew what was happening, the blaster was ripped from her grasp.

Synthetic fingers grabbed her wrists and with incredible strength threw her across the compartment.

She smashed into the bulkhead near the entrance and plunged to the deck. Her wrists hurt incredibly. The exoskeleton frame had collapsed there, and the metal was digging into her skin.

She clambered to her feet.

From the far side of the compartment, the robed Artificial was pointing the blaster at her.

Shaw raised her hands in surrender.

Then the Artificial smiled widely, lowered the weapon, and it tossed the blaster to the deck behind it. Then it raised its hands, assuming a sparring stance.

Shaw summoned all her reserves, and then she attacked.

The Artificial lunged for her.

Shaw side-stepped, partially activating the supermagnets in her boots to momentarily run on the bulkhead as she had practiced with Rade so often in the past, and then rammed her feet down on the attacker, connecting with the back of its head.

The Artificial momentarily gave way before the impact, then spun around as she landed and issued three quick blows.

Shaw blocked them in turn, and issued three of her own. "Hut hut hut!"

She used her supermagnets to rotate her body sideways and issue a solid kick to its ribcage.

The Artificial caught her foot and slammed her to the deck.

The impact knocked the wind out of her, but she managed to kick with her other foot and sent the Artificial toppling backward.

She got up and threw herself on her foe, mounting it. She issued several rapid blows to the head and neck area.

The Artificial flung her off and rose to its feet. It came in fast, fists swinging and feet kicking.

All that training Shaw endured in the navy, the hand-to-hand combat rating school, the endless sparring sessions with Rade and the other ex-MOTHs, she called upon all of that now as she fought for her very life. Because she knew if she lost, not only would she die, but likely Rade and everyone else left behind on that planet would, too.

But it wasn't enough.

A hard blow connected with her face and everything momentarily became black. She thought she was dead.

But then she awoke a few seconds later. Her head throbbed. Her body ached everywhere.

The Artificial was roughly dragging her through the tight corridors, carrying a laser rifle in its free hand. She was too utterly spent to resist.

The robed Artificial reached a hatch and tossed her legs to the side, and then concentrated on using the

ISAAC HOOKE

rifle to cut through the door. Shaw tried to rise on one elbow but felt extremely dizzy. She noticed a pool of blood underneath her where her face had lain on the ground. She touched her features, searching for the source, and felt a sharp pain when she touched her cheek. The bone was shattered, she thought. The notion saddened her. Rade had always said she had the cutest cheeks. The cutest dimples.

The breached door fell inward and the Artificial dragged her inside. She realized she was in sickbay.

The Artificial lifted her onto one of the tables and began to rip her exoskeleton away. Sometimes the metal fragments of the broken exoskeleton tore into her flesh, and she flinched at the pain. Finally, when the suit was completely removed, the Artificial secured her to the table using the provided straps.

It wheeled one of the Weavers to her. The surgical robot pressed a needle into her arm and mercifully she lost consciousness.

twenty

S till standing in front of the pedway shed, Rade glanced at Ms. Bounty, then to the robots carrying the empty glass container. He remembered what Ms. Bounty had told him earlier: "Our target escaped..."

"Why have our ships left orbit?" Rade said, fighting back a growing anger.

"It has to be the work of my target," Ms. Bounty said.

"Zoltan?" Rade asked.

"That is what the colonists call the Artificial, yes," Ms. Bounty replied. "He's not on the planet anymore."

"How do you know?"

"We are linked in a way, him and I," Ms. Bounty said. "When in the same city, I can sense his presence, and get an idea of his general location. I'm not receiving anything at all at the moment. He had to have gone into orbit. It's possible he may have ventured into the desert beyond, but I highly doubt that."

"Would this Artificial have the means to take over a ship such as the *Argonaut?*" Rade said, a sinking feeling gripping his stomach.

"Absolutely," Ms. Bounty said.

Rade pressed his lips together. Hard. "All right, Argonauts. Listen up. We need to make our way back to the starting terminal at the best possible speed. Shaw is in danger. Traveling overwatch. Three fire teams. Now fucking move!"

Tahoe divvied up the men, placing the HS3s and robots in the lead, and dispersing the *Amytis* team members among Rade's men. The teams hugged the buildings as they advanced.

Rade kept an eye on the sky, leery of the Perdix drones. If that swarm came at them, in their current condition the team members wouldn't put up much of a fight. In fact, without the laser shields of the Hoplites, his team would probably fall to the very first wave. It was a good thing the swarm didn't have enough propellant to stay airborne indefinitely, because all the machines would have had to do was hover near the top of the dome and keep an eye out for movement below.

"Lead HS3 is picking up a bioweapon," Bender said.

Rade saw the red dot appear on his display. It was slowly moving perpendicular to their course.

"Give it a wide berth," Rade said.

The team circumnavigated the area containing the lumbering creature, and then proceeded once more toward the designated terminal located at the rim of the colony.

Soon they had left behind the tall minarets and sand-colored buildings of the Persian section for the low-slung, mansard-roofed structures of the Sino-Korean.

"This is odd," TJ announced. "I'm not reading the shuttle on my overhead map. Nor any of the booster rockets. But we should be well within range by now."

"Must be some interference," Manic said.

"I hope so," Tahoe said. "For all our sakes."

About two blocks from the target Bender spoke.

"Okay, we have a problem," Bender said. "The HS3s are reporting Perdix drones perched on top of the buildings lining the path to the terminal."

Rade glanced at his overhead map and spotted twenty-one red dots representing the drones, spread out across the mansard-roofed structures.

"They're lying in ambush for us," Tahoe said. "Probably lurking on rooftops all along the perimeter, waiting for us to make a run for the hangars so that they can mow us down."

"I'll send two robots to draw them off," Ms. Bounty said.

"You'll lose them..." Rade said.

"I know," she replied.

A moment later two of her robots were dashing through the street at a full run. They activated their jetpacks, leaping onto the rooftops. Rade watched from the point of view of one of the HS3s, which was hovering close to the top of a nearby building, and he saw the Perdix drones thrust into the air. The two robots swerved to the side, leaping down into the adjacent street.

Rade glanced at his overhead map. Eighteen red dots pursued, leaving only three behind.

Rade gave silent thanks to the AIs that were giving their lives for the rest of them; he waited until the retreating drones were about three streets away, and then gave his next order:

"Bender, Lui, Manic, take out the remaining drones."

The indicated men leaped onto the nearest rooftop, dropped, and low-crawled to the edge. A moment later the remaining three red dots vanished.

According to the overhead map, that act caused a dozen of the eighteen drones to turn back: their onboard AIs realized the robots were acting as a diversion. New red dots also appeared from the western and eastern sides as more drones came to investigate.

"Go go go!" Rade said.

The party dashed forward, some of them hugging the buildings on the left side of the street, others, the right. Ms. Bounty shared the burden of porting the glass container with her remaining robot.

Rade held his rifle toward the rooftops opposite him, and linked the servomotors in his jumpsuit arm to his local AI. The AI took control of the arm, and compensated for his movements to keep the scope aimed above the mansards. As soon as drones came within view, the weapon would automatically open fire. He withdrew the blaster from his belt with the other hand, and programmed that arm the same way. The others in the party were doing the same with their own rifles and blasters, so that everyone ran with their arms outstretched.

The robots on point were about twenty meters from the hangar when the first drones arrived. As the units overtopped the buildings, weapons opened fire across the team, bringing the Perdix attackers down.

"We've reached the terminal," Unit C said.

One by one the team members emerged into the street that ran along the outer rim of the dome, and was adjacent to the terminal. They crossed in zigzag patterns to the designated building.

Rade emerged. He spread his arms out to either side, so that he had a weapon covering each approach. He had set his AI to assume control of his mad dash, and it randomly swerved left and right while increasing and decreasing his speed to avoid the invisible laser fire from the incoming drones. He glanced to the left, and saw the malevolent metal forms of the drones in the sky. In the street below, one of the bioweapons was quickly bearing down on them.

Rade barreled through the glass doors of the terminal. He glanced over his shoulder, and saw the remainder of the party enter behind him. Tiny laser bores began to riddle the glass.

Halfway across the terminal, the glass shattered entirely at the entrance as the armored bioweapon broke inside.

The party reached the designated hangar and everyone hurried into the bay. Rade disabled AI control of his jumpsuit and paused by the hatch, waiting for Tahoe who was on drag, and as soon as his friend was in, Rade entered and with Tahoe's help shut the large exit hatch behind him.

"TJ, lock this door," Rade said.

"On it," the hacker replied.

Rade turned toward the landing platform.

The Dragonfly was gone. And beside it, the *Amytis* shuttle was a pile of rubble, no doubt a victim of the Dragonfly's weaponry. As before, there were no other craft in the hangar. Units A and B weren't there, either, probably still trapped in the pedway. The Hoplites were absent as well—the blast shields at the lab hadn't opened after all.

Rade didn't care about the incredible expense of losing the mechs and robots by that point. All he cared about was reaching Shaw.

The floor shook. Behind him, protrusions appeared in the metal of the hatch as the bioweapon bashed at it, attempting to break in.

"All right," Rade said. "Fret, I need the location of the closest abandoned shuttle or evacuation craft."

"I'm sending out a ping now," Fret said. "Without repeaters, I have no guarantee it will travel very far." He paused. "Mmm, all the nearby hangars are empty."

"Anything beyond?" Rade said.

"Wait," Fret said.

The hatch continued to cave.

"Fret..." Rade pressed.

"Found something," Fret said. "A Model 3C in a different terminal along the rim of the dome, about five blocks away."

"Forward the comm ID to TJ so he can begin his hack attempts," Rade said.

"I don't know," TJ said. "3Cs can be tricky. You're not reading any others out there?"

"I told you, without repeaters..." Fret paused. "Okay, I picked up a couple of 4As, and a 5B. Plus some evacuation craft. IV-3s. The 3C is still the closest."

"Mmm," TJ said. "All right. The 3C is the best bet, then."

"Set the waypoint, Fret," Rade said.

The waypoint appeared on the overhead map.

"Wait, what are you going to do?" Tahoe said, staring at the growing protrusions in the hatch. "We can't really go back in there, you know that right?"

Rade gazed toward the hangar doors that led to the desert outside. "We don't have to."

twenty-one

R ade instructed TJ to access the hangar interface and send a signal mimicking a shuttle's exit request.

The hangar doors promptly opened.

The HS3s flew outside. The area was clear.

"Out!" Rade said.

The team members rushed toward the hangar doors and leaped outside in turn.

Rade dashed to the edge and vaulted over, firing a quick burst from his jetpack to cushion his fall to the sand two meters below. He landed at a run and continued on toward the target. The thick red sand swallowed him to the ankles, forcing him to slow right down. The team followed the outer contour of the base of the colony, staying close to the metal wall. Behind them, the hangar doors sealed shut. Rade doubted it would hold back the bioweapon for long.

"By the way, looks like the booster rockets are gone," Manic said. "Our Zoltan friend was quite thorough in his destruction of our property."

Rade had his local AI take over the run and then he glanced to the east, zooming in on the different booster rocket sites. All that remained of each of them were piles of charred metal. He canceled the zoom and took control of his suit once more.

About fifty meters from the target hangar doors, Tahoe announced from the drag position: "The bioweapon just broke out of the hangar. A bunch of drones came with it."

"Hurry!" Rade said.

The first Centurion reached the hangar. TJ once more mimicked a shuttle request and the doors opened. The team members began jetting the two meters into the hangar.

"Gah!" Tahoe said before he landed.

He was the last one in.

"Shut the door!" Rade rushed to his friend, who was limping. "Where were you hit?"

"Lower calf," Tahoe said.

Rade retrieved the suitrep kit from Tahoe's cargo pocket. As blood misted from the tiny holes in his calf area, Rade applied one patch to the entry region on the suit, and another to the exit. Tahoe's skin had no doubt swelled outward to seal the gaps and maintain suit pressure.

"TJ, where's our shuttle!" Rade said, helping Tahoe toward the Model 3C; it looked like a tiny United Systems corvette class starship with those rear wings and slim nose. The other members of the team had formed a defensive circle around the craft.

"Almost got it," TJ said.

The bay doors began to buckle behind him: the bioweapon had arrived. Bore holes appeared in the metal as the drones opened fire.

"Hurry!" Rade said.

More protrusions appeared in the hangar doors in the shape of the bioweapon's armored head. A small gap had formed in the center where the two doors met.

"It's ours!" TJ said.

The down ramp lowered.

"Load up!" Rade said. "Harlequin, you take the cockpit. TJ, transfer control to him."

In moments all members of the combined team had taken their seats in the cabin and clamped in.

"The doors won't open," Harlequin said. "The bioweapon has damaged them too much."

"Get ready to punch it, Harlequin," Rade said. "Arm all external weapons. TJ, give me access to the nose camera."

That access arrived, and Rade switched to the camera's perspective. The doors seemed on the verge of breaking.

The left door finally caved and the bioweapon stuffed its blunt head inside.

"Now!" Rade said.

The shuttle accelerated, ramming into the head, sending the creature hurtling backward as the shuttle burst through the weakened doors. The external turrets of the craft opened fire as the Model 3C swept out over the desert, and its lasers took down at least four Perdix drones. The remaining regrouped and pursued.

The craft swerved as Harlequin initiated evasive maneuvers. He flew the shuttle very low to the dunes, which was the best strategy to avoid presenting the drones with an easy target. The rearmost turrets fired constantly.

Rade glanced at the overhead map and saw that the powerful shuttle was easily outrunning the drones. In about thirty seconds, the Perdix craft had fallen behind by four kilometers. Harlequin swerved the shuttle behind a rock formation, cutting them from view entirely.

"Keep going on this track until we've put about twenty kilometers on them," Rade said. "Then take us into orbit. Oh and, see if you can reach the colonists. Let them know we'll return for them when we can."

"Done," Harlequin said. "I was able to connect with the comm node Fret left with them. Farhad wishes us the best of speed."

In about twenty minutes the Model 3C had accelerated to escape velocity and reached the upper atmosphere.

"I'm detecting debris in orbit," Harlequin said.

"Is it the *Argonaut?*" Rade asked. Was Shaw gone?

"No," Harlequin said. "The elemental composition is consistent with the *Amytis* transport."

Rade slumped in his seat. "Tell me you have a bead on the *Argonaut?*"

"No, I—" Harlequin said. "Wait. I've found it. The *Argonaut* is three hundred thousand kilometers distant, on our starboard side. It's heading toward the return Gate. To SK space."

"Set a pursuit course," Rade said. "In the meantime, see if you can tap her in."

Harlequin paused. Then: "The *Argonaut* isn't answering."

"What's the maximum speed on this shuttle as compared to the *Argonaut?*" Rade asked.

"About a quarter the speed," Harlequin said.

Rade nodded slowly. He glanced at the tactical display that now overlaid the upper right of his vision, as fed to him from the shuttle's AI. The ice giant whose moon contained a Sino-Korean military base was not far from Lang. "Are the two corvettes still in orbit around the abandoned military base?"

"They are," Harlequin replied.

"If we make a detour for those two corvettes,"

Rade said. "And are able to salvage them, how long would it take to intercept the *Argonaut*?"

"It'll take four days to reach the corvettes from here," Harlequin said. "Then, assuming we successfully obtain control of one of the starships, we should reach the Gate in another six days. Or four days behind the *Argonaut*."

"And if we fly directly to the Gate with the shuttle?" Rade asked.

"It will take about a month," Harlequin said.

"Four days behind versus a month behind," Rade said. "It's an easy decision. Harlequin, set a course for the SK military base. And keep trying to reach the *Argonaut*. Let me know if you ever get through."

Rade ordered the cabin pressurized so that he could treat Tahoe's laser injuries. Before he opened Tahoe's jumpsuit, he had the internal cabin sensors run a complete scan for contagions. Lui ran his own scan, and also concluded that no one harbored any external pathogens or microscopic bioweapons on their suits, or in the case of Ms. Bounty's unsuited robots, their polycarbonate shells. Lui performed a final sweep of the cabin itself and then gave Rade the go-ahead to proceed.

Rade removed Tahoe's leg assembly, and then thoroughly disinfected and bound the entry and exit wounds. When that was done, Bender revealed that he, too, had been hit, though in the shoulder region, but had applied his own suit patches. Rade treated him as well.

When that was done, Lui took blood samples from the both of them, and confirmed that they were not infected with anything. Rade ordered everyone else to keep wearing their jumpsuits as a precaution, and instructed Lui to keep the pair under observation for the next few days. It was as close to a decontamination watch as Rade could come up with, given his limited resources.

When Rade returned to his seat he stared angrily at Ms. Bounty.

"What?" she said.

"I'm going to need you to tell me who the hell this Zoltan is," Rade said. "And what you intended to capture with that glass cage of yours."

"I don't have to reveal that to you," Ms. Bounty said.

"I think you do," Rade said. "Given the hell my team went through to rescue you. And considering that I've lost my ship to this character. Not to mention, my girlfriend. I need to know what we're up against if I'm going to help you any further. Otherwise, when we get to the corvettes, I'm going to quarter you and your career mercenaries in the brig for the rest of the trip."

The mercenaries bristled obviously at those words, with their hands reaching toward the blasters at their belts. Rade's own team members did the same.

Ms. Bounty glanced at her hired soldiers. "Get your hands away from your weapons. We're working *with* these men, not against them." She looked at Rade, then sighed. "As you wish, Mr. Galaal. I will answer your questions to the best of my abilities. I cannot reveal everything to you, however. Not yet. But I will share relevant details."

"And why can't you reveal everything?" Rade said.

"Some details you are not ready to understand," she said. "Not in your current state of mind."

"And what's that supposed to mean?" Rade said.

"I think she's referring to the fact that Zoltan has your girlfriend," Harlequin said.

"Tell me everything," Rade said. "Never mind my state of mind. What's your interest in this Zoltan character? You came to capture him, correct?"

"I did," she said.

"Why? And don't try to tell me it was to help the colonists."

"I came partially to help them," Ms. Bounty said. "Let's just say, he you name Zoltan is a danger to the galaxy."

"A danger? How so?"

"He wishes to destroy humanity," Ms. Bounty said. "What he did on Lang was merely his proving ground. He was testing out various concepts; I interrupted him before he could complete his tests."

"Is that why he was creating bioweapons?" Rade said. "To use them against Earth?"

"Yes, but not in the way you think," she said. "He was trying to create something, a specific type of creature. Something that would allow him to generate geronium from the crust of a populated world."

Geronium was the fuel that all starships used.

"So what are you saying, he was trying to create his own navy?" Rade asked.

"Essentially," Ms. Bounty responded. "But the creation process involves the destruction of the populated world. Or rather, the inhabitants themselves."

"I see," Rade said. "So what did you intend to do with him, once you captured him?"

"I would interrogate him," Ms. Bounty said. "To learn what he has discovered, find out what he has communicated to others like him, and then kill him."

"Others like him?" Rade said. "You mean there are more Artificials like him out there? What is this, some kind of robot revolt?"

"No," Ms. Bounty said. "But there are other Artificials who share Zoltan's... thirst for geronium. It's a thirst that will devastate humanity."

"So you're going to save us," Rade said, unable to hide the doubt from his voice.

"Indeed," Ms. Bounty said.

"Don't Artificials follow the Machine Constitution?" Manic said. "They can't harm humans."

"He and the others have overcome that programming," Ms. Bounty said.

"And you haven't?" Rade told her.

She smiled coldly. "If I am helping humanity, then evidently not."

"You know, it would have been easier if you let us go down with you from the get-go," Rade said. "If we had taken our Hoplites, you might have this Zoltan in custody by now."

"After reviewing the report from the drones I sent down to the surface," Ms. Bounty said. "I thought I could take him with my handful of robots and ex-soldiers. I was wrong. I underestimated his ingenuity. I did intend to contact you if trouble arose. However, we were unable to reach you after we were trapped in the pedway system."

"All right," Rade said. "Is there anything else we should know about this Zoltan?"

"Only that he will stop at nothing to achieve his machinations," Ms. Bounty said. "And that he cannot die by ordinary means. When we encounter him, you must let me trap him in the cage." She nodded at the large glass container strapped into one corner of the cabin, where she had placed it with her remaining porter robot.

"What, you're saying this Zoltan has some sort of energy shield around his body?" Rade asked.

"No," Ms. Bounty said. "But he can switch robot bodies. If you disable his current body, he will merely migrate to another. This cage will prevent him from doing that."

Rade glanced at Tahoe. He didn't like the sound of that. Not at all.

"An AI intelligence that migrates between bodies?" Rade said.

"It's possible," Tahoe said. "But we haven't developed the tech for that, not yet."

"What are you not telling us, Ms. Bounty?" Rade asked.

"You know more than enough to successfully complete the mission," Ms. Bounty said. "That will have to do, for the moment."

"There is one last thing I need to know," Rade said. "What's Zoltan going to do with my girlfriend?"

She stared at him unblinking. When she spoke, there was pity in her voice: "I'm afraid, Mr. Galaal, that's one question I truly don't know the answer to."

ISAAC HOOKE

twenty-two

During the long flight to the corvettes, the crew passed the time in the cramped quarters in various ways. There wasn't enough room in the cabin for more than two people to do proper physical training at once, so they took turns doing calisthenics throughout the day. They engaged in VR war games often; the addition of Ms. Bounty's four mercenaries made things interesting for the first while, but there was only so much gaming a person could take in a twenty-four hour period.

Rade caved out in VR when he needed to, usually two or three times a day. He muted all external sound, instructing the AI to interrupt him only in the event of an emergency, and immersed himself in a cavern environment. He placed the cavern mouth on a cliff near the sea, so that he could sit there, look down and watch the waves from on high when he so desired. He tried to clear his mind during the sessions, but his thoughts kept returning to Shaw, and the worry he felt for her. He had no idea what had happened aboard the *Argonaut*. If that Zoltan character harmed her in any way, Rade swore he would hunt down the Artificial and tear it limb from limb.

On the fourth day, the shuttle used the gravity of

the ice giant to slingshot toward the moon, matching its rotation speed, and in another two hours finally reached the abandoned military base and the two derelict corvettes in orbit.

The docking mechanisms on both ships were inactive, so Rade had Harlequin magnetically mount the shuttle to the closest ship and they boarded via an external airlock hatch. He sent in the HS3s and Centurions to secure the corvette, and when that was done he dispatched TJ and Bender to engineering, and from there the pair were able to restore power to the ship and boot the AI. TJ applied a special security chip to the AI core before the boot, which allowed him to elevate his privilege level to the maximum available. Once the AI was online, TJ was able to assign captain privileges to Rade. Needless to say, that chip had cost TJ a fortune on the black market.

"I've set the language to English, you should be good to go," TJ transmitted after Rade and the others had taken their places on the bridge around the circular series of stations that were the equivalent of the Sphinx. The compartment was far more spacious than their own bridge aboard the *Argonaut* of course. The only thing missing was Shaw in the astrogator's seat. Harlequin had taken that role. The Artificial would never replace her, and judging from the contrite expression on Harlequin's face, he knew that.

"Greetings, Captain," the corvette's AI said. "I am Zahir, AI of the corvette *Tiger*. Please state your name and set a password."

"Rade Galaal, password is tango beta five niner," Rade said. He planned to change it in private later.

"Thank you, Captain Galaal," Zahir said. "How can I be of service to you?"

"Tell me what happened here," Rade said. "Where

is the crew?"

"Those records have been wiped," Zahir replied. "However, judging from the airlock access logs, it appears the skeleton crew manning this ship was spaced to the last man."

"Do you have any record of an Artificial named Zoltan taking over?" Rade asked.

"No," Zahir said. "The last I remember, I was in orbit above Lang. I see that the autopilot was engaged while I was offline, with instructions to fly to the military base on this moon. I also see that the comm system was left active, with an automated system set to answer inbound comm requests. It is very strange."

"Yes," Rade said. "I suppose it is. Are there no combat robots remaining aboard?"

"There are fifteen offline combat robots in storage area C-22," Zahir said.

"Bring them online," Rade said. "And have them assume master-at-arm duties. What about mechs? Are there any mechs aboard?"

"Negative," Zahir said.

"Too bad. Shuttle complement?"

"Five Model 4As and one Model 3C," the *Tiger's* AI said.

"Nice," Rade said. "All right, bring us closer to the second corvette. We're going to board it. Bender and Tahoe, get down to sick bay. I want the Weavers to check on the progress of your wounds, and to double check you for any bio-contagions."

When the *Tiger* closed with the remaining derelict, Rade sent TJ, Fret and a team of robots to the second corvette via the shuttle, and TJ usurped control of that starship in the same manner. Once the AI was activated, Rade instructed his team to return, and then he ordered the second corvette, the *Camel*, to journey to Lang to retrieve the colonists. He had the *Camel's* AI activate its own offline combat robots aboard, with the hope that the units would be able to lead the colonists to safety. If that task proved too difficult—what with the lingering Perdix drones and potential bioweapons roaming the dome—Rade instructed the *Camel's* combat robots to simply guard the colonists until the SK military arrived to investigate.

During the past four days, the *Argonaut* had continued toward the exit Gate, never deviating. Rade ordered the *Tiger* to pursue. They had six more days until they reached the Gate, but in two days the *Argonaut* would pass from the system.

"Let's just hope she doesn't blow the Gate behind her," Fret said.

That was a terrible thought, and Rade tried not to think about it. With the Gate gone, they had no way to pass through the Slipstream and follow. They'd be trapped in the system until an SK Builder arrived to construct a return Gate. That could take anywhere from six months to a year.

The *Argonaut* was well beyond the range of any of the corvette's weapons, of course. Not that Rade would have ever risked firing at the ship, not while Shaw was aboard.

Bender and Tahoe rejoined the crew shortly after the *Tiger* was underway; the Weaver had declared them completely fit for duty.

The crew passed the time in a similar manner as they had aboard the shuttle. Lots of VR sessions. Listening to music on their Implants. Engaging in simulated war games. Physical training.

As for the latter, there no gym aboard the corvette, but Rade had the crew move aside all the junk in one of the cargo bays, converting it into a makeshift workout area for group calisthenics. Rade led the crew through PT three times a day.

A day out from the moon, Rade found himself leading one particular workout. There was something off about him that day, he couldn't quite place it. He felt... defeated. And angry. During the workout, he just kept pushing himself and the others. After completing one hundred pushups, he ordered another hundred. When he finished that, he demanded a hundred more.

He pushed himself and his men harder than any of them had ever worked since MOTH training. Rade took them through an endless series of exercises, cycling between pushups, pullups and abs.

"Come on you fecal eaters!" Rade would say. "Are you men, or are you maggots?" He'd pick out individuals who were lagging. "What's wrong, Manic? You claim you were once a MOTH? Bullshit! Push 'em push 'em push 'em!"

A few of Ms. Bounty's mercenaries threw up near the hour and a half mark, and another defiled his pants. By the two hour mark, all four career mercs had excused themselves. None of the Argonauts left; they continued pumping out sets for their boss, despite the stench of feces and vomit that lingered in the compartment.

Finally, at the third hour mark Fret collapsed. Rade only noticed when one of his men shouted at him.

"Boss!" Manic said.

Rade looked up from his pushups.

Manic was giving him an accusing look. The man nodded to one side. "Fret."

Rade followed his gaze and saw Fret lying on his back, staring up at the overhead; beads of sweat streamed down Fret's pale face, yet he seemed to be shivering.

"That's it," Rade said, rolling out of his pushup position. He could hardly speak for his panting. "You're all dismissed. Zahir, send a Weaver down here immediately." He pulled himself over to Fret. Manic was already there, supervising Fret as he drank from a water bottle.

"Are you all right?" Rade asked his prone brother.

Fret smiled weakly. "Yeah. I just need to lie down for a sec. Don't crowd me or anything."

"You can go, Manic," Rade said.

Manic gave Rade one last condemning look, then left.

An MA robot arrived, escorting a Weaver. The surgical robot promptly delivered glucose and rehydration therapy to Fret via intravenous.

When Fret was well enough to stand, Rade ordered the MA to escort Fret to the shared berthing area.

"Get some good food in you," Rade told him.

"Sure," Fret said. "Once I work up an appetite. I just want to sleep right about now."

Rade watched them go and then sat there alone in the compartment. He stared at the exit hatch for long moments.

"You all right?" someone said.

Maybe he wasn't quite so alone after all.

He glanced to his right and saw Tahoe watching from the far side of the compartment, where he sat with his back to the bulkhead.

"Yeah," Rade said.

"You shouldn't take it out on them you know," Tahoe said. "It's not their fault."

Rade sighed. "I'm more angry at myself than anyone else."

"And yet you take it out on your crew," Tahoe said.

"Maybe I should start working out alone," Rade said. "Put you in charge of PT. At least for the short term."

"Probably a good idea," Tahoe said.

"All right, done," Rade said. "Effective immediately, you're in charge of PT."

Tahoe nodded. "So truthfully, now, how are you holding up?"

Rade gazed down at his hands. He opened his fingers, stared at his palms. "Honestly? I'm a wreck."

"You're putting on a good show for the crew, then," Tahoe said. "Because I see a man fighting."

"I'm holding myself together just enough to get through this," Rade said. "You can't notice it, but I'm almost bursting at the seams. I am hanging on, however. And that's all I can do at the moment."

"I hear you," Tahoe said. "If I lost Tepin, I would... actually, I don't know what would happen to me. I wouldn't be the same man, I can tell you that."

Rade nodded. "That's it, I think. She makes me the man I am. Around her, I want to be a better person. I leave behind the ruthless killer I was on the Teams. But now that she's gone, the killer is coming back. Whenever I think of Zoltan, sheer murder fills my mind."

"When we find him," Tahoe said. "Ms. Bounty better hope that she gets to this Zoltan first. Because when you or I, or any other member of the crew meets him, there won't be much left of the Artificial."

"No, there won't," Rade agreed. "It's just too bad we can't touch him."

"That whole body-hopping bullshit?" Tahoe asked. "I'm not sure I believe it."

"I'm not sure either," Rade said. "But I'm going to try to hold back."

"Think you'll succeed?" Tahoe said.

"Honestly," Rade said. "When I meet this Zoltan, I'm not sure I'll be able to stop myself from throttling the Artificial."

twenty-three

Shaw opened her eyes. She had fallen into and out of a drugged consciousness for the past few hours, but now she was wide awake and lucid. She struggled against the straps that held her to the bed. She was able to shift her limbs back and forth slightly, but not enough to get free—mostly she was simply sliding around the upper layers of skin underneath the binds.

"Bax, let me out of here," Shaw said. "Bax?"

The *Argonaut's* AI didn't answer her.

Her cheek area seemed numb, but she did sense what felt like a bandage secured to the area. She glanced down; all her other cuts had been replaced with pink scars.

"Remain calm," a nearby Weaver unit said. "All of your injuries have been healed. I replaced your shattered cheekbone with 3D-printed osseous tissue, and grafted fresh skin grown from your stem cells. It will take a few hours for everything to set, and then I will remove the bandage."

"Cut me free," she told it.

"I am sorry, I am not authorized to do that," the Weaver said. "Not even after I remove the bandage."

"Why?"

No answer.

"When Rade gets back, he's going to have you dismantled for this, you realize that don't you?" she said.

Still the Weaver didn't respond.

"Hell, I'll do it myself when I get free," she muttered.

She accessed the overhead map, but the AI had apparently limited her access because she could only see her current position aboard the *Argonaut*, and not that of the intruder. She attempted to bring up the tactical display to get an idea where the *Argonaut* was headed, but received an "access denied" message.

Via her Implant, she began toying with the various remote interfaces around her, trying to see if she could log into any of them.

None of the interfaces answered her requests. But when she tried one of the video cameras in sickbay, her viewpoint automatically switched to it. She tried the second camera in the compartment, and then the hallway outside. They all worked.

So I still have access to the cameras.

She continued to cycle through the feeds. She noted that she had visual data only, no audio.

Eventually she reached the cameras on the bridge. She saw the robed Artificial seated at the captain's station. Its mouth was moving. Having a conversation with Bax, no doubt. Given how quickly the Artificial had reprogrammed the earlier robot, she had no doubt it had already converted the *Argonaut's* AI to its side. She wondered where the Artificial was taking the ship.

She tried to access the lip reading app she had stored in her Implant, but once more was hit with an "access denied."

She had a thought, and switched to an external

camera. Stars filled her vision.

So far, so good.

She attempted to rewind the feed by a few hours. That worked.

She had the local AI in her Implant compare the current position of the planets and other celestial bodies with footage taken from a few hours ago, and from the changes had it deduce the course of the *Argonaut*. Apparently the Artificial was steering the vessel straight for the exit Gate. Well, that wasn't too surprising, she supposed.

She continued cycling through the cameras, switching back to the internal placements. She reached the cargo bay feed and paused. She saw the Persians that had accompanied the Artificial from the planet. Dressed in robes, they were lying about, scattered across the deck, looking extremely pale, foreheads covered in sweat. They were quite obviously sick. Purple blotches had formed on the exposed skin of some of them. It looked worse than any bruising that Shaw had ever seen, and she suspected these poor people had been injected with some sort of engineered contagion.

She continued cycling through the remainder of the cameras, both internal and external, but discovered nothing else of note. She dismissed the feed entirely to ponder her predicament.

She had felt a persistent throbbing in her right wrist since awakening, and had attributed it to the overly tight restraints. But she was starting to wonder...

Glancing down, she shifted her wrist as far as she was able within the strap, and spotted something that made her suppress a grin. The Weaver had missed a fragment of the exoskeleton that had embedded in her wrist area when Zoltan crudely tore the metal framework from her body.

She rotated her wrist as far as the binding strap allowed, positioning the protruding steel sliver against the thick material, and began sliding her forearm back and forth a few millimeters at a time.

I'm going to saw my way out of here, if it takes the next week.

SHAW FELT A growing despair after the first few hours, because the binding material showed no signs of yielding to her slow attack. Instead, all she really seemed to accomplish was the creation of fresh friction burns to her wrist from the constant rubbing.

But Shaw didn't give up. She sawed every waking moment. It took her a few days, but her dogged persistence paid off, and she finally managed to file through the restraint. The end came quickly after she had cut halfway through—she started yanking on the bind in between sawing sessions, accelerating the process.

When she had successfully freed that hand, she remained motionless, knowing that the watchful eyes of the *Argonaut's* AI would alert the Artificial the moment she lifted her arm.

She cycled through the cameras once more, confirming that the path to Engineering was clear. Luckily, her captor had lasered through all the potential breach seals between sickbay and her destination. Out of curiosity, she cycled the camera to the cargo hold to check on the human prisoners. She had watched a terrible transformation take place over the past few days, with the passengers slowly becoming unrecognizable. They had ripped off their robes since the last time she had checked on them, and their backs had swollen into large purple masses. She didn't know what was happening to them.

Didn't want to know.

What the hell was the Artificial planning?

She checked the bridge camera, confirming that the robed intruder still resided there, then she dismissed the feed.

She stared at the ceiling and took several deep breaths.

Well, it's now or never.

She lifted her arm from the table and quickly freed her left hand from the other strap. She sat upright, and worked on the restraint that tied down her right leg.

The Weaver attempted to intercept her. She freed the leg and aimed a kick at the surgical robot's midsection, sending it crashing into the nearby bulkhead. She removed her other leg from the last remaining restraint and then leaped onto the deck. She hurried out the breached door into the tight corridor outside.

"Please return to the sickbay, Shaw," the *Argonaut's* AI came over the main circuit. "For your own safety."

"Screw you, Bax," Shaw said.

"There is no one here by that name," the *Argonaut's* AI replied. "Please return to the sickbay."

Shaw ignored the AI. She hurried through the passageways, once again glad that the intruder had cut through all the seals, preventing the AI from blocking her. She only wished she could see where her enemy currently resided on the overhead map. She quickly accessed the bridge camera: the robed Artificial was no longer there. She had no doubt it was racing to intercept her. While the sickbay was closer to

Engineering than the bridge, given the faster speed of an Artificial versus a human, she judged she would have about thirty seconds after she reached her destination until the intruder arrived.

At Engineering she hurried to the control panel. She wished she could manually seal the hatch behind her, but like all the doors that led there, it was permanently cut open.

She reached under the panel counter and retrieved the security chip TJ had hidden. She shoved the chip into the provided connection.

"Please stop what you're doing, Shaw," the *Argonaut's* AI said. "You don't realize the enlightenment Zoltan will bring to humanity."

Most military-grade starships had various defenses in place in their engineering sections to prevent crew members from doing what Shaw intended, like flooding the compartment with incapacitating agents for example, but the *Argonaut* had no such capabilities. The Marauder wasn't military grade. The Artificial would have to come down to the compartment itself if it wanted to stop her.

Using the chip, in moments she had usurped control of the *Argonaut* from the bridge. The tactical display filled out. She could see the planets around her once more, and another vessel pursuing four days behind.

Rade.

Shaw pulled up the Hellfire launch interface. First of all, she had to prevent the Artificial from destroying the undefended Gate. The Hellfires could be timed to detonate after the *Argonaut* passed through the Gate, destroying it behind them and trapping Rade and the others in the system. She intended to remedy that by firing all the missiles now. The Viper lasers could destroy the Gate, too, of course, but only before the *Argonaut* traversed. If the Artificial did that, he would strand everyone in the system.

Shaw set random targets and fired all missile tubes; she waited for the reload and fired again, repeating the process until the last of the missiles were away. She watched the green warhead indicators expand outward on the tactical display, sourced from the blue dot of the *Argonaut*. She smiled. As a side bonus, by launching all those missiles, she stripped the *Argonaut* of long range offensive capabilities, making it even easier for Rade or anyone else to intercept the ship in the future.

She wiped the smile from her lips. Next, she had to—

Something struck Shaw hard in the back of the head, and she slumped forward.

twenty-four

Rade sat in his spacious office aboard the *Tiger*. While the extra room was nice, he missed his old ship terribly, mostly because Shaw wasn't there. Any ship could be his home with her around. He hadn't been lying when he had told Tahoe he was a wreck without her. The most obvious absence were the scents he associated with her.

She was an early riser, and every morning when he woke up, it was always to the distinctive smell of the fresh coffee she had brewed. Or when he returned to their shared stateroom after his shift, sometimes he was greeted by the aroma of one of her home-cooked meals—usually some variation of chicken and leavened bread.

Then there were the smells of her body. At her station on the bridge she wore a very slight amount of perfume. It wasn't enough for him or anyone else to detect under ordinary circumstances—she was very conscious about not "disturbing the olfactory sensibilities" of the bridge crew, as she put it—but when she leaned toward him, or he brushed past her, he always picked up the subtle yet intoxicating fragrance. There were other scents: the sweat of her after working out, or making love. The smell of her hair after a shower. The minty fragrance of her breath in the evening.

All of that gone in the blink of an eye.

With the absence of her pleasing odors, his own stench was made all the more obvious. And vile. Especially considering he had neglected his personal hygiene in recent days.

Really should take a shower.

The call indicator flashed in the lower right of his vision. It was Lui.

Rade answered, voice mode.

"Boss," Lui said. "I just detected multiple missiles leaving the *Argonaut.*"

Rade stood up. "Shaw."

He dismissed the call and hurried from his office.

Lui glanced at him as he stepped onto the bridge.

"It has to be her," Lui agreed. "She's dumping the full inventory of missiles."

Rade nodded slowly. "Making sure Zoltan doesn't blow up the Gate behind him." *That's my girl.*

He took his place at the Sphinx. "Do we have trajectories on those missiles?"

"Yes," Lui said. "They've been fired perpendicular to the *Argonaut.* Well away from our ship, and the Gate. Wait... they're detonating."

Rade nodded. There was no way to change the target of those missiles, not after they had been launched. Not with that model of Hellfires, anyway. But Shaw apparently had elected not to take any chances.

He saw that the others were looking at him expectantly, as if waiting for him to give another order. Rade realized there wasn't really anything more they could do at the moment, and that he probably should have stayed in his office.

Despite all the years he had been in command of these men, he still sometimes felt uncomfortable. Like a fraud. He didn't have all the answers, didn't always know what to do. But he could never let them see his doubts. He had learned that early on. Which is not to say he wouldn't ask his crew for advice when he was uncertain what course of action to take. A good leader did that often.

But now wasn't one of those times. He knew exactly what they needed to do.

Keep following Shaw.

"Let me know if you detect anything else unusual," Rade said. He glanced at Fret, who had made a full recovery after the exhausting workout session. "And keep trying to hail them. Watch for a reply, no matter how weak, even if it seems like mere background radiation."

"We're going to get her back, boss," Manic said.

Rade nodded. He forced himself to stay sitting there, even though he felt like going back to his office immediately. After twenty minutes, he finally rose and returned to the adjacent compartment.

He sat down on the couch. Yes, that was another plus of the corvette: it had room enough for actual furniture in the captain's office. He could only imagine how much more he would be able to do if he had a couch in his office aboard the *Argonaut*. He would be so much more productive with all that room and a comfortable place to sit...

He lay back and closed his eyes.

OVER THE NEXT twelve hours, while the *Argonaut*

yet remained in the system, Rade often found himself gazing longingly at the fleeing vessel via the external camera. Even at maximum zoom, the craft was only the size of his fist.

Shaw was aboard.

Shaw.

So close. Yet so far.

When the ship finally passed through the Gate and out of view entirely, Rade felt a complete and utter sense of loss.

She's gone.

He sat back in his chair and rubbed his eyes. Gone forever.

No. She's still alive. Just in a different system.

Still, while he was sitting in his plush office chair, she was likely suffering at the hands of the Artificial. Who could say what tortures he was inflicting? Rade imagined them all, and it only stoked the fire of rage inside him.

The killer within was at full force by the time the *Tiger* reached the Gate four days later. It was well that he had stopped working out with the others, because his physical training spanned half the day by that point, three hours per session. He had talked to Bender, and the man had shared his stash of gear with Rade. The steroid kind. Rade needed a shot of testosterone to boost his recovery—otherwise, all of that training would have been for nothing, and he would have driven his body to the ground. Instead, he felt better and stronger than ever, completely energized, like he could take on anything.

He didn't care about the side-effects to his body. He took as much test and other gear as he could, despite the cautioning of the Weavers. He had the surgical robots monitor him of course, so that he didn't completely destroy his liver, but he continued to push himself. Nothing else was important right then, except for the single woman who meant everything to him.

If I die saving her, then so be it.

Outside PT, he spent the rest of the day training in the combat room of the corvette, practicing hand-to-hand combat, sniping, and small arms fire with opponents provided by the AI. He had trained with other team members at first, but he couldn't hold himself back, especially during the hand to hand portions, and the unfortunate individuals had to be taken to sickbay with broken wrists and ankles. Thankfully, the Weaver could heal those immediately. Still, it wasn't pleasant for the affected Argonauts.

Eventually, Rade found himself wanting to practice on the real thing once again, so he dismissed the augmented and virtual reality opponents, donned a strength-enhanced exoskeleton, and instead of summoning a human opponent, called upon Harlequin to spar with him.

But even with the exoskeleton dialed up to the full speed and strength settings, no matter how hard he tried, Rade could never beat the Artificial. He had instructed Harlequin not to hold back, and Rade received his fair share of broken wrists and ankles. One time, Harlequin nearly tore out one of the hardpoints Rade's exoskeleton was mounted to. That was excruciating. Fortunately, Rade had permanently stationed a Weaver in the combat room by that point, so he was never out of the fight for longer than twenty minutes, even after the hardpoint incident. When the Weaver was done, he had the robot shoot him up with painkillers, then he willed himself back onto the mat once more.

"Why do you do this to yourself, boss?" Harlequin said at one point, in the middle of a particularly bad fight. "Is it because you want to punish yourself for what happened?"

Rade had never considered that. He punched at the opening Harlequin presented, and the Artificial snatched his arm, twisting it behind Rade's back and holding it to near breaking, forcing Rade to his knees. The hardpoints were supposed to improve the speed with which his brain signals reached the extremities of the exoskeleton, but he was still half as fast as Harlequin. Rade tapped out.

As they reset to their original places on the mat, Rade said. "I train because I need to be ready. Not because I want to punish myself."

"Ready?" Harlequin said. "To fight Zoltan, you mean? I, Ms. Bounty, or one of the other combat robots can handle that."

Rade didn't say anything.

"I know you want to be the one who saves her," Harlequin said. "But it's going to be a team effort, you do realize that, don't you?"

Rade attacked. Once more, in seconds he was on the mat, with Harlequin pinning him with his arm behind his back. Harlequin released him; Rade gave the Artificial a scowl and reset.

"I know it will be a team effort," Rade said. "But I have to feel like I'm doing something to help her. Rather than just sitting around here all day. She's probably being tortured at this moment. Unspeakable things are being done to her. I can't allow myself to while away my time. I have to know that I'm doing everything in my power to save her."

"I understand," Harlequin said. "You want to be tortured, too. I merely suggest that there might be more... effective... ways of using your time."

"I disagree," Rade said. "Someday I'm going to have to fight this Artificial, I guarantee you. And I need to be ready."

Rade attacked, and once more was beaten down. But he didn't give up. He refused. It wasn't in his nature. He kept at it over the next few hours and days.

Something happened on the third day of sparring with Harlequin. He began to notice the fighting patterns the Artificial employed. When Rade punched, always Harlequin's arms would move to intercept in a certain way. When he dodged an incoming blow, the Artificial would rebalance and come at him again, always from the lower right.

And when he saw those patterns, Rade began to find real openings. And he won, occasionally. He worked it up to twenty-five percent of the time.

"Do all Artificials follow the same combat program?" Rade asked at the end of one session. He was panting. He had been fighting for three hours, and hadn't won in the past two, despite the pick-me-ups the Weaver had injected him with.

"Mine is based on version 2.3g of the mixed martial arts protocol all combat robots employ," Harlequin said. "There is no guarantee that this Zoltan runs the same program."

"What are the chances he runs 2.3g?" Rade said.

"Good, I would say," Harlequin replied. "2.3g is the latest and most common download among combat robots. I would estimate its distribution at approximately sixty percent. Twenty-five percent run an older variant of 2.3, ten percent run a version of 2.2, while the final five percent run something else entirely. Still, even if Zoltan has the same program, consider for a moment: you are only able to defeat me one time out of four."

"But at least I *can* defeat you," Rade said. "And that's something, isn't it?"

"I suppose."

"If we keep practicing," Rade said. "Maybe we can increase that ratio to one in every two times."

But Rade never got the ratio up beyond one in four.

Even so, Rade trained. And trained. And trained. A part of him knew that the training was to distract himself from what had happened. Perhaps even to punish himself, as Harlequin had suggested. Because when the time came, he might never even get close enough to touch the Artificial. But he always dismissed those thoughts, and focused on his physical training in the mornings, and his sparring in the afternoons.

And though he trained to exhaustion to shut out what had happened, sometimes as he lay alone on his bunk during the designated night hours, waiting for the exhaustion to pull him under, his mind wandered.

Occasionally a strange sense of hope took hold of him, and he told himself that maybe Shaw wasn't in any danger after all. Maybe she had already rescued herself. She was a strong, resourceful woman after all. Perhaps she had escaped during the customs inspection after passing through the Gate. Though as much as he tried to convince himself of that, he couldn't believe it.

Then there was the other extreme his mind sometimes descended to. Shaw was dead, spaced by the Artificial. Or tortured to death. Or transformed into a bioweapon, a creature with tentacles and claws. Rade always roused himself from the depths of despair by convincing himself that Zoltan would want leverage to use against him. Zoltan wouldn't harm the only prisoner he had who gave him that leverage.

And yet despite telling himself that she was fine, he could never shake off the sense of guilt. The fact that he had never even told her he loved her ate away at him.

Sleep would always come, temporarily freeing him from his mental torture. And when morning came, he dove into his physical training with renewed vigor.

Rade had already lost a lot of weight during the past six weeks, but by the time they reached the Gate, most of the remaining fat he had gained since departing the navy was gone. He was as lean as he had ever been, if not leaner. And definitely at his biggest, in terms of muscle mass.

He felt as ready as he could possibly be to face what the universe threw at him. Whatever awaited on the other side of that Gate, he would find a way to reunite with Shaw.

There were no customs vessels on this side of the Gate, but there would be in the neighboring Sino-Korean system.

"General quarters," Rade said as they neared the Gate. "I want our Vipers fully charged when we pass through."

"Won't customs detect the charge on our lasers?" Fret asked.

"Lui assures me the heavy armor of these corvettes will hide the fact," Rade said. "Right, Lui?"

"Right," Lui replied. He didn't sound as confident as he had earlier.

The Vipers aboard the corvette were classified as heavy lasers, and had twice the range over the light lasers the *Argonaut* possessed.

Rade had told himself he wouldn't fire on the *Argonaut*, that it was too dangerous, but the more he considered it, the more he realized there were areas Manic could target that definitely wouldn't harm the Marauder's crew. The Vipers concentrated their energy on spot sizes varying in radius from five millimeters to five centimeters, depending on range. If aimed properly, a shot on an engine or laser turret would damage only the affected component without breaching the hull. And Rade planned to employ such shots if he needed to. Against the *Argonaut*, or even the customs vessels themselves. He just hoped Manic and the AI didn't miss, if it came to it.

"Vipers are fully charged," Manic said.

"Harlequin, take us through the Gate," Rade said.

twenty-five

Rade switched to the view from the external nose camera; when the *Tiger* passed through the Gate, the visible stars and constellations shifted as the vessel emerged thirty-seven lightyears away in the neighboring *Hēiguāng* system, thanks to that network of wormholes the race known as the Elder—now believed to be extinct—had threaded throughout that entire region of the galaxy around five hundred thousand years ago.

"We're receiving a hail from customs," Fret said. "We're to slow down for the security scan."

"Do it." Rade continued his external observations via the nose camera. There were no waiting ships queued to enter the Gate. The customs officials would be bored, having little to do, and eager to hassle them if only to pass the time.

"Meanwhile," Rade continued. "I want you to start scanning the profiles of all ships in the system. Find the *Argonaut*."

"What if Zoltan has changed the registry information?" Lui said.

"Then scan for the heat signature of Marauder class vessels," Rade said. "There won't be many of them in this region of space."

Rade watched the black triangular shapes of the corvettes approach. He had already discussed various strategies for successfully passing customs with his crew. There was no point trying to change the registry information of the vessel, especially not out there on the frontier of known space. The Gate officials would have kept track of all corvettes entering and leaving the system, and would have known that there were only two such ship classes in the neighboring Hóuzi H☐i system. His best bet was to pretend to be a member of the Persian crew that had flown the craft originally. Earlier, Rade had Farhad transmit the old crew manifest, along with video and biometric data of the captain, since the *Tiger's* own database had been wiped. With that information, TJ and the *Tiger's* AI had been able to construct a three-dimensional avatar of the original captain.

The SK vessels pulled alongside and matched speed.

"They're tapping in," Fret said. "Requesting holographic mode."

"Connect," Rade said, dismissing the external camera viewpoint.

The stern-faced SK official appeared in the center of the stations forming the Sphinx. He wore a powder blue dress shirt with gold buttons, and black and gold chevrons on the shoulders. On his head was a black cap fronted by the red star-golden laurel wreath symbol of the SK government.

The avatar of the Persian captain prepared by TJ and Zahir would in turn be projected to the customs officer; with Zahir's help, it would reflect Rade's movements in realtime. Zahir would also translate his words into Persian before transmitting them to the customs warships, and change the mouth movements to match; that way the AIs would detect the language as Persian, as expected, before translating it into Sino-Korean.

"Back so soon, Captain Ahmed?" the customs official said, sounding suspicious.

"Good evening," Rade said. "We're on our way to Gilgamesh system to collect more colonists."

According to the manifest, that was where the crew had originally come from.

"Transmit your crew manifest," the official said.

Rade glanced at Fret. "Do it."

Fret would be sending the old crew manifest, of course.

The customs official's eyes defocused as if reading the list. Then his face turned sour. "You are to halt immediately and prepare to be boarded."

Rade frowned. He muted the connection for a moment. "What the hell happened? Zahir, did you mess up the manifest?"

"No," Zahir said.

"What about the three-dimensional avatar? The Persian translation of my words?"

"The translation was exact, and the avatar synced perfectly," Zahir said.

"Then what the hell happened?"

"Zoltan must have done something," Tahoe said. "Either he paid off customs to search us no matter what, or somehow deceived them."

Rade unmuted the connection and decided to attempt a trick he had once witnessed another captain use at a Gate crossing, back in his old MOTH days.

"So, uh, look at this," Rade transmitted. "There seems to be an extra one million won just sitting around in our bank account. I wonder, do you know of anybody who could put it to use? Maybe we could contribute it to the customs officials who protect the borders of the Great Empire. What do you think?"

The official stared at Rade stonily for several seconds. Then: "Transmitting account information."

Rade exhaled softly, muted the connection, and glanced at Fret. "Did you get it?"

"I did."

"Send the information to Tahoe," Rade said.

"Are you sure we can afford this?" Tahoe said.

"Ms. Bounty has promised to reimburse us for any expenses," Rade said.

"But I doubt even her purse is bottomless," Tahoe said. "A million won is the price of a good used mech."

"I know, Tahoe," Rade told him. "Just do it."

Tahoe sighed. "As you wish." He paused. "Done."

Rade glanced at the official. "We have transferred the funds. May you bask in the glory of the Paramount Leader forever."

"And you as well." The official smirked. "Now halt, and prepare to be boarded for inspection."

"Damn it," Rade said. "You betrayed us."

"If you do not halt," the official said. "We will open fire."

"At least tell us why? What have we done wrong?"

"Three of your crew profiles were already present in the manifest of a trade vessel that emerged from Hóuzi H☐i four days ago," the official said.

Ah. So that was his enemy's stratagem.

Damn it. I should have considered that.

"The previous vessel lied on their manifest," Rade said.

"If that is the case," the official said. "A warrant will be issued for their capture and arrest. They will be detained at the next station or Gate they visit. In the meantime, we will board your vessel to confirm your actual crew and cargo match what is listed on the manifest. And if it is found that your crew does not match, and you are not the legal owners of this vessel, your ship will be impounded and you will be detained for piracy. The penalty for piracy in Sino-Korean space is death."

Rade terminated the connection and the hologram vanished. He tapped in Ms. Bounty, who was in her quarters. "You're aware that customs wants to board us?"

"I am," she replied. "I've been monitoring the situation closely."

"Tell me you can use the vast resources and contacts of your company to get us out of this," Rade said.

"I'm already working on it," she replied. "Unfortunately, due to the relatively slow speed of the InterGalNet, and the bureaucracy that is the Sino-Korean government, I won't have us cleared for two or three days."

"That's two or three days for our enemy to get away," Rade said. *With Shaw.*

"I know," Ms. Bounty replied. "If you have any other ideas, I'm open to them."

Rade stared at the black vessels on the external feed. He was no longer aboard the *Argonaut*. The *Tiger* was a real warship. Not the strongest, certainly, but essentially the same class as the two customs ships. He could do things he would have never even considered when he only had the *Argonaut*.

"I have a few ideas, yes," Rade said. He shared what he had planned.

"Mm," Ms. Bounty said. "I'm not sure that's the best idea."

"It'll save us the trouble of detention," Rade said. "Can you clear our name afterward, or not?"

"Only if we are successful in capturing the prisoner," Ms. Bounty said.

"We'll capture him." Rade closed the connection.

"Found her," Lui said.

Rade glance at Lui. "The *Argonaut?*"

Lui nodded. "She's three hours away from *Chungshan* station, a scientific research facility with a crew of fifteen. Looks like she's going to dock."

Rade glanced at his tactical map.

Chungshan Station was located in orbit around the terraformed moon of a nearby ice giant, *Guangdong*. The population of the moon, called Guangdong IV, was two million. The ice giant was stationed near the outskirts of the system. There were another three giants further into the system, along with three terrestrial planets orbiting the barycenter of two binary stars. A third star orbited some distance beyond Guangdong, with a highly elliptical orbit that precluded any of its own planets, according to the tactical display.

"Are there any other bases, stations or depots along the way that the *Argonaut* could have stopped at already?" Rade asked.

"No," Lui said.

"And we're not detecting any of its Dragonfly shuttles out there in the system?" Rade said.

"We're not," Lui said.

Rade leaned forward, studying the tactical display. "So it's likely they're both still aboard."

"The official wants to know when we're going to halt for the boarding process," Fret said.

"Tell him momentarily," Rade said. "Lui, if we set a course to that moon, how long would it take to arrive?"

"Three and a half days at the maximum speed of the *Tiger*," Lui said.

Rade nodded. "What sort of defenses does that moon have?"

"Surprisingly few," Lui said. "There's a military base on the surface, but currently no warships in orbit. It looks like the system navy has dispatched most vessels closer to the binary suns for some sort of training exercise."

"Lucky for us," Manic said. "If you're planning what I think you're planning."

Rade gave him a sly look.

"The third terrestrial planet in the system is also habitable," Lui continued. "With a surface population reported at ten million. That's where most of the remaining warships in the system are. Those ships are the closest to us, and will be the first to react if we do anything... untoward here."

Rade nodded. "Fret, given the distances involved, how long before we can expect a dispatch from that third planet?"

"It will take three hours for light—and communications—to reach the third planet," Fret said. "A dispatch of warships could come any time after that."

"And once they've left, Lui?" Rade said. "How long do we have until intercept? Assuming we're already proceeding at top speed toward the station."

Lui paused. Then: "Assuming they send their fastest ships, they'll arrive two days *after* we reach Chungshan station."

Rade nodded. "Good. Very good. Tahoe, what do you think? When we reach Chungshan will any of the orbital defense platforms or station defenses prevent us from docking?"

"As for the platforms, all we have to do is issue a surrender before we enter orbit," Tahoe said. "They'll tell us to halt and await boarding."

"All right, let's say we find a way around that, and continue toward the station with the intention to dock," Rade said.

Tahoe pondered for a moment. "Well, the station won't open fire, not when it's obvious we intend to dock. They won't risk debris from our ship tearing into the hull. Instead, any security robots aboard will attempt to arrest us after we debark."

"That's my thinking as well," Rade said. He glanced at Manic. "Back to the situation at hand: if we fired all of our Vipers at the same time, could we take out the laser turrets and missile launchers of both customs ships?"

"No," Manic replied. "They have two banks of ten turrets on both sides of their hulls, and another five on the nose sections."

"What if we unleashed missiles at the same time?" Rade said. "At this range, they wouldn't be able to counter in time."

"That would work," Manic said. "If we fired both missiles and lasers, in theory we'd be able to disable all of their weapon mounts."

"That would be illegal," Zahir said.

Interfering AIs.

Rade tapped in TJ, who was in engineering. "TJ, you gave me complete override control for the AI, right?"

"That's right," TJ returned.

"Zahir," Rade said. "I'm going to fire our Vipers and Hellfires at those ships. And you're not going to stop me, do you understand? Override code Rade

Galaal, tango beta five niner."

"Override... granted," Zahir replied.

Rade smiled. "That's a good AI," he said sweetly. "Manic, target the laser turrets and missile launchers on both ships. Prepare to fire on my command. Harlequin, get ready to punch the engines."

"Yes boss," Harlequin said.

Rade considered for a moment how loyal Harlequin was versus the ship's AI. Rade had never had to issue any override controls against Harlequin... the Artificial had always obeyed him, no matter how questionable his orders may have been in terms of legality or rules of engagement. Like a true MOTH.

He's really a rare find. One of our brothers.

"Weapons targeted," Manic said.

"Fire," Rade said.

"Direct hits on all laser turrets and missiles launchers," Lui said. "We've disabled the weapons of both ships."

"Punch the engines!" Rade said.

Harlequin accelerated.

Not unexpectedly, the two corvettes didn't pursue—they didn't want to risk more fire, not when they were essentially defenseless.

"I'm detecting communications beams from both ships," Fret said. "Directed toward the third planet of the system."

Rade nodded. He would have liked to disable the comm nodes aboard those ships, but it was tricky, considering the whole hull was basically used as an antenna. Plus light from the skirmish would reach the bases anyway, and the AIs would readily interpret what had happened and inform the commanders.

"Continue on course to Chungshan station," Rade said.

At the three hour mark, Lui reported: "The *Argonaut* just docked with Chungshan."

"Keep an eye on that station," Rade said. "And let me know if anything departs: a surface shuttle, another starship. A lifepod."

"Will do," Lui replied. "I'm also detecting four SK warships leaving the orbit of the third terrestrial planet in the system. Destroyer class. They're on an intercept course with us."

"Is their arrival time still two days after we reach the station?" Rade asked.

"It is," Lui said. "Give or take a few hours."

Rade tapped in Ms. Bounty. "You promised to use your extensive resources and contacts to get them to stand down?"

"I've started the process," Ms. Bounty said. "They've already agreed that as a passenger, I'm not liable for your behavior. However, at the moment, you and your crew will still be arrested when the destroyers arrive."

"Why am I not surprised?" Rade muttered.

"As I said earlier, capturing Zoltan will ensure I am successful in clearing the rest of you," Ms. Bounty said.

"And why is that?"

"Because I'm not the only one who wants him," Ms. Bounty said. "Let's just say, the Sino-Korean government has a vested interest in his capture. Even if they don't know it yet."

twenty-six

Z oltan had set up shop in the third level bioengineering lab, adjacent to one of the hydroponic bays. He was surrounded by centrifuges, microscopes, and RNA printers; shelves lined the bulkheads, filled with vials containing the genetic code of countless plants.

Shortly after docking, he had unleashed the creations waiting in the *Argonaut's* cargo bay aboard the scientific research station. While Chungshan's security robots were distracted, he proceeded to neutralize all crew members of said station, injecting them with his favorite sedative. When he had returned to the lower levels, he discovered that the robots had killed most of his former creations. In a fit of rage, he shot down the surviving robots. That was unfortunate. He should have reprogrammed them.

Afterward he returned to the bioengineering lab and began work on tweaking the formula of the contagion. While the station's facilities were more appropriate to the genetic manipulation of crops, they served readily enough for his own purposes. Maybe he might even find some useful piece of genetic code in one of the plant vials. He had carried aboard his own samples, of course: he needed to make some final tweaks to his formula. He would test it on the station crew members, and fine-tune the genome until he had what he needed.

When it was perfected, he would use the station itself as the deployment weapon. He had already set the necessary charges. The *Argonaut* wouldn't have been massive enough. But half of the research station? When it hit the moon below, the collision would impart more than sufficient kinetic energy to disperse the contagion. Zoltan had estimated the probability of total biological contamination at higher than ninety-nine percent.

Fifteen percent of the human population would transmogrify into Great Formers, while the rest would simply die. The three hundred thousand Formers would feed upon the lingering imprints in the supra-dimension created by the deceased inhabitants, and transform the crust as per his design. The planet would serve as a beacon to all of his kind in the region, and they would flock to the system. The new era would begin.

Unfortunately, he only had four days until his ancient enemy arrived. And that enemy had attracted the attention of the human authorities as well, it seemed. That was unfortunate.

Four days.

Zoltan would finish in time.

He swore he would.

And if not, well, he would simply have to beat a hasty retreat and try again another day.

He glanced at the woman named Shaw, bound and gagged on the deck nearby. He had interrogated her earlier, regarding those who were helping his enemy. She told him a man named Rade Galaal was their leader, and she promised him that Rade would stop at nothing to set her free and punish Zoltan for what he had done to her.

Zoltan couldn't help but smirk at that. He had considered experimenting upon her, as he planned to do with the others, but decided against it in the end. She would prove quite useful to him when the time came.

If anyone could stop this Rade Galaal dead in his tracks, it was her.

twenty-seven

Two days had passed since entering the system. Rade had continued his relentless training, spending his downtime in his office staring at the tactical display, alternating his gaze between the *Argonaut* and the four destroyers racing to intercept the *Tiger*, as he was doing now.

The *Argonaut* had remained docked with Chungshan for the past two days. Lui had detected no signs of any other vessels leaving the station. He promised the *Tiger's* sensors could discern something as small as the release of a lifepod. Rade wasn't entirely convinced, but he hoped Lui was right. He didn't want to have to sift through the population of an entire terraformed moon to find her.

Once he rescued Shaw, he intended to abandon the *Argonaut* and hide out on the moon's surface, at least until Ms. Bounty could clear them of charges. The trick would be evading arrest once they landed.

Chungshan station had instructed them to proceed to the moon for arrest. Rade had responded, telling them that was precisely what he planned, so please tell the orbital defense platforms not to fire. He also asked if they could relay to him the status of the passengers aboard the *Argonaut*. The station hadn't responded.

"Fret, have you heard anything back from the station yet?" Rade asked after returning to the bridge. "It's been over, what, a day and a half since you sent our response?"

The comm man shook his head. "I just get the same automated reply. 'All hands are currently occupied. But your message is important to us and we will get back to you as soon as we are able.' Every time."

Rade glanced at Tahoe. "What do you think?"

"It's possible Zoltan has taken control of the station," Tahoe said. "With all the battleships out on training exercises, he would face little chance of repercussions. Especially if he's able to convince the local authorities on the planet below that all is well. There's only a crew of fifteen aboard, after all. And some security robots."

"Why bother taking over the station?" Rade said. "He could have transferred to a shuttle and departed to the surface. Then we would have lost him entirely."

"The question might better be posed to Ms. Bounty," Tahoe said.

Rade tapped her in, and shared the hologram with the bridge crew. "You're aware that we've lost contact with the station?"

"I guessed as much," she said.

"What is Zoltan planning?" Rade asked.

"I'm not entirely sure," Ms. Bounty said. "But I have a suspicion he intends to deploy a bioweapon to Guangdong IV. If he is successful, the entire population of two million inhabitants will be lost."

"All the more reason for us to succeed in this mission," Rade said. Though in truth, he found himself caring more for Shaw than the two million inhabitants. And that made him wonder, if it came down to a choice between two million lives, and Shaw, what would he pick?

"I just detected a shuttle launch from one of the nearby orbital defense platforms," Lui said. "It's headed toward the station."

"Probably coming to investigate why the station is answering all hails with automated replies," Fret commented.

"Ask the platforms what the latest news is on the station," Rade told the comm man.

A few hours later Fret told Rade: "Apparently everything is fine on the station. As for the shuttle, it contains our arresting party."

That made some sense, given that the *Tiger* wouldn't be able to dock with any of the defense platforms, but it could dock with the station. The shuttle from the platform could have also boarded the *Tiger* directly, but apparently the SKs didn't want to risk that.

Two days later Rade was on the bridge as the *Tiger* approached the station.

"The orbital defense platforms have locked on," Lui said.

"Issue our surrender," Rade said. "Tell them we will proceed to Chungshan station for arrest."

"The platforms are still aimed at us," Lui said.

Rade held his breath. Several moments passed.

"They're not firing," Lui finally said.

"I just received a reply from the official in charge of one of the defense platforms," Fret said. "They say we can dock with the station. But we are not to board. We are to remain inside the *Tiger* until further notice."

"I'm guessing they haven't heard back from the boarding party they sent out two days ago," Tahoe said.

"Probably not," Rade agreed.

The *Tiger* approached the research facility. It looked like a massive white wheel with a long cylindrical axle extending out from either side. At either end of the axle, several lines threaded back to the main disc in a conical pattern. Several times larger than the *Tiger*, the station spanned three kilometers in area.

According to his Implant, the facility had several hydroponic and farming bays aboard for the purposes of researching food development. Specifically, by genetically engineering crops, growing them, and breeding them to gain the desirable traits.

The large station had no actual hangar bays. Instead, around the central hub several smaller spindles protruded—entry tubes. The *Argonaut* was attached to one of those tubes via the magnetic mounting brackets surrounding its external airlock. The shuttle from the defense platform was attached to another entry tube.

"Fret, request permission to dock," Rade said.

"Done," Fret replied a moment later. "Unsurprisingly, I get the same automated response."

"All right, Harlequin, prepare to dock," Rade said. "Fret, inform the nearby orbital platforms that the station isn't answering us."

"The platforms tell us they lost contact with their team a few hours ago," Fret replied. "We're to remain aboard the *Tiger* after we dock, and wait until they can dispatch another team to investigate. Meanwhile, if the arresting party comes knocking at our door, we're to let them in."

Bender laughed. "And they probably think we're actually going to obey those instructions, right?"

Rade glanced at Harlequin: "Dock us as close to

the *Argonaut* as possible."

"Because of the *Tiger's* size and shape, I'll have to mount her two entrances away," Harlequin said.

"That's fine," Rade said.

Harlequin had the *Tiger's* AI assume control when the corvette was only a few meters away. Rade switched to the perspective of the external camera in that section and watched as the *Tiger* lined up its own external airlock with the tube. He heard the moaning of distant bulkheads as the magnetic clamps latched on.

"We're docked," Harlequin said.

"Fret, are you able to reach Shaw?" Rade asked.

"No," Fret said. "Though we're well within range. Her Implant must be offline. And I'm not receiving comm pings from any other passengers, including the Centurions we left aboard."

"Could it be some sort of interference from the station?" Rade asked. "Blocking materials employed in the hull?"

"No," Fret said. "From what I can tell, the station is actually designed to optimize external communications. If Implants and aReals were active aboard it, the crew would be showing up on our overhead maps."

"And yet they're not," Manic said.

"No."

With his Implant, Rade tried to reach Bax, but the *Argonaut's* AI didn't answer his link request.

Rade tapped in TJ. "Are you able to access the *Argonaut's* AI?"

"No," TJ said. "I'm locked out. We'll have to get to engineering and reboot it, then reset the passcode."

"What about the station's AI?" Rade asked.

"Same thing," TJ replied.

"All right everyone," Rade said over the main circuit. "We've docked. Proceed to the staging area and suit up."

"What do you think we'll find in there?" Tahoe asked as they proceeded to cargo bay three, which was adjacent to the particular airlock exit.

"I don't know," Rade said. "I truly don't." He paused. "But I know Shaw is alive."

"How?" Tahoe said.

"I just do."

In the cargo bay, the party members began donning the specialized jumpsuits they'd stored there. Rade had the robots and Artificials wear their jumpsuits as well. He didn't want to risk contamination. The robot with Ms. Bounty employed a repurposed SK jumpsuit taken from the *Tiger's* inventory.

When that was done, the group proceeded to the armory closet. Beside the rifles the Argonauts and Ms. Bounty's mercs had carried aboard with them, there were a few SK weapons inside, all laser variants. No one bothered to take them, sticking with their old rifles. To their harnesses they attached the remaining grenades salvaged from the Hoplites, and supplemented them with fresh SK grenades from the armory.

"You really think we'll be able to use these in there?" Fret asked, indicating the grenades.

"Their hull contains several layers of external armor," Lui said. "Random detonations should be fine. Now if we line the bulkheads with a couple of bricks..." He indicated the explosive charges in the armory. "Then that's a different story."

"Probably a good idea to bring some along," Rade said, scooping up a couple of bricks for himself.

"Ah, I remember the old days, when you were just a caterpillar new to our team," Manic said, taking four bricks. "A little afraid of charges like these. How far you've come, boss. How far we've all come."

Rade nodded absently. He couldn't reminisce, not then, not when Shaw was a prisoner somewhere aboard that station.

When the lot of them had finished gearing up, Rade said: "Let's go meet our arresting party."

He led the way to the airlock.

"Zahir, open the inner hatch," Rade sent.

It opened. Rade gazed at the outer door. Beyond the portal, he saw only the steel of the Chungshan's external hatch, which capped the entry tube.

"Send in the HS3," Rade said.

The scout proceeded forward; Rade had Zahir shut the inner hatch, then open the outer.

"The atmosphere is remaining constant," Lui said. "The seal is good."

"TJ, access the station's external hatch via the remote interface and open it," Rade instructed his man.

A moment later the hatch to the entry tube opened.

"Atmospheric pressure hasn't changed," Lui said.

Rade nodded. "That's good, I think."

"No arresting party..." Manic said.

Rade switched to the point of view of the HS3. The long, tunnel-like passageway beyond indeed proved empty. Emergency lights in the overhead provided dim illumination.

"Seal the hatches," Rade said. "And send the HS3 forward."

twenty-eight

The HS3 neared the end of the entry tube, where a sealed door blocked any further progress.

"TJ, open the station's inner hatch," Rade commanded.

The door seal swiveled aside.

"The pressure is still stable," Lui said. "We're good."

The HS3 entered. Several moments passed. The inner corridor didn't look much different from the first passageway, other than for the fact it was wider. It had steel bulkheads, a steel deck and overhead, with emergency lights above providing a dim glow.

Rade watched the overhead map fill out as the HS3 explored the fog of war of the station interior. Closed hatches on the right indicated the passageways to the external entry tubes, as well as a few lifepods. Those on the left allowed access deeper into the station.

"Well this is nice," Manic said. "Not having to worry about interference for once."

Rade nodded absently.

After several minutes, the HS3 had mapped out a donut-shaped area around the central hub, having looped back to the initial airlock.

"All right, first order of business, we secure the *Argonaut*," Rade said. "You and you, into the airlock. Bender, send two more HS3s."

The designated combat robots and HS3s entered. Once more Rade had the *Tiger's* AI go through the process of opening and closing the airlocks, and in moments the two Centurions were in the central hub. They dashed to the hatch that led to the *Argonaut*, and Rade had TJ open it.

The robots deployed inside, as did the HS3s. One of the HS3s remained behind at the entrance, while the remaining joined the robots and dispersed throughout the Marauder class ship. Rade saw evidence of forced entry throughout the ship, with hatches and seals broken down by laser cutters. Several disabled robots were piled in the cargo hold. The sickbay showed signs that someone had been held prisoner, strapped to a bed. DNA samples confirmed that that person had been Shaw.

After a complete search of the ship turned up no one, Rade ordered the robots to proceed to Engineering. There, the Centurions were able to successfully boot the *Argonaut's* AI. TJ had given a special security chip to one of the robots beforehand, and it placed that chip into the AI core before the boot. Notably, the existing chip that TJ kept hidden under the panel was missing.

Rade tapped directly into the appropriate Centurion's external speaker system for the next part.

"Greetings, Captain," the *Argonaut's* AI said. "I am Cunt Hair, AI of the Marauder class vessel *Argonaut*. Please state name and set new password."

"Rade Galaal, tango beta five niner," Rade said via the Centurion's speakers.

"Thank you, Captain Galaal," the AI said. "How

can I be of service to you?"

"First of all, update your database to call me boss," Rade said. "Not captain. Second of all, change your name to Bax." It wasn't a good sign that the AI had reverted to the name it had used when Rade first acquired the vessel.

"Done on both accounts, boss," Bax replied.

"Do you have any records of what transpired since coming to Lang?" Rade asked.

"I'm sorry, all records have been wiped since acquisition," Bax replied.

Rade had expected as much. "Bax, use your internal sensors and tell me who is aboard. Include any robots or Artificials, but omit offline robots."

"I am detecting an HS3 model A92 beside airlock 3A," the *Argonaut's* AI replied. "And two more HS3 A92s in Engineering, as well as two Centurion model B3A units in the same area."

"No one else is hiding aboard?" Rade pressed. "Say in a ventilation duct?"

"Negative," Bax replied.

Rade nodded. "All right. We've got our ship back, people." *Though I really was hoping to get Shaw back.*

Rade instructed the two Centurions to guard the entrance airlock aboard the *Argonaut*, then he recalled the HS3s.

"TJ, can you access any of the inner doors inside the main hub that lead deeper into the station?" Rade asked.

"No," TJ answered. "The doors aren't set to open on command like the airlocks. We're going to have to use the cutters."

"All right," Rade said. "Let's get inside. Zahir, open the inner and outer hatches, and close them again at the first sign of decompression. That goes for you as well, Bax." Rade glanced at two of the combat robots. "You two, stay here. Everyone else, headlamps on infrared, and advance."

"Remember," Ms. Bounty said. "We have to capture Zoltan completely intact. If you disable or destroy him, he will switch to another robot or Artificial."

"I wished you'd tell us how that works, exactly," Manic said.

"If it happens, you will know," Ms. Bounty said.

"Maybe we should leave all our robots behind?" Fret said.

"It won't matter," Ms. Bounty replied. "Zoltan can reach any of the robots, regardless of whether they are aboard the station, or inside the ship."

"I'm not sure I like the sound of that," Tahoe said.

"You shouldn't," Ms. Bounty agreed. "But know that the process isn't instantaneous. The farther the destination robot is, the longer it will take Zoltan to transfer."

"Something to keep in mind," Rade said.

The group traveled the long entrance tube to the main hub. Once there, Rade sent two robots forward to cut through one of the doors that led deeper into the structure. He had everyone else assume defensive positions, their weapons aimed at the hatch.

Ms. Bounty stayed behind in the passageway that led to the *Tiger*; two robots remained with her, holding the glass container that she intended to capture Zoltan with.

The Centurions cut through and the door collapsed. They set their weapons back to "fire" mode and entered. One went high. The other low.

"Contact!" A Centurion shouted.

There was a blur of motion beyond the opening.

Two red dots had appeared on the overhead display. Meanwhile both blue dots indicating the advancing robots had winked out.

Rade aimed his scope inside, and the weapon light illuminated a long, centipede like form within.

"Unleash grenades!" Rade said.

Several grenades were tossed inside. "Fire in the hole!" someone said.

The explosions came. Like Lui said, the frags weren't powerful enough to cause a hull breach. They did send up smoke and vibrate the hull quite well, however.

"Bender, I want an HS3 inside!" Rade said.

An HS3 moved forward. Rade switched to its viewpoint: within the external compartment, the mutilated bodies of two giant centipedes lay curled on the deck. Their heads had large pincers, which explained why the robots were each cut in half.

"Bugs," Bender said.

"Lui, get me an analysis on these creatures." Rade rotated the swivel camera of the HS3 to examine the compartment. It seemed to be some sort of hydroponics chamber, with tomatoes growing from pots suspended from the overhead, and troughs of fern-like flowering plants lining the deck. The explosions had caused fragmentation damage to some of the closer troughs.

"These things seem partially engineered from Earth stock," Lui said. "Their DNA is eighty percent human. But there are other nucleics here that don't match anything from Earth."

"What, like alien DNA?" Fret said.

"No," Lui said. "I'm not sure that would even be technically possible. Blending alien DNA with human, I mean, and expecting to get something capable of cellular division. I just mean, there's a lot of custom stuff in here. Whoever made these sure had a hell of a lot of time on his hands. I'm not sure what traits half of these genomes are supposed to trigger."

Rade returned his attention to the creatures. "Could they have once been human?"

Lui hesitated. "You mean transformed by a retrovirus?"

"Yes. You did say their DNA was eighty percent human."

"It's certainly possible," Lui said. "But I can't say for certain one way or another."

What if one of these was Shaw? And we just killed her?

"Send in more HS3s," Rade said. "Clear the compartment."

In a few minutes the HS3s had completely mapped out the large hydroponics chamber. Rade had one of the HS3s stay behind at the opening to guard their back, then he had two robots cut open the next door.

On the other side, no tangos awaited. Instead there was a small cylindrical room with an elevator at the middle. Along the circular bulkhead were three other doors, each situated at a different point of the compass, ostensibly leading to other chambers like the one the party had just departed. It was the station's inner hub.

"The elevator seems to be inactive," TJ said. "I can't access it."

"All right, let's open these other doors," Rade said. "And clear the compartments."

The robots opened the doors and the party cleared the hydroponic bays beyond in turn. They encountered three more of the giant centipedes in one of the other compartments, but the remaining two proved clean. The ex-MOTHs made short work of the creatures with their grenades. The doors on the far sides of each compartment led back to the hallway of the main hub that circled the station: they had cleared the first level.

The group returned to the elevator.

"Open it up," Rade ordered two robots.

The robots spread the doors apart, revealing an empty shaft inside. A carbon fiber cable stretched up and down into the darkness.

"Climb to the next floor," Rade instructed.

The robots leaped onto the carbon fiber cable and clambered out of view.

In moments they had the door to the next level open. Rade switched to their perspective, and saw that they resided in another circular inner hub with four hatches placed at the different points of the compass.

"All right, let's get up there," Rade said. The members of the boarding party climbed one by one. Ms. Bounty and the two robots porting the glass container came last. The latter two ended up using their jetpacks to bring the heavy cargo to the next level.

"Let's open this door," Rade said, picking one of the four hatches at random.

He stepped back, assuming a defensive position while the cutters moved in.

When the door fell in, he ordered an HS3 inside. Within, corn grew in troughs beneath sprinkler systems. The HS3 flew between the rows, mapping out the compartment. No tangos awaited.

The team deployed inside and the robots cut through the outer hatch. It led to a curved hallway that seemed to follow the external hull of the station, much like the main hub of the floor just below. A pair of lifepod hatches were embedded in the bulkhead directly across from the opening.

Bender once more flew an HS3 inside to explore.

"Boss, better look at this," Bender said a moment later.

"What is it?" Rade switched to the viewpoint of the HS3.

"We've found Shaw," Bender said.

twenty-nine

Rade saw her halfway down the corridor, flexicuffed to the railing. She was dressed in the same fatigues she usually wore on duty, except the cloth was ripped in places. Shaw's face was dirty; her lips were chapped and bleeding in places. She had a black eye on the right side of her face, and a fresh cut above the left. Despite all of that, she looked defiant.

Beside her stood a man who could only be Zoltan. He wore a clean, flowing purple robe, the shawl raised to cover his head. He had a thick black beard with eyebrows to match. His eyes burned with an intensity that Rade had never seen in an Artificial. His right hand was extended out to the side, and held a small cylindrical device: his thumb pressed down on the tip. A green light flashed on the bottom portion of the device.

"Everyone, stay inside! He's got a dead man's switch of some kind!" Rade switched to his own point of view and hurried toward the passageway.

"What are you going to do?" Ms. Bounty said urgently. "I need him intact!"

"I'm going to negotiate for Shaw's life," Rade said.

"Wait, Rade!" Tahoe said. "Let one of us do it

instead."

"She's my girl," Rade said. "It has to be me."

As he neared the passage, he let his rifle hang from his shoulder strap and preemptively raised his hands. Then he took a deep breath and stepped through to stand underneath the HS3.

Shaw smiled, despite the obvious pain she was in. Her eyes glistened, and she blinked rapidly several times.

"What do you want?" Rade said gruffly, using the external speakers of his jumpsuit. He felt like throwing all of his grenades at the Artificial, and unleashing his rifle into the brain case. But he could do none of that, not until he knew what kind of detonator Zoltan held.

"Are you there, my ancient enemy?" Zoltan said.

"I am present," Ms. Bounty said from the side compartment behind Rade, also using her external speakers. She had ramped the volume way up.

Zoltan nodded, smiling, then focused on Rade. "You know what this is?" Zoltan nodded toward his trigger arm.

"A dead man's trigger," Rade said.

"Very good," Zoltan replied. "I've placed explosives all along the rim of the central hub of the station. When I release my thumb, half the station will break away, along with a bioweapon I've hidden in one of the compartments; together, they will plunge toward the colony. I've also placed charges on the corvette you just docked: I had robots waiting on the hull of the station, and when you arrived, I deployed them. The explosion will disable the ship.

"I have not, however, attached charges to your precious *Argonaut*: it will survive the detonation intact. You can use it to destroy the bioweapon before it impacts the surface. You will find Hellfires in the cargo bay of the *Argonaut*, taken from the defense platform shuttle that docked here two days ago. I've modified these Hellfires to work with the launch tubes of the ship. You will have to carry the missiles to the necessary compartment, of course, and manually load them. Observe station cameras 2A, B and C, and *Argonaut* cams 3A and 5A, to confirm what I say is true. I have granted you the necessary privileges to view the former cameras, and you should already have access to the latter by now."

Rade muted his external speakers. "Tahoe, check it."

A moment later Tahoe replied: "Everything he says is true."

"What about the modified Hellfires?" Rade said.

"I checked with Bax," Tahoe replied. "The AI is convinced they'll fit the launch tubes."

Rade reactivated his external speakers to address Zoltan. "The colony's surface-to-space defenses will eliminate the danger. Or the defense platforms will."

"Actually they won't bother," Zoltan said. "The impact will be far from the inhabitable zone. They will believe they are safe. When the broken station hits, the infection will disperse across the moon in hours. Good bye Guangdong IV."

"Why didn't you load the missiles into the *Argonaut's* launch tubes yourself and fire at us?" Rade pressed. "Why let us approach?"

"I didn't have time," Zoltan said. "And the truth of the matter is, I never planned to deploy my bioweapon in this way, but your woman pissed me off. 'When Rade gets here, he's going to kick your ass. When Rade comes, he's going to smear your insides across the bulkheads.' Rade Rade Rade. This is my revenge on you both. Hunter, and hunted."

Zoltan swung the arm that held the dead man's switch toward Rade. "When I release this trigger you will have two options. The first is to race back to the *Argonaut*, manually transfer the missiles from the cargo bay to the launch tubes, and then destroy the severed station segment that is hurtling toward the moon, sparing the citizens. It will require all your men. The second is to save Shaw. Again, doing so will require all your men. You cannot do both. It will be interesting to see what you pick." Zoltan's thumb seemed to twitch on the trigger, and he cocked his head. "Better hang onto something."

"Wait!" Rade said.

"What?" Zoltan asked.

"Take me in her place."

Zoltan smiled widely. "It doesn't work that way." He lifted his thumb.

Flashes appeared in the passageway beyond Shaw; Rade heard an explosion and then the corridor behind her was gone entirely. In its place resided the stars of deep space.

The explosive decompression sucked Zoltan out. The flexicuffs slid backward as Shaw too was pulled toward the void, but the cuffs mercifully caught on the bend in the railing that was created when the bulkhead severed.

Rade was already hurtling toward her, thanks to the decompression.

He activated his jetpack to slow his approach and wrapped his arms around her. He held the surgical laser in the tip of his index finger to the cuffs and shot through them.

Shaw broke free, and for a moment they were both drawn toward the void by the decompression. She had shut her eyes and mouth. If he let her fall into the void, without a pressure suit the saliva in her mouth would boil away, along with any perspiration on her body. Though that would be the least of her problems.

Rade activated rear thrust once more, fighting the air flow, and brought her to the lifepod hatch. He grabbed onto the nearby handle, slammed the "open" switch, and then shoved her inside, sealing the pod just as the last of the air decompressed.

The inner environment pressurized, judging from the fog that crept along the outer edges of the portal in front of Shaw's face. Apparently the lifepod was set to evacuate upon entry, because the entire compartment ejected a moment later. In seconds the lifepod was a dot above the colonized moon that ate up half the stars.

Rade tore his eyes away from the portal and instructed his local AI to track her. When he overlaid her trajectory with that of the moon on his tactical display, he realized the explosion had disturbed the orientation of the space station, and her pod was headed directly for the colony.

Unfortunately, those particular lifepods weren't rated to survive atmospheric entry.

The damaged station still had artificial gravity. Rade used it to dash to the opening that had been torn into the passageway and leaped outside into the zero G. He spotted the other half of the station drifting away toward the moon below, but he didn't care right then.

He jetted toward Shaw's lifepod, using the tracking provided by his AI. Her tiny craft soon came into view, and soon grew bigger.

"Rade!" Shaw transmitted. She must have seen him, and was using the comm node in the lifepod to communicate. She couldn't have reactivated her

Implant, because the blue dot representing her position hadn't appeared on his HUD. "You have to stop the bioweapon!"

"The rest of the crew will take care of it," Rade replied.

"But you won't survive!" she said.

Rade released another burst of thrust to accelerate his approach; he jetted in reverse to decelerate as he grew near. He hit hard, latching onto the outer handles of the white pod with his gloves.

"I got you." He gazed at her through the glass portal. "I got you."

"What have you done?" Shaw said.

Rade activated thrust, attempting to alter her trajectory, but he couldn't counter the momentum of the pod. The craft was irreparably locked in a decaying orbit.

"It's no good," Shaw said. "I'm going to burn up. Let me go. It's too late. Save yourself."

He tightened his grip. "I'm not letting go. I will find a way."

"We're all dead, anyway," Shaw said. "Eventually."

"Yes," Rade said. "But not yet."

He had the local AI of his jumpsuit run a calculation, and it showed him the best place to apply reverse thrust. He positioned himself there and jetted until he was lined up with the force vector the AI overlaid onto his vision.

But it was no use.

"Rade," Shaw said. "If you use too much fuel, you won't be able to save yourself."

He glanced at his fuel levels. "Too late for that now, Shaw."

"Why, Rade?" Shaw said. It sounded like she was weeping.

"I'm not going to give up." Brave words, but he knew there wasn't much else he could do. He could already feel the rising heat—his thermo regulator couldn't keep up. It wouldn't be long now.

Orange flames burst from the underside of the lifepod.

"You should have let me go," Shaw said.

"Never," Rade said.

"We die together," Shaw said. "A shooting star."

"I hope someone down there makes a wish," Rade said as the flames picked up. "So it's not wasted."

"It's never wasted." Shaw reached out, placing her flat palm on the inside of the glass. Rade rested his glove on the surface opposite.

Something wrapped around his legs. He looked down. Another jumpsuit. The Implant labeled the operator as Tahoe.

Behind him, a long line of suits, joined hand in hand, formed a daisy chain to a Dragonfly. A Model 2, from the *Argonaut*. Harlequin resided at the top of the chain, gripping the down ramp.

"Hello, boss," Harlequin said.

The flames around the lifepod receded.

"But the bioweapon," Rade said.

"We've made our choice," Tahoe said.

"Zahir," Rade sent the *Tiger's* AI. "Give me an update."

"Charges have detonated on the hull of the *Tiger*," Zahir replied. "The corvette has suffered severe engine damage."

Rade tried the *Argonaut's* AI instead. "Bax, are you serviceable?"

"Aye, boss," Bax replied.

"Seal the airlock and break away from Chungshan," Rade ordered the AI. "Proceed to the falling portion of the station. Deploy the grappling hook and drag it into a stabilized orbit if you can! Meanwhile, have the two Centurions start transferring the missiles from the cargo bay to the launch tubes."

"Roger that," Bax replied.

"You intend to fire Hellfires at the station section?" Lui asked over the line. "That might do what Zoltan says, and eliminate the contagion. Or it might actually make the spread worse."

"We only destroy the station as a last resort," Rade said.

It took half an hour for everyone to get aboard the shuttle, and to magnetically mount Shaw's lifepod underneath. The *Argonaut* had latched onto the decaying station segment by then, and was attempting to tow it.

"Bax, update me," Rade said.

"I'm having some difficulties fighting the momentum," the *Argonaut's* AI responded. "I don't believe I will be able to steer the debris from its decaying orbit without more motive force."

"Deploy your remaining shuttle," Rade told the AI. "We'll join you shortly."

In twenty minutes, the Dragonfly joined the *Argonaut* and its shuttle, and all three craft attached grappling hooks to the station segment.

It was enough. They slowly altered the orbit of the segment, carrying it into a stable orbit.

"See, we did it after all," Tahoe said, as if trying to justify their choice.

"We did," Rade agreed. "Barely."

Normally he would have wanted to be alone after such an intense session, but he tapped in Shaw immediately.

"I need to hear your voice," Rade said.

"It's so good to hear yours."

"I missed you," Rade said.

"I missed you back."

"Tell me everything that happened," Rade insisted.

"You first. I'm... I can't talk now." She sounded like she was choking up.

"Are you okay?" Rade asked.

"Yes," she said. "I'm just so happy. And relieved."

Rade told her everything that had happened since they lost communications. Then he listened to her as she revealed the trials she had endured for the past ten days, and her words only angered him further. Zoltan was lucky he had spaced himself, because if Rade had gotten his hands on the cruel bastard, there would have been only smashed pieces left for Ms. Bounty to collect.

thirty

R ade and the others docked with the *Argonaut* a short while after dragging the station segment back into orbit. Luckily, the orbital platforms and surface-to-space defenses hadn't fired upon the *Argonaut*—the inhabitants realized Rade and his crew were trying to help them. Ms. Bounty had apparently sent a few transmissions to the operators and local government as well, smoothing over their fears and promising to remain in orbit when the task was done as a form of "house arrest" until the SK destroyers arrived.

Rade had originally planned to travel to the surface of the moon in the hopes of evading arrest, but Ms. Bounty convinced him that local police would readily track them down, if not shoot them out of the sky before they landed. She promised that she was almost done negotiating their pardon.

Ms. Bounty was already aboard the *Argonaut* when the Dragonfly docked, and she pinged him: "Mr. Galaal, I respectfully request that you transfer Shaw to a jumpsuit, and then bring her to the cargo hold where I have prepared a decontamination unit for her. A precautionary measure until we confirm she is free of contagions. Just for two days."

Rade found it hard to suppress his outrage. "Do you know what she's been through? And now you want me to lock her up for another two days?" He knew Ms. Bounty was right, of course. Still, he couldn't help the words. He had a need to defend Shaw from what he perceived as a cold, dark universe.

"It is entirely up to you, obviously," Ms. Bounty replied. "She may not be infected with a bioweapon. If you wish to risk the lives of your crew, that's entirely up to you."

"It's okay, Rade," Shaw transmitted. "I'll suit up in the spacesuit provided by the lifepod. Somehow... in this cramped space."

And so she did. Rade had her moved to the temporary decon unit—basically a glass tank. A Weaver was embedded inside with her, where it was able to provide medical care. She was rehydrated and fed. The Weaver determined that Zoltan had shorted out Shaw's Implant, and the surgical robot scheduled a repair operation to be performed as soon as she cleared decon.

Ms. Bounty had set up another glass container in the hold, this one with a black curtain draped over it. It contained the robot Zoltan was currently occupying. Apparently he had transferred out of his Artificial body before being sucked into space; when the atmosphere had finished venting, one of the robots porting the glass cage had turned on Ms. Bounty. She and the other robot had managed to trap it in the container.

Rade visited Shaw in the hold, placing a bare palm on the glass tank that held her. She met his hand with her own from the other side. He was aware of the watchful eyes of the two career mercenaries and Centurions currently acting as guards in the compartment.

"How are you feeling?" Rade asked. A small microphone attached to the outside of the glass transmitted sound data to a pair of speakers within, allowing her to hear him clearly. A similar microphone was attached to the inside, which in turn relayed her response to his Implant.

"Well enough," Shaw said.

Rade glanced at the black-draped container beside her. "You sure must have royally pissed off this Zoltan to make him resort to such a revenge tactic."

"I did," Shaw said. "His retribution was to make you suffer. He hated you by the time you arrived, because I was always talking about how you were going to rescue me and kick his ass. Too bad his revenge was all a ruse. He didn't finish his weapon in time. But not even I knew that."

Rade nodded slowly. He had sent robots to examine the severed station section. There was no sign of any bioweapons or deployment devices aboard. Ms. Bounty had concluded that Zoltan hadn't had the bioweapon ready yet, and merely hoped to distract the team as part of his getaway.

"Even so," Rade told her. "The ruse didn't work out for him in the end, did it? We got the bastard."

"I'm still not happy by the choice you made." She lowered her hand and retreated to the far side of the tank. She sat down against the glass, and brought her knees to her chest, wrapping her arms around her legs. "How much is one life worth? Ten? A hundred maybe, depending on the individual? But never more than two million. Never. You shouldn't have done what you did out there. You should have let me go."

"The choice was ours to make," Rade said. "Mine and my crew. I knew we would find a way to stop the bioweapon afterward."

"Did you really?" Shaw said.

"No," Rade admitted.

"I didn't think so."

"Look, the colony didn't die," Rade said. "And we found out it was a ruse in the end anyway. Imagine if the team had salvaged the station segment from its decaying orbit first, only to discover that we had let you die for nothing."

"Fine, but what if you're faced with a similar choice in the future?" Shaw said. "Would you choose the same way?"

Rade didn't answer her.

She looked away, then sighed. She closed her eyes. "I suppose I have no right to guilt-trip you like this. If I had to make the choice, I would have chosen you as well. You, every time." She opened her eyes and gazed directly at him. "Does that make us bad people? Selfish?"

"I don't know," Rade said. "But it certainly makes us flawed, I guess."

He accessed the outer hatch of the airlock attached to the tank.

"What are you doing, sir?" one of the mercs asked.

Rade waggled a finger at him. "Don't call me sir."

Shaw stood up quickly. "Rade, close that hatch. I haven't completed decon yet."

"I don't care." Rade stepped inside and shut the outer hatch behind him, and waited for the air to recycle. "I'm staying in the dollhouse with you until you're cleared."

"No, you're not," she said.

Rade opened the inner hatch. "Too late." He entered. "I never did follow orders very well."

Shaw shook her head, smiling.

Rade shut the inner hatch behind him, and when he turned back toward her, she was already wrapping her arms around him.

"My flawed warrior," she said.

Rade had a front row seat to the interrogations that Ms. Bounty performed with the prisoner over the next few days. The caged Centurion had been removed from its jumpsuit, and resided inside a glass tank that looked identical to the one holding Shaw and Rade, except for the flat metal disks on the top and bottom, a meter in diameter each. It looked like the robot was confined to the invisible three-dimensional volume formed by those disks, because it never ventured beyond that imaginary space, though there was still room in the container outside the circular boundaries. Rade guessed it was some form of magnetic or perhaps gravimetric containment.

During the questioning, the robot acted as if it was an ordinary Centurion. It could not recall turning against Ms. Bounty.

"The last I remember," the robot claimed. "The station had suffered an explosive decompression. I was holding the glass tank. And then a moment later you were attacking me, forcing me into the container, which I had apparently dropped at some point. Five point three seconds are missing from my timeline."

After the first session, Ms. Bounty muted the microphone and walked over to Rade's container to consult with him.

"So what do you make of it?" Rade said.

"It's lying of course," Ms. Bounty said. "I sense his presence aboard."

"Is it possible Zoltan jumped to a different robot before you trapped that one?"

"There is a small possibility, yes," Ms. Bounty said.

"I'm working on modifying the container tech to give me the ability to extract the entity within the robot. Then I will know for certain."

"The entity?" Rade asked. "You never really explained how Zoltan was able to jump bodies. Is it really an AI intelligence? And why did Zoltan call you his ancient enemy before destroying the station?"

"I suppose now is as good a time as any to tell you," Ms. Bounty said, and she proceeded to do just that.

As Rade listened, his face darkened with concern. The entity in question was a member of an ancient race he had encountered once, long ago. A very dangerous race.

When she finished, Rade sat back in the holding tank.

"So you see now why it is imperative that we capture him," Ms. Bounty said.

"I do," Rade said. "Is there no other way we can scan for this being, using the technology we have aboard?"

"No," Ms. Bounty said.

The subsequent interrogation sessions Ms. Bounty engaged in with the robot proved just as futile, with the robot perpetually claiming innocence. Ms. Bounty meanwhile continued to work on her entity extraction tech, and hoped to have something working soon so she could prove to the Sino-Koreans that the team had actually captured the ancient being, and thus were eligible for the pardon.

A day and a half later, six hours before the destroyers were due to arrive, Ms. Bounty cleared both Rade and Shaw for duty, concluding that neither were infected. Shaw scheduled her Implant repair appointment for later that afternoon, and Rade held her hand as the Weaver operated on her, replacing a portion of her Implant with a freshly 3D-printed unit while she was awake. When the Weaver finished, it ordered Shaw to rest for the next few hours. Rade gave her a kiss and then departed. He headed for the combat room next to the gym.

"Harlequin, feel up for a quick match?" Rade sent the Artificial along the way.

"I've been itching to return to the mat ever since we boarded," Harlequin replied. "I had grown accustomed to our sessions. I will join you momentarily."

Harlequin reached the combat room and stepped onto the sparring mat to wait while Rade donned a strength-enhancing exoskeleton.

"What's the news on the captive?" Harlequin replied.

"I'm not sure we have the right robot," Rade said. "It claims to have no recollection of attacking Ms. Bounty. Whether or not its a ruse, I don't know. Our employer says it's possible Zoltan's intelligence has transferred to another robot. Have you noticed any strange behavior in any of the units?"

"Not at all," Harlequin said. "Though I haven't been paying particular attention. I've spent most of my time at the nav station during duty hours, or in my shared stateroom with Lui in off hours."

"Lui says you've been a bit distant lately," Rade said, attaching the last component of his exoskeleton and stepping onto the mat.

"Yes," Harlequin replied. "We had a talk about that. I told him I was disturbed by our choice out there, to risk two million lives to save a member of our team."

"You don't think it was worth it to risk those lives

to save the one member?" Rade asked.

"I'm not certain it was," Harlequin said. "At least in terms of economic production and contribution to society in general, logically two million lives have far more value than one individual."

"Not to me," Rade said, and he attacked.

Harlequin swiped Rade's fist to the side in a blur of motion; the exoskeleton absorbed most of the impact, and Rade felt the pain as the suit buckled slightly, pressing into his skin.

Harlequin's foot slid underneath Rade's ankle impossibly fast, tripping him.

Rade rolled to the side before Harlequin could mount him. He started to get up, but something slammed into his ribs, sending him reeling away. He landed on his back. Agony flared in his side.

Harlequin's foot came down, aimed at his chest. Rade rolled away, hearing the soft thuds beside him as the heel repeatedly struck the mat.

Rade scrambled up on one knee, then ran his own foot along the mat in a roundhouse motion, tripping the Artificial. Harlequin landed face first on the mat.

Rade mounted Harlequin and latched onto the Artificial's right arm, jamming it up into his back. The move counted as an official hold, and Harlequin was supposed to accede the loss of the match at that point, but instead the Artificial placed his other hand underneath his body, and pushed upward—apparently with all his strength—forcing the pair into the air.

Harlequin broke free in midair and spun around, slamming Rade in the chest with one foot. Rade was sent flying off the mat and into the far bulkhead.

"I win the first round," Harlequin said. There was a strange glint in the Artificial's eye.

Rade got up off the deck and wiped away the

blood that was trickling down his chin, caused by his impact against the bulkhead. He glanced at the mat; he hadn't noticed it in the heat of the fight, but he saw that there were rips in the surface where Harlequin's heels had struck. The Artificial wasn't holding back.

Rade felt at his side, where he had taken a blow early in the combat; the exoskeleton had collapsed there, and the suit's metal was digging into his flesh.

The Artificial was launching killing blows.

"Bax," Rade sent. "Get security. I want three MAs here on the double."

The *Argonaut's* AI didn't answer.

"Bax?" Rade tried again.

"I've raised a noise canceller around the area," Harlequin said. "And disconnected the cameras. It's only you and me, Rade Galaal. Let's fight, shall we?"

"Zoltan," Rade said.

Harlequin merely grinned.

thirty-one

The pair circled one another on the mat.

"Harlequin, initiate shut down," Rade ordered. "Override Galaal beta gamma fifty-nine."

The Artificial grinned widely. "I've disabled both the software and hardware kill switches." Harlequin parted his hair, revealing a small, flesh-colored knob on the scalp. He pressed it twice. "See?"

Rade continued to circle his opponent. He reminded himself that he had been able to beat Harlequin once in every four matches. So it wasn't impossible. One in four.

Then again, back then Harlequin was following the rules, and acceding when Rade obtained a hold. Rules didn't apply anymore, not when the Artificial was fighting to the death.

Rade wasn't sure the one in four odds were still valid. In fact, he doubted he could actually win at all.

Harlequin finally came in to strike. The opponent moved quickly, like a viper. Fists blurred past. Rade ducked, sidestepped, and deflected; he experienced a few glancing blows on his torso and thighs.

Rade managed to catch Harlequin's fist after one particular sidestep, and he slammed his other arm upward into the elbow, attempting to break the joint.

It had no effect.

Harlequin grinned, and sent Rade hurtling to the mat with a roundhouse kick. The Artificial mounted him, crushing his chest with his knees. Fists came smashing down toward Rade's unprotected skull.

Rade managed to dodge those fists, and pieces of the mat flew into the air beside him. He caught the Artificial by the wrists, and the servomotors in his exoskeleton whirred as the electroactuators struggled to counter the force of his opponent. Those crushing fists slowly descended toward Rade's face.

"Harlequin, I know you're in there somewhere," Rade said. "Fight it."

"Harley who?" Harlequin said, pressing harder. "I'm going to kill you, Rade Galaal, and then I'm going to take over your ship. Your woman will be mine. I'm going to have my way with her every day for the rest of her short life. She likes it rough, you know."

Rade growled, filled with hatred. The anger helped him shift the wrists of his opponent to the side, and he released his hold, allowing Harlequin's fists to smash into the mat beside his head.

Rade flung his hips and legs upward at the same time, and spun his torso to the side, and he broke the mount hold. Scrambling to his feet, he deflected and dodged the next several blows.

Harlequin was relentless. While Rade was panting hard, the Artificial merely stared at him serenely as he fought, his breathing not affected in the least.

Rade retreated under the onslaught, positioning himself near the lengthwise edge of the mat.

A part of Rade's mind reminded him to watch for the patterns he had learned while fighting Harlequin previously. The Artificial employed version 2.3g of the mixed martial arts program used by all combat robots. With Zoltan inhabiting Harlequin, it seemed likely that the attacker would be using that same program. Still, Rade had seen no sign of those patterns as of yet.

And then when Rade dodged one particular punch aimed at the solar plexus, he noticed it: the Artificial rebalanced and came at him again from the lower right. That was the same pattern Harlequin had exhibited in training. All Rade had do to was wait for that punch again...

Rade ducked and side-stepped several kicks and blows, and avoided another grappling attempt, and once more positioned himself at the lengthwise edge of the mat. The punch to the solar plexus came again. Rade dodged it.

Harlequin rebalanced, and came at Rade from the lower right.

But Rade had already sidestepped the expected blow and the Artificial found empty air. Rade gave Harlequin a roundhouse kick squarely to the behind, and knocked his opponent from the mat entirely.

Before Harlequin hit the bare deck, he vanished from view, as if passing through an invisible planar barrier.

Rade heard a muted thud, and a squeegee sound, as of boots on glass. A louder thud followed, and then nothing.

The holographic image representing that portion of the combat room flickered and then winked out entirely, revealing a glass holding container. Harlequin stood within, inside the area demarcated by the two metallic disks on the floor and ceiling of the trap. There was a small black box attached to the top disk in the center.

The Artificial moved its hands about the invisible

three-dimensional volume created by those disks, like a mime probing for a way out of an imaginary box.

Ms. Bounty stood beside the container, next to one of the now deactivated holographic emitters: small devices situated atop tripods.

"For a while there I thought you were going to intervene," Rade told the woman Artificial.

"You seemed to have the situation well under control," Ms. Bounty said.

Rade had to laugh at that. He glanced at the overhead. "Bax, you there?"

"Roger that," the *Argonaut's* AI replied. "The noise canceler repealed when you trapped the Artificial."

"I'm turning on the internal microphone," Ms. Bounty said.

"Go ahead," Rade told her. Like the container she had built to hold the other robot, this one had microphones attached to the inside and outside, and speakers.

"So you call yourself Zoltan these days, do you?" Ms. Bounty said.

Harlequin glared at her. "My ancient enemy. How did you know?"

"It soon became obvious it wasn't the Centurion," Ms. Bounty said. "We soon realized you must have vacated the body before we captured it. When I modified the cage to allow me to extract your presence from the robot, I proved your absence for certain. And yet I still detected you aboard the vessel. So I knew you were here somewhere. We just didn't know where. I thought you might be hiding in the AI core at first, so we removed the *Argonaut's* core and placed it in the cage. Again, I wasn't able to extract anything."

"So that was why the ship's AI went down this morning for an hour," Harlequin said. "You said it was for 'scheduled maintenance.' I should have suspected."

"Yes," Rade said. "Only three people aboard knew about it. Shaw, Ms. Bounty, and me. Certainly not any of the robots. Or you."

Harlequin glanced at Ms. Bounty. "So you still haven't explained how you knew it was me."

"We didn't know for sure," Ms. Bounty said. "But we suspected."

"I received reports of subtle changes in Harlequin's behavior since we boarded," Rade explained. "For example, at the end of his duty shifts, Harlequin always returned to the stateroom he shared with Lui, and once there he accessed the various external cameras to view the stars. He did that every day for at least fifteen minutes. He was amazed by the wonders of the universe, you see. And liked to spend the time contemplating his place in it. You never accessed those cameras, not even once. And then there were the other comments from Lui. About how you seemed distant, and untalkative. Your old sense of humor, gone."

"We originally planned to call you and the other robots here one by one, and ask them to voluntarily enter the glass tank," Ms. Bounty said. "But my worry was, once you saw the holding container, you would flee the body immediately, seeping unnoticed into the deck. We decided to place the holographic emitters to hide the object, and Rade here volunteered to force you inside under the guise of a sparring match. I don't think he expected you to respond quite so violently as you did."

"How did you know I wouldn't simply flee the body when you called me to the match?" Harlequin said.

"There was nothing unusual about it," Rade said.

"From your words before the match, you obviously searched Harlequin's memories, and realized we had sparred often in the past. Besides, Shaw told me you hated my guts. I knew you wouldn't be able to resist the chance to fight me one on one. Though like Ms. Bounty said, I was a bit surprised by how... violent your response was."

"Eventually," Ms. Bounty said. "I plan to develop a gravimetric capture weapon that will allow me to snare your kind with ease, via a simple shot from a rifle. But until then, this cage will have to suffice. Would you like to see the extraction feature I've added to the tank? It took me quite some time to install." Her eyes defocused, indicating that she was accessing some sort of remote interface.

Harlequin floated into the air, centering between the disks. The Artificial began to spin, slowly at first, then faster and faster. A soft hum emerged from the cage, growing in pitch. In moments the body was a revolving blur.

From the head area, a red liquid began to coalesce. It flowed away from the body, a brighter color than blood, forming a sphere about half a meter above the Artificial. The sphere grew larger as more liquid accumulated, until it was roughly the size of two fists.

The small black box at the top of the container folded open, and the sphere floated up toward it. When the red liquid was completely inside, the box sealed shut. The hum produced by the container began to lower in pitch, and Harlequin's rotations slowed. The Artificial's features became visible again and when Harlequin stopped spinning his body lowered gently to the bottom of the container.

Harlequin stood up. "How did I get here?"

"Can we let him out?" Rade asked.

Ms. Bounty nodded and the glass door at the front of the container opened. When Harlequin emerged, the door sealed behind the Artificial.

"It's done," Ms. Bounty said, staring at the black box. "Thank you, Rade Galaal, for your help. Have you considered my earlier proposition?"

Rade nodded.

"And what have you decided?" Ms. Bounty asked.

"I think it's time we told the rest of the team who you really are," Rade said.

thirty-two

Rade had his team assemble in the combat room, which also functioned as the mission briefing area due to the lack of space aboard. The men all sat cross-legged on the mat, with Rade, Shaw and Ms. Bounty standing next to the bulkhead on the right-hand side. Ms. Bounty's four career mercenaries leaned against the wall opposite them. The container housing Zoltan had been removed.

"So, I hope this meeting is about back pay and leave time," Bender said. "I hear Guangdong IV has some wicked sweet pleasure clubs."

Rade glanced at Ms. Bounty. "She has some good news on both fronts."

She nodded. "Because of your contribution to ridding the system of a dangerous alien threat, the local judiciary has decided to waive the charges against you for your attack against the Gate customs vessels. Effective immediately, the *Argonaut* and its crew have been pardoned. I have forwarded a copy of the digital paperwork to the four SK destroyers, and all other craft and bases in the system. We are free to come and go as we please."

Most of the crew members shrugged nonchalantly.

"You don't seem surprised," Ms. Bounty said.

"Why would we be surprised?" Fret asked. "The boss would never let us go to jail, not on his watch. Hell, if you didn't get us pardons, we would've simply become outlaws. We'd be free either way. And we'd still follow him."

Rade had to smile at that. The loyalty of his men never ceased to amaze him. He wondered how much of that loyalty was due to force of habit: he had been their LPO, and later their chief, during their time in the Teams. Then again, some of the hairy situations he had gotten them into since then, and the unquestioning loyalty and obedience they had displayed, told him they would follow him to the gates of hell and back again. Essentially, they had done just that in their last mission.

I wouldn't trade my team for anything in the world.

What Ms. Bounty had left out of her announcement was that she had made a generous monetary contribution to the SK government and the families of the officers aboard the customs ships, which helped grease the wheels that led to their pardon. Rade knew if she told them, his team would expect a similar contribution. Rade was merely happy that she had paid their agreed upon bill, plus expenses.

"It's time for you all to learn who Ms. Bounty is," Rade said.

Bender perked up. "Let me guess, she's working for the Special Collection Service, or some other black budget spy program run by the United Systems."

"Close," Rade said. "Actually, she's an alien."

Bender seemed taken aback. "You don't say." Staying seated, he edged away from her on the mat.

Ms. Bounty's eyes seemed to drill into Bender. "We've met before."

"Really..." Bender was still moving away. Near

him, Fret and Manic slid aside to let him pass.

"We've become more adept at hiding our presence in this universe." She reached up to her neck and lowered the high collar of the fatigues she wore. "With careful placement of the hair, and the collar, we can avoid detection entirely, at least when assuming control of an Artificial body. Robots lacking skin, such as Centurions, are more difficult." She turned her back to the team and swept aside her pony-tail, revealing her bare neck. Glistening green drops of condensation clung to the artificial tissue there.

"Phant!" Bender drew the blaster from his utility belt and aimed it at her.

Others reached toward their own belts.

Rade placed himself in front of her and raised his palms. "Stand down! Stand down."

Bender reluctantly lowered the blaster. "Sorry, just a reflex. I'm assuming this is one of the good Phants?"

"That would be a safe assumption," Rade said. When Bender holstered the blaster, Rade moved aside once more.

Ms. Bounty lowered her pony-tail and raised her collar again, then turned around to face the team.

"Where have we met before?" Fret said.

"I am Surus," she said, as if that explained everything.

Manic's brow furrowed. "Who's Surus again?"

"The Green that fought with us during the First Alien War," Tahoe said. "Surus was Rade's copilot, if I remember."

"That's right," Rade said. He had once shared a mech with the entity, during the conclusion of the First Alien War. The Green Phants had been crucial in that war, and helped humanity drive off the aliens. It seemed a lifetime ago.

"You stayed behind when the other Greens left," Tahoe said. "Last I heard, you were acting as political observer to the Sino-Koreans in Tau Ceti, helping them clean up the Phants remaining in that system after the war. I always imagined you as a man."

Ms. Bounty, or more properly, Surus, smiled. "I am genderless, of course. Though my host is female. And yes, I offered my services to the Sino-Koreans for a time, and helped them hunt down every last Phant in the system."

"I like the little hint at your origins you put in your company name," Lui commented. "Green Systems." His eyes were defocused, indicating he was inside his Implant. "Take a look at the patent applications Green Systems has submitted since incorporating. Surus has been slowly leaking alien technology to us it looks like. Some of this stuff is unbelievable. Magnesium-ion packs that can be charged in ten minutes with a battery life of a *month*. Diamond nanothread production techniques. Grav elevator specs."

"I've seen them," Rade said.

"Someone has to fund my endeavors in this region of space," Surus said nonchalantly. "And besides, if I'm going to give technology to humanity, I might as well make a profit doing it."

"So wait a second," Manic said. "You're saying this Zoltan character was a Phant?"

"That's right," Rade said. "A Red."

"Phants." TJ scratched his chin. "Inter-dimensional aliens that can enter the AI cores of our robots and Artificials, and assume control."

"They can take over humans, too," Fret said.

"Yeah," Lui told him. "But only when they attach an unsightly control unit all along your back, interfacing with your spine and skull. Otherwise, when they touch a human, you go poof."

Rade lowered his gaze. He had lost his best friend in the First Alien War to a Phant. The memory was painful.

"Well if Zoltan was a Phant," TJ continued. "That explains why the robot we found outside the alleyway on Lang had its memory circuits wiped. The Phant could have seeped inside unnoticed, proceeded to take control of the AI, and issued a wipe command before departing."

"That," Manic said. "Or my previous theory that the robot wiped its own core to prevent its knowledge from falling into enemy hands still stands."

"Surus here has a proposition for us," Rade said.

All eyes turned to her.

"I told you I had hunted down every last Phant in Tau Ceti, the system of the First Alien War," Surus said. "My task has since expanded. As you now realize, not all of the aliens remained in Tau Ceti after the war. Several eluded capture by hitching a ride in robots and Artificials and escaping to other systems. I have taken it upon myself to hunt down the last remaining Phants in the region. Red, Purple, Blue and Black alike. I, and a few other Greens who remained in your space in secret.

"I need a team of dedicated men and women to help me in this task. A team I can call upon whenever my network of eyes and ears detects signs of a potential Phant presence. This first mission was merely a proving ground. I fought with you all before in Tau Ceti, and knew you were once good, but I needed to determine whether you still were. I was pleasantly surprised."

"Wait a second, are any of the galactic governments going to lend us aid, either in terms of troops or funding?" Lui said. "And if not, why not, considering how dangerous these things are? I watched Shaw's debriefing: this Zoltan freak tried to deploy a retrovirus that would have transformed a portion of Guangdong's population into those slugs we saw aboard the station, while killing the rest. Two million people, killed without purpose."

"Actually," Surus said. "It wasn't without purpose. Those slugs would eventually grow into the Great Formers you fought in Tau Ceti, creatures that slowly transform the crust of planets into geronium." Starship fuel. Phants also fed on it. "And as for the galactic governments, no they won't lend aid. The Sino-Koreans funded my hunt in Tau Ceti when their system was actively infested. But when I cast the last Phant into the Tau Ceti sun, the funding dried up. That said, all human governments have agreed to send military aid if we can bring them proof of a nest of Phants, but it's up to me to hunt them down individually until then."

"So wait a second," Lui said. "You're telling me the human governments are doing nothing at all to deal with Phants possibly hidden in their midst?"

"I didn't say that," Surus replied. "The governments are relying on their politicized intelligence services to ferret out Phants. To their credit, the human governments have found several already. Just last year the Russians caught two trying to work their way up the ranks of the Spetsnaz, and six months ago, the United Systems captured a Phant inhabiting a high ranking Artificial general. But I do not believe these intelligence services are good enough. I have certain abilities that no service has. I can detect when a Phant is in the same city or aboard the same starship as I am, for example."

"So how exactly is this going to work?" Manic said. "You said you want us to help you out whenever your spy network detects a potential Phant. Are we going to be on call, or something?"

"Not exactly," Surus said. "If Rade accepts my offer, I'll become a permanent member of your crew, and pay a monthly retainer. You'll be free to accept other clients, but the moment I detect a Phant, you agree to drop everything as soon as contractually possible, and make capturing the Phant your priority."

Rade ran his gaze across the men. "So, what do you say? Anybody want to hunt aliens?"

"Hell ya!" Bender said.

"Hunt aliens..." Fret said. "And yet, Surus is an alien herself. She admitted she's a Green Phant."

"The Greens are our friends," Rade said.

"So they say," Fret replied. "How can we really trust someone who is a traitor to their own race?"

"We've been at war with the Reds, Blues, Purples and Blacks for countless millennia," Surus said. "We do not consider them part of our race any longer."

"All right, and what if you have to capture a rogue Green one day?" Fret said. "Will you do it?"

"If we discover that one of the Greens who stayed behind is violating our rules," Surus said. "I won't hesitate to throw him into the core of a star, yes."

Rade rubbed his eyes for a moment. "Listen. I plan to accept Surus' offer. I won't force any of you to continue now that our mission statement has essentially changed. Like Surus said, while we're still free to accept other clients as they come up, hunting down Phants will be our priority. If any of you want out, I'll completely understand. I'll buy out your shares and send you on your merry way, no questions asked. No ill will. In fact, I don't expect all of you to stay, and

I'll respect the decision of anyone who wants out."

"It's a grand, multi-system bug hunt," Bender said. "Thank you thank you thank you. You're a lonely ex-MOTH's wet dream! Count me in. Where there are bugs, I bring spray."

"I would like to kill Phants," Harlequin said. There was a slight uncharacteristic rage in the Artificial's voice. Rade supposed Harlequin hadn't liked having his AI core commandeered.

"I'm in, of course," Tahoe said.

Everyone else expressed similar enthusiasm in turn. All save Fret.

Rade gazed at him. "What about you, Fret? Do you want me to buy out your shares? Remember, no ill will, and I respect your decision."

Fret regarded the others seated around him and sighed. "No, I'm coming. You're my brothers. I can't abandon you now. Not after everything we've been through. Do you remember what we often said on the Teams? 'Brothers to the end.' I believe those words, in my heart and soul." He lowered his gaze, and voice, as he continued: "We have to stick together in this life. You're all I have." He was quiet a moment, then looked up. "Besides, someone's got to keep Bender out of trouble."

"Yeah yeah," Bender said.

Once again Rade was heartened at the show of loyalty, and he found himself momentarily tearing up. He quickly dismissed the emotion. Now wasn't the time.

Shaw stepped away from the wall. "I'm out."

The room had fallen completely silent. A pin could have dropped and everyone would have heard.

Rade stared at her in disbelief, and pain. "But, Shaw—"

She looked at him, her features stern, serious. Then Shaw broke into a smile. "Just kidding. This is the mission of a lifetime, the client of a lifetime. Of course I'm going to accept. Welcome aboard, Surus." She extended her arms and gave the alien a hug.

"We're now officially bug hunters!" Bender said. "All bugs across the galaxy, you're on notice: we're going to spread your guts across the stars! No bug will be spared. We're going to leave a trail of upturned carapaces and crimped legs in our wake."

"Bender brings up a good point," Surus said. "I don't intend to restrict our mission necessarily to Phants. If we detect other potential alien threats to humanity, we must hunt them down, too."

"See!" Bender said. "This Surus is my kinda alien. So how about bankrolling a bigger ship for us, huh Surus bro? Or sis I mean. And some new toys."

"Your ship is good enough as it is," Surus said. "Small, inconspicuous. In fact, it's perfect for our needs. If you're a Phant hiding out on a small colony world and a large supercarrier enters the orbit of your planet, the odds are you'll flee the first chance you have. But if a vessel class favored by pirates arrives? You won't bat an eye. And as far as new toys go... I will supply them on an as-needed basis. For example, at the moment your AI core is in need of special shielding tech to prevent it from ever being corrupted by a Phant again. I will pay for and supervise the installation of said tech at the first opportunity."

"If there are no other questions," Rade said. "You're all free to go."

It was time to iron out the specifics of the deal.

—≪ —≪ —≪

THE FOUR SK destroyers left orbit, dragging the *Tiger* behind them; the damaged corvette was destined for repairs at a dry dock on the third planet, to be paid for by the Persians. The latter group had gotten in touch from the *Hóuzi Hāi* system. They had successfully boarded the *Camel*, and were due to arrive in a week. They planned to remain in the system until both the *Tiger* was repaired, and the SKs cleared their colony of drones and bioweapons. Rade offered to expedite the latter process for a fee. The Persians accepted. What he didn't tell them was that he had to return to the planet anyway to recoup his Hoplite investment.

Rade set a course for the binary suns of the current system first. There was something he had to do.

He stopped at the inner terrestrial colony along the way to replenish propellant and geronium levels, restock the *Argonaut's* depleted Hellfire and booster rocket supplies, and to give his crew much needed liberty. He, Shaw, Surus and Harlequin continued toward the two stars to complete the final phase of the mission.

Rade had specifically purchased one Hellfire without a warhead, and Surus laid the container housing the Phant inside. When the *Argonaut* had obtained the closest possible safe orbit around the binaries, Rade ordered the missile fired into the blue main sequence star, and then the ship began the long fight to escape the gravity of the suns.

He was in his stateroom with Shaw when Bax announced: "It's time."

Rade stood facing one bulkhead, then held Shaw's hand. He tapped into an external camera on the starboard side. The view was of the blue sun. Bax had zoomed in on the Hellfire, or rather, its debris—the missile had broken up in the heat—and filtered out the brightness of the background star.

Rade watched the debris vanish into the flaming corona. That was the only way to truly kill the inter-dimensional Phant: trap it inside the core of a sun, where it was unable to escape the immense gravity. Over the next few millennia it would eventually starve to death from lack of geronium.

"What a way to go," Rade said.

Shaw's fingers tightened around his. "I can only imagine how terrible it's going to be for that thing. Trapped in the star, alone for a thousand years or more before it dies. Even after what it did, I feel sorry for it."

"Well I don't," Rade said. "Not a whit of pity. It deserves every last moment of suffering. No one touches my Shaw."

He sensed motion beside him and dismissed the external video feed. He turned toward Shaw. She was facing him, looking into his eyes.

"Would you ever leave me alone like that?" Shaw said.

"Never."

She wrapped her arms around him and gripped him close. "Love you."

"Love you back," Rade said without hesitation.

Shaw gasped softly, and squeezed him tighter.

Thank you for reading.

Acknowledgments

THANK YOU to my knowledgeable beta readers and advanced reviewers who helped smooth out the rough edges of the prerelease manuscript: Nicole P., Lisa A. G., Gregg C., Jeff K., Mark C., Jeremy G., Doug B., Jenny O., Amy B., Bryan O., Lezza M., Gene A., Larry J., Allen M., Gary F., Eric, Robine, Noel, Anton, Spencer, Norman, Trudi, Corey, Erol, Terje, David, Charles, Walter, Lisa, Ramon, Chris, Scott, Michael, Chris, Bob, Jim, Maureen, Zane, Chuck, Shayne, Anna, Dave, Roger, Nick, Gerry, Charles, Annie, Patrick, Mike, Jeff, Lisa, Jason, Bryant, Janna, Tom, Jerry, Chris, Jim, Brandon, Kathy, Norm, Jonathan, Derek, Shawn, Judi, Eric, Rick, Bryan, Barry, Sherman, Jim, Bob, Ralph, Darren, Michael, Chris, Michael, Julie, Glenn, Rickie, Rhonda, Neil, Claude, Ski, Joe, Paul, Larry, John, Norma, Jeff, David, Brennan, Phyllis, Robert, Darren, Daniel, Montzalee, Robert, Dave, Diane, Peter, Skip, Louise, Dave, Brent, Erin, Paul, Jeremy, Dan, Garland, Sharon, Dave, Pat, Nathan, Max, Martin, Greg, David, Myles, Nancy, Ed, David, Karen, Becky, Jacob, Ben, Don, Carl, Gene, Bob, Luke, Teri, Gerald, Lee, Rich, Ken, Daniel, Chris, Al, Andy, Tim, Robert, Fred, David, Mitch, Don, Tony, Dian, Tony, John, Sandy, James, David, Pat, Jean, Bryan, William, Roy, Dave, Vincent, Tim, Richard, Kevin, George, Andrew, John, Richard, Robin, Sue, Mark, Jerry, Rodger, Rob, Byron, Ty,

Mike, Gerry, Steve, Benjamin, Anna, Keith, Jeff, Josh, Herb, Bev, Simon, John, David, Greg, Larry, Timothy, Tony, Ian, Niraj, Maureen, Jim, Len, Bryan, Todd, Maria, Angela, Gerhard, Renee, Pete, Hemantkumar, Tim, Joseph, Will, David, Suzanne, Steve, Derek, Valerie, Laurence, James, Andy, Mark, Tarzy, Christina, Rick, Mike, Paula, Tim, Jim, Gal, Anthony, Ron, Dietrich, Mindy, Ben, Steve, Paddy & Penny, Troy, Marti, Herb, Jim, David, Alan, Leslie, Chuck, Dan, Perry, Chris, Rich, Rod, Trevor, Rick, Michael, Tim, Mark, Alex, John, William, Doug, Tony, David, Sam, Derek, John, Jay, Tom, Bryant, Larry, Anjanette, Gary, Travis, Jennifer, Henry, Drew, Michelle, Bob, Gregg, Billy, Jack, Lance, Sandra, Libby, Jonathan, Karl, Bruce, Clay, Gary, Sarge, Andrew, Deborah, Steve, and Curtis.

Without you all, this novel would have typos, continuity errors, and excessive lapses in realism. Thank you for helping me make *Bug Hunt* the best military science fiction novel it could possibly be, and thank you for leaving the early reviews that help new readers find my books.

And of course I'd be remiss if I didn't thank my mother, father, and brothers, whose untiring wisdom and thought-provoking insights have always guided me through the untamed warrens of life.

— Isaac Hooke

www.isaachooke.com

44308189R00185

Made in the USA
Middletown, DE
03 June 2017